FAMILY

A WRITING BLOC ANTHOLOGY

WRITING BLOC

CONTENTS

OTHER ANTHOLOGIES BY
WRITING BLOC

Escape!
Deception!
Passageways: Nine Tales. Nine Unique Literary Worlds.

Print ISBN: 978-1-7373536-4-5

Digital ISBN: 978-1-7373536-5-2

Cover by Kaytalin McCarry

Formatted by G.A. Finocchiaro

Edited cooperatively by all the authors (Cari Dubiel, lead)

Curated by Mike X Welch

❀ Created with Vellum

FOREWORD

Two-thousand twenty-one, aka year *two* of COVID-19, was a helluva year.

In the United States we had an administration change. These always bring uncertainty and, to some, angst to the fore. Lots of people went back to work, some to brand-new jobs. Plenty of people continued to play chicken with the pandemic, either by avoiding vaccination, scoffing at the idea of wearing a mask, or just flat-out refuting the science. The rhetoric stopped being about 'flattening the curve' for our health care workers and more about 'our freedom.' The year started out with a full-fledged insurrection. The only thing certain was uncertainty.

So what remained constant in 2021? What did we hold close, closer, closest to our hearts at a time when it seemed like the fabric of society itself threatened to unravel around us?

Family.

Family is why we did what we did, be it getting out of our comfort zone and getting a new job, or taking a job we didn't want but were forced to by circumstances, or standing pat where we were despite our desire to go elsewhere.

Family is who we desperately tried to keep healthy. Who we

thought of when we put on our mask, with a resigned sigh, before going into the grocery store. In some cases, family was who we put our feelings aside for and got vaccinated. Family is who we pointed to when we justified what we were doing, regardless of what it was.

Lots of people lost members of their families; some lost their entire families. A fortunate number welcomed new members to their families, the pandemic adding an extra layer of anxiety on top of the inherent ones. Some people quietly formed new families.

Writing Bloc chose the theme of Family for this year's anthology because of how important, versatile, and universal the concept is. Even if you completely lack a family, it's something you can write about. You can be estranged from it, enveloped in it, searching for it, or building it; there is virtually no end to the possibilities that the idea of Family inspires in an artist.

Writing Bloc is a group that I consider to be family. Cari Dubiel is mother to every book published by our dogged independent collective, regardless of author. I do my best to be the "fun uncle," keeping the brothers and sisters, cousins, nieces and nephews in formation for the family photographs. Reliable aunts Becca Spence Dobias and Jacqui Castle do their invaluable work on the Writing Bloc podcast, website, and myriad behind-the-scenes tasks. Prodigy cousin G.A. Finocchiaro selflessly puts the words in the right order and makes them look great. Granddaughter Kaytalin Platt usually ends up as our go-to cover artist, and her work is stunningly beautiful. Every member of Writing Bloc helps keep this ship afloat.

For 2021, Writing Bloc has been like a life raft to many of the authors in our collective. Without the opportunity to work on both *Passageways: Nine Tales, Nine Unique Literary Worlds* and this volume, *Family*, a majority of authors in our fold have expressed to me — both privately and publicly — that they wouldn't have written a word otherwise. And personally, if I hadn't been in a position to wrangle these incredibly talented authors, to view their work and offer advice, criticism, or sometimes just a shoulder...well, I promise you that my 2020 and 2021 would've been pretty miserable.

Please be aware that some stories in this collection contain adult language, sexual situations including assault, and plenty of violence. That said, there should be something for absolutely everyone contained herein.

From the Writing Bloc family to your family — whatever form it may take — we hope you enjoy this collection of tales by some of the most talented indie authors writing today. Thank you for reading.

Mike X Welch - 1/30/22
Writing Bloc *Project Manager of Books*

CASTAWAY FAMILY

T.C.C. EDWARDS

The reporter approached the alien as she entered through the airlock. The alien was one of the Eunda who lived in the neighboring colony dome. Among her own kind, her name was a designation of her work and rank within the social hierarchy, but she had chosen the name Sorra for her meetings with humans. She pushed a small floating cart in front of her, loaded with several glossy-black cases and canisters. The reporter waited while Sorra took in the colony, her squid-like head turning as she gazed up at the idyllic holographic sky under the closed dome.

Sorra held out a tentacle in greeting. William Flynn, the reporter, mentally commanded his glasses to begin recording as he gently clasped the tentacle. The glasses were a gift from the architects of this colony dome and were based on the original recording visor that Flynn had hoped to use in a different life at the New Gaia colony in the Tau Ceti system.

That life had never begun. Instead, Flynn and the other passengers of the colony ship *Tereshkova* were at this colony provided by alien hosts, and they were farther from Earth or Tau Ceti than any human could imagine. The hosts were kind, though, and had maintained this comfortable "Human Dome" for the colonists for the last five months.

"Great to see you too, Sorra," Flynn said. "This is everything?"

Sorra looked down at the cart. Her "eyes" were four circular patches of photoreceptive skin on the front of her rounded head, and they were nearly the same shade of blue-white as the rest of her body. The display in Flynn's glasses shifted the contrast between her "eyes" and skin — he had never been able to see them without the glasses.

Sorra then looked up to Flynn, holding four tentacles in front of her. She gestured, tracing designs in the air. Tiny black spikes poked out of the skin on her arms, and electrical sparks formed and danced between the spikes. Flynn's glasses registered the movements and the electrical pulses, generating a translation in English which he heard through the earpieces built into the glasses.

"This is all I want to take," Sorra said. "The rest is left behind. It reminds me of my mate and my family, who passed beyond."

Flynn nodded solemnly. "I know I've said it before, but I'm sorry you lost so much."

"And again, I say 'no need.' I have taken the time since the attack to devise a new purpose."

Flynn nodded his understanding and gestured for Sorra to walk with him. He thought about that attack, the single enemy ship that had almost destroyed Base 472, this alien colony that was supposed to be secret and safe. It was only the unexpected presence of the humans that had kept the enemy from succeeding. The *Tereshkova* had appeared in this galaxy, in the middle of a war, by the most unlikely chance. And yet, the humans aboard had turned the tide of battle over this colony.

Sorra and Flynn walked along the wide stone road under the colony dome. On their right side, colonists looked and waved as they tended to the vegetables that grew in the neatly tilled dirt on that side of the dome. On the left side of the road, water glistened under the dimming evening light. The pond – or small lake, Flynn had never known what to call it – stretched across nearly a quarter of the space and met with the wall on the far side.

Ahead, the road gave way to a square surrounded by eight blocky buildings. Each was drab gray and clearly designed for practicality rather than aesthetics. With twenty dorms in each building, there was more than enough space for the 190 humans who lived there.

Flynn took Sorra through the archway of the nearest building – the buildings had no outer doors, as there was no one to keep out and the weather never changed. In the lobby, Helena Clarke and Dena Lee stood next to a round table in the middle of the common area. Clarke gestured to four plates of sushi on the table as she greeted Flynn and Sorra. Flynn helped Sorra push the cart with her belongings next to one of the several empty tables, then the two joined Clarke and Lee.

"Hello, Sorra, welcome home," Clarke said. "Dinner's ready!"

"I guess that means the synthesizer's working," Flynn said, nodding at Lee. "Good job, Dena."

"Heh, thanks," Lee said. "I guess fixing the protein vats gives me *something* to do."

"What are you complaining about?" Clarke said. "I'm a pilot. No one needs anything flown right now, so what do I do? I farm! Me, a farmer!"

"Not many people want a reporter either, it turns out!" Flynn added. "I'd settle for getting people to vent and rant."

"Wait, you're recording right now, aren't you?" Lee asked.

"I requested a record," Sorra interjected before Flynn could answer. "A sample of our interactions may help your people accept me."

Lee and Clarke each took an extra second as they listened to the translation in their own earpieces. Like most of the colonists, they had opted for simple earpieces rather than glasses like Flynn's.

"Then let's have a good interaction," Clarke said. "Have some 'sushi,' everyone – I tried some already, it tastes … close enough!"

Flynn, Lee, and Clarke grabbed nearby chairs and sat at the table, while Sorra bent her lower tentacles in a sort of crouch. Flynn knew that she was comfortable this way but noted Lee and Clarke's questioning glances. They turned back to the food quickly enough. There were chopsticks ready for the three humans, but Flynn knew Sorra couldn't use them. Instead, she held up one tentacle, and the tip of it split into three short fingers. She picked up a piece of "salmon" sushi first and placed it in her beak.

"This is pleasant!" Sorra said after chewing. "The real fish must taste wonderful!"

"It sure does," Lee agreed. "I bet you'd love real seafood. Wish we could take you to Earth!"

"Yes, I want to swim your waters," Sorra said before grabbing more food.

Flynn still marveled at her appetite. He had tried a Eunda staple called *gorda*, which Sorra had assured him was compatible with human digestion. It was a viscous liquid made by blending sea creatures that lived on the Eunda homeworld. The stuff was thick and smelled so strong, Flynn had barely managed a sip before his gag reflex had taken over. Sorra, however, could digest nearly anything – it was a gift the Eunda had, along with their ability to breathe in nearly any atmospheric or aquatic environment.

Other colonists came and went through the lobby as the four finished the sushi, each taking a moment to regard the Eunda before going to their dorm rooms. Though everyone had seen Eunda and other aliens before, not many humans had had the chance to spend more than a few minutes talking with one.

"This was blissful," Sorra said when the meal was finished. "But now I must rest."

"Ah, your room," Flynn said as he stood. "We have a place right here on the first floor for you."

"Thank you. Human Lee, Human Clarke: I express gratitude for this experience."

"Thank you, Eunda Sorra," Clarke said with a nod. "See you tomorrow."

"Good night," Lee added.

Sorra gestured at them, then stood at her full height. She turned to follow Flynn, and they went to a room at the far side of the lobby. The dorm was a standard room, but Flynn and Lee had removed the double bed and replaced it with a wide tub filled with saltwater. They had also swapped the bright white light fixture in the room's ceiling with a softer orange-yellow light according to Sorra's specifications. The light cast a sunset glow across the drab walls and over the still water in the tub. Though the room was a bit hot for his taste, Flynn breathed in the humid, salty air and felt the muscles in his shoulders soften at the relaxing effect of the setup.

Sorra went ahead of Flynn, climbing into the custom bathtub.

"Ah, so good to be in salty water, Human Flynn. Oh, you employed a good mix of salt!"

Flynn smiled. "Three percent salt: half potassium chloride, half sodium chloride, just like you said."

"It is therapeutic," Sorra said. "I shall sleep well. About … twelve hours by human measurement."

"Ah right, your day is about thirty-six hours, isn't it?"

"Indeed. We sleep for a third of it – humans are similar?"

"We are. Eight hours out of twenty-four, usually."

"Such a short day. How do you accomplish your works?"

Flynn had to laugh. "Good question! We manage, though. Usually!"

Sorra waved her tentacles in a gesture that translated as a laugh – apparently the idea of "not enough hours in the day" transcended both Eunda and human cultures.

* * *

"Thanks for staying with me, Helena."

Clarke smiled from her place on the chair next to Flynn's bed. It was one in the morning by the colony's clock, but she showed no signs of fatigue. Lee had gone to bed soon after Sorra, leaving Clarke and Flynn to their hours-long talk. As always when they talked, the subject drifted to Darya Fitzgerald, Flynn's fiancé. Like Flynn, Fitzgerald was a reporter, and she had been recruited to help document the lives of the New Gaia colonists. A few years before that, though, Fitzgerald had met Clarke for a series of interviews about her military experience, and the two had become close friends.

"I miss her too, Flynn," Clarke said now. "Darya and I talked a lot –

she always loved my test flight stories. Remember when she sent me her homemade cookies?"

"Yeah, she loved cooking – hell, I bet she still does. I hope she's found a good oven at New Gaia and some people to try out her creations!"

"Oh yeah, sure. People like me who hate cooking – her baking was a godsend when I couldn't be bothered to make dinner."

Flynn chuckled. "She'd be so happy to know that! God, I wish she were here."

"Yeah, me too. Or that we could go to her. Do you think she'll stay in New Gaia?"

Flynn opened his mouth but rethought his answer. He and Darya had planned to spend the first years of their marriage working in New Gaia, collecting and sending their reports of the colonists' lives to audiences on Earth. They had assumed they would be together, and Flynn hadn't considered what she'd do without him.

"I think she'll stay," Flynn said after a moment's thought. "She'll have no trouble making friends among the colonists. I think one day she'll have another man in her life."

"You would be okay with that?"

"Not right now, no. But later, if we can't get to her. I want her to be happy. Even if that means she eventually meets someone else."

"And how about you, Flynn?" Clarke leaned in close, squeezing Flynn's hand.

Flynn sat on his bed regarding her, taking in her deep brown eyes. All he would have to do is caress her cheek, and she would happily stay with him in his bed. But she wouldn't *stay* with him. She wouldn't marry him – that wasn't her way. One night, maybe even a month of passionate nights, but she would eventually want a different lover or want to take a break from romance entirely. Darya, if Flynn ever saw her again, might condone the affair as a result of their separation. But Flynn wouldn't as easily forgive himself. Not yet.

"Not now," Flynn said. "She has my heart, and I have you as a friend."

Clarke nodded, her smile betraying no disappointment. "Sounds good to me. You keep her in your heart, Flynn. I'll always be here to talk."

* * *

SOMETHING squished underneath his chest as he woke. Flynn's eyes shot open, but he couldn't comprehend the glowing mess on his bed. There were two more spots on the ceiling, casting yellow-green light from above, but it was too dark to make sense of what he saw.

"Lights on!" Flynn said.

The room lights came on, at last forcing the stupor from his head. He sat up, and a strand of glowing goo stretched and snapped as he pulled his chest up from the bed.

"Ugh!" He brushed at it instinctively and immediately wished he hadn't. It was warm and stuck to his fingers like syrup.

Okay, calm down. Stop brushing at it already. Deep breaths.

He looked to the ceiling, slowly allowing his eyes to take in the crawling things on the ceiling. Each one was about a centimeter long with antennae that curled back along their glowing green shells. The two above Flynn had left trails of yellow slime that led back to an air vent in the ceiling. There was a third trail, thicker than the other two, that went from the vent and ended above Flynn's bed. He looked again at the mess on his bed and shirt, noticing tiny, unidentifiable organs among the thick paste that was left. He shuddered and gagged but managed not to throw up.

Flynn moved carefully around the messy bedsheets and rose. He picked up his glasses and put them on. The display came to life immediately as his glasses reacted to his brainwaves.

CAUTION: Eunda larval stage beings detected. Locate brood mother immediately. Avoid skin contact.

The message flashed across the bottom of Flynn's vision as his display outlined the creatures with blinking red auras. *Avoid skin contact*, Flynn thought, examining his goo-covered fingers. *Now you tell me.*

A knock sounded at his door.

"Flynn, this is Holloway. We, uh, need your help out here."

Flynn quickly went to the small bathroom in his dorm, washing his hands before he answered the door. The stuff washed off, but it left yellowish patches where it had touched his skin. The knock sounded again, and Flynn sighed and went to the door.

Damien Holloway stood there, looking down at Flynn and the mess in his room. "Christ, they're in here too!"

Flynn let the taller man pass. Holloway looked to the ceiling, examining the creatures but clearly restraining himself from touching them.

"Sir, I've got no idea where they're from," Flynn said. "I just woke up — looks like I squished one in my sleep."

"It's just 'Holloway' now; I'm not captain anymore."

"Right." Flynn shook his head. Old habits, he thought. Holloway had been the Chief of Security on the *Tereshkova* before an attack had left the original captain dead. He had served as acting captain for the voyage to this colony. Here in the Human Dome, Holloway was back to his original role as a security officer, though that had mostly meant negotiating spats between colonists.

"I've seen a dozen of these things so far," Holloway said. "They've come out of the vents in several dorms in this building. They have anything do with our Eunda guest?"

"We need to ask her," Flynn said as his own reasoning followed Holloway's.

The Eunda and other aliens of Base 472 rarely stayed in the dome, visiting only when the life-support systems needed maintenance. The humans didn't know the Eunda very well, and so they couldn't know what to expect.

Holloway and Flynn moved through the hallway and down the stairs. Sorra's door was already open, and Doctor Ankit Chandra was standing next to the tub of saltwater.

"Flynn, Holloway, you're here, good," the doctor said, gesturing for Flynn to come closer. "She isn't responding. I need you to help me get her to the clinic."

Flynn looked at Sorra, who lay in the tub unmoving. His glasses showed a readout next to her body, indicating that she was alive but in a comatose state. Behind Flynn, the doctor gestured to Holloway, and the two unfolded a stretcher that Chandra had brought into the room earlier. Flynn carefully lifted Sorra from the bathtub, and Holloway and the doctor carried her out through the lobby.

The clinic was a one-floor building between the eight larger dorm buildings. Like the dorms, it had no outer doors, just a wide archway that Holloway and Chandra could easily carry Sorra through. They found an empty bed, and Flynn again lifted Sorra. Chandra picked up a handheld scanner, another device provided by the Eunda hosts. The device could accurately diagnose any of the dozens of species known to the Eunda, including the most recent addition to its database, *homo sapiens*.

"She just gave birth!" Chandra said excitedly. "She has produced a brood of twenty to twenty-five Eunda spawn. We should bring the young here immediately – they'll have the best chance of survival in high-salinity water at twenty degrees Celsius."

"Her bathtub water," Flynn said. "We can use that – but why couldn't her babies just stay in it?"

Chandra frowned. "We'll ask her later."

The doctor gestured for Holloway to stand back, then came to Flynn. He ran the scanner over the stain and Flynn's chest and examined Flynn's hands.

"God, I'm sorry about this," Flynn said. "I killed one of her kids!"

"You didn't know," Chandra said. "We'll talk this out with Sorra. But first, I'll need to examine your chest. "

Flynn held still as Doctor Chandra cut open his green-stained shirt with a small pair of scissors and removed it. There was a patch of red, irritated skin from his collarbone to his left pectoral. Chandra ran his scanner over the skin and regarded the readout.

"Okay, I understand what I'm seeing now. The larval secretion has stayed in the outer layer of skin – I don't think it has spread any deeper, but we'll need to check again in a few hours. Eunda and human physiology are quite different, so it's unlikely you'll get seriously ill. The secretion produces a strong numbing effect, which is why you don't feel anything now. I can't prevent the nasty itching you'll get soon, but I have a good analgesic cream I can prescribe for it."

"All right. I'll get it from you later. For now, we better round up those larvae – I mean, unless I need to stay here."

"I think you're safe to go, but come back immediately if you feel anything strange."

"I'll help you," Holloway said to Flynn

"Yes, but please," Chandra implored, "wear gloves when you handle them!"

* * *

THE TWO IN Flynn's room were dead. The larvae lay on Flynn's bed, each one shriveled into a tight ball, their pale green bodies no longer glowing. Flynn, now wearing the drab gray replacement shirt and the thin gloves that Doctor Chandra had given him, picked them up anyway. Holloway held out a clear cylindrical container with a small amount of Sorra's bathwater, and Flynn placed them into it.

Holloway had ordered everyone to open their doors and leave the building so that he and Flynn could quickly find the missing larvae. Over the next hour, they found sixteen of them, on beds, desktops, or on the floor. None had made it far from the building's vent system – and not one was still alive. Flynn's glasses helped him scan the building, and they soon finished the search.

They went back to Sorra's room, and Holloway put the specimen collection aside as he and Flynn examined the wall next to Sorra's bed-bathtub. Several trails of slime led up the wall to the vent. Flynn had started the search by removing the cover of the vent, but no larvae had stayed near their mother. None were trapped within the vent system either, according to Flynn's scans – each larva had found an exit from the vents before perishing.

"Have we got them all?" Holloway asked, echoing the question now in Flynn's mind.

"We have sixteen. There could be twenty-five. God, why didn't Sorra *tell* me?"

"Flynn, it's ... well, it's not *okay*, but ..." Holloway stammered, but then continued more steadily. "We didn't know. There could still be ones still alive here. Just think – where else could they go?"

Flynn considered the question and looked around the room. The bathtub was still half-full, so the water hadn't gone down the drain – *wait*! There was a secondary drain next to the tub. Flynn knelt and examined the drain carefully.

There! A trail of slime led to the drain, so thin it was barely visible even with his glasses on. The slime, thick as it was, must have eventually gone down the drain with the larvae.

"The filter!" Flynn said as he realized. "We have to check the filter for this building."

Holloway looked surprised, but he nodded and picked up the collection tank as Flynn left the room.

The bathwater, like the wastewater from the sinks and showers, would go through a filter station before draining into the colony's pond. Flynn hoped he was right that the larvae had ended up in this simple cleaning system, rather than in the more elaborate septic system. He didn't want to think about *that* possibility until absolutely necessary.

They exited into the stone square between the dorm buildings. The displaced residents were waiting in a loose crowd, all eyes turning to Flynn as he examined the people one by one, his glasses helping him find any patches of irritated skin. Lee and Clarke were among them, each explaining the situation to restless colonists.

"Sorry to interrupt, Dena," Flynn said as he approached her.

"Oh, Flynn, good! Any luck getting them all?"

"Holloway's found sixteen – but I really need you right now. You've checked the greywater filters before, right?"

"Of course, why?"

"I need you with me now, please."

* * *

Lee led Flynn to a row of eight small metal boxes set at the edge of the pond. She knelt, opened a panel on one of the boxes, and reached in. After a brief twist of her wrist, an object came loose, and she brought it out of the box. She held out a round metal filter, and sure enough, there were four alien shapes inside it. But instead of worm-like forms, they were pale green cocoons with sticky fibers that held them to the inner side of the filter.

"Flynn!"

Holloway's voice came from somewhere behind him as the world shifted. Pain shot through his chest, and Flynn found himself crouching on the ground before Lee. Holloway, who had returned from Doctor Chandra with a new container after delivering the found larvae, came around in front of Flynn's wavy vision.

"You need to get to the doctor, now," Holloway said.

"Flynn, just take it easy," Lee added, clasping Flynn's hand.

"Uh, yes. Yes, of course …" Flynn looked up at Lee as his vision twisted and swam.

Lee put the filter into Holloway's container and threw Flynn's arm around her shoulder. He let her lead him through a drunken haze of stone buildings. Somewhere along the way, Clarke was there too, lifting his other arm. He heard Chandra's voice from somewhere in the distance as his back somehow found a comfortable bed. Clarke's voice assured him everything would be okay as he drifted off.

* * *

"No, no, don't you get up yet!"

Flynn couldn't remember sitting up, but he was sitting now. His chest burned, but he couldn't remember any fire either. Doctor Chandra was in front of him. The doctor gently pushed Flynn down to the bed (*when had he gone to bed?*), and he obliged.

"Flynn, I need you to lie down a little longer. You've done a great job, but you need to rest."

Great job? That sounded nice. *But what had he done?*

He was awake again. Helena Clarke was there, smiling at him from above. She held something small in her hands – no, not *something,* *someone.* Flynn raised slowly and sat on his clinic bed. Memory came back to him – chasing the larvae, seeing so many that had died, finding the filter, his burning chest. There was still a dull ache somewhere above his heart, but at least his skin wasn't itchy now. Somewhere in his brief respites from medical sleep, it had itched terribly, but Chandra had always been there to stop his scratching.

"Helena," Flynn said finally, "I'm glad you're here. What – Who is that?"

Clarke shifted position so that Flynn could better see the form in her arms. It was a Eunda, a tiny version of Sorra, except this one's skin was a darker shade of blue. Clarke gestured to a place across the room, and Flynn's gaze flicked to the door..

Sorra was now at the entrance to the clinic. She carried two more baby Eunda in her tentacles as she walked toward Flynn.

"Three?" Flynn asked softly. "Only three babies survived?"

"It is joyous, is it not?" Sorra said, "Three from a brood. Truly the seas are kind!"

"Wait," Flynn said, shaking his head, "Are you saying – Eunda babies don't usually survive?"

"Fortune favors us when one metamorphoses. If two grow, we are blessed. Three is a rarity indeed!"

Flynn looked to Clarke, who smiled at his questioning glance.

"She's happy to have three – and you helped raise one of them."

"I did?" As soon as he said it, a sharp pain struck, as if something was inside his upper chest trying to get out. He grunted and reached for the wound, but Doctor Chandra brushed past Sorra to clasp Flynn's hands.

"No. You must not touch it. The skin won't mend if you keep touching it."

"Wait," Flynn said, again shaking his head in bewilderment, "There was a *larva* – in my *chest?*"

"Yes," Chandra said, "There must have been *four* in your room, not just three. Two of them fell onto you while you slept. I think you turned onto your chest – it was enough to wake you, but not fully.

You squished one of the larvae, but the other likely got caught between your shirt and skin. With nowhere to go, it ate into the top layers of skin."

"And I didn't feel *any* of this?"

"The larval secretion," Chandra explained. "It was stronger than I realized, and the layer of it on your skin was enough to mask the larva inside from my scans. It numbed most of the pain. I intend to study the secretion fully – it could make an amazing painkiller."

"Eunda larvae search for warm bodies when they leave the mother," Sorra added. "The larvae were acting on instinct when they searched your domicile structure. Some larvae try to eat into larger creatures without killing them and grow inside, while others feed on plants and small things until they can grow. The mother sleeps for a long time when spawning comes. I was exhausted!"

"And you didn't know you were pregnant?"

"No. My mate and I entangled the day before he died, but there was no way to know of success until spawning came."

"In fact," Doctor Chandra added, "I suspect your little seafood dinner sped things up. Our synthesized food is more nutritionally dense than Eunda food, I think. It will take a lot of study to be sure, but it seems Sorra's metabolism received a huge shock, which triggered her spawning."

"See, it's all our fault, Flynn!" Clarke said jokingly.

Flynn smiled and shook his head. "You ... you're *enjoying* this, aren't you?"

"A *man* gave birth. You bet I'm enjoying it."

"I did not ..." But Flynn laughed instead of finishing the claim. The pain in his chest, the absurdity of an alien growing in his pectoral, and the joy of a parent glad that at least three children were with her now — it was too much, and all he could do was laugh.

* * *

"So, what should we name her?"

Helena Clarke held the small Eunda on her lap as she sat on the bench. Flynn sat next to her as they looked out over the pond.

"Her?" Holloway's gruff voice came from beside Flynn. "Do I want to know how you can tell it's a *her?*"

Flynn looked to the next bench over, where Holloway and Lee sat and Sorra stood next to them. Sorra held her two young ones, clicking her beak in a soft regular pattern as they slept in her tentacles. If she heard Holloway, she didn't react to his question.

"Two males, one female," Clarke said. "Ask Sorra how she knows – I'm sure she'll be happy to tell you."

Holloway looked to the peaceful Eunda mother, and Flynn regarded her as well. She hadn't counted the losses of the larva that had died. Rather, she had counted the gains – two who had grown from the cocoons in the water filter, and one who had grown inside Flynn's chest. Three – enough for a miracle.

"She really wants *us* to name her," Flynn said. "It's such a big responsibility!"

"Well, you are the surrogate father," Lee said. "Plus, Sorra wants to stay with us. I guess she just likes us humans!"

Flynn smiled at that. He looked toward Clarke to find her smiling at him. He imagined Darya sitting next to him, looking at him that way, and it came to him. The perfect name.

"Eleanor," Flynn said. "I want to name her Eleanor."

Clarke nodded knowingly. "Darya Eleanor Fitzgerald. Eleanor's her middle name."

"That's so sweet," Lee said.

"Yeah. A bit too much sweetness for me," Holloway grunted. But even he allowed a smile to touch his lips in approval of Flynn's choice.

Flynn, Clarke, and Eleanor sat for a while after Lee and Holloway excused themselves and went their separate ways. Sorra came over to the three of them, gesturing to Flynn that their time with her daughter was almost over.

"We can see her again tomorrow," Clarke said. "Sorra hopes you'll help a bit with raising her. And hey, don't worry, I'll help too."

"I never would have thought you the mothering type."

"You're right. But I am the aunting type!"

Flynn laughed. "Okay. Sure, let's do what we can."

Clarke smiled warmly at him before looking down at the little Eunda in her charge. She was still, sleeping peacefully in Clarke's arms. Clarke looked back up at Flynn. Flynn looked back and smiled, proud to be part of this family in this home away from home.

PEARLS AND SWINE

SUSAN K. HAMILTON

They fear me.

The sour stink of it pervades the air as I pass by. A few stand to block my way, but their courage is fleeting. A single glance from beneath my hood strips away their bravado, baring their souls, their deficiencies, their darkest secrets, and they wilt, opening a clear path for me. One that leads straight to the gallows.

Straight to her.

Standing barefoot on the rough-hewn boards, harsh rope around her throat, the girl is maybe twelve summers old. Her stained cotton shift is tattered at the hem and the sleeves have been torn—one from the shoulder, the other from the elbow. Dark spatter stains the front, spectral memories of blood and sweat. Her hair is lank, her arms thin like reeds. But there is a spark in her. I can feel it.

Her wrists are bound in front of her and that stirs my anger. I know the Magistrate here. He is a cruel man and has bound her this way so he can laugh as she hangs, scratching at her throat as she strangles. Stopping at the base of the gallows, I pull in the edges of my cloak, and the midnight indigo hem swirls around my feet. They all think I am here to witness her death and collect her corpse once they cut her down—I am, after all, a Sister of the Moon. I shepherd the souls of the dead to the Dark Goddess.

But that is not all the Sisterhood does, and they will be reminded of that soon enough. What they are not certain of are my guards, who remain at the edge of the square, silent and attentive. Above their collective restlessness, I hear a whisper. "Why does a Sister of the Moon bother with a penniless waif?"

I turn. The speaker's apprehension is palpable; he knows I've heard him. "She Who Is The Darkness cares not for your gold or land, your titles or ambitions, if you are rich or poor." I point at him. "She will collect your soul one day, and you will be grateful if a Sister attends to *your* passing."

The muffled response that follows holds contrition. But I am not here today to guide his soul to the Goddess' embrace. This soul I seek —her soul—has called me across the miles, just as my soul once sounded a clarion hail to another Sister. I am here to give her a choice.

"That one," I say, pointing at the girl. "That one is mine."

"What?" The Magistrate is barely able to sputter the word.

His confusion does not surprise me. It is rare for a Sister to spare the condemned. To offer them a new life, a new family. It happens a handful of times in a generation, but it is my right, a privilege given by The Darkness Herself. I will brook no interference from this buffoon.

"She is mine—if she so chooses."

"Absolutely not!" A shrill, indignant declaration cuts off the Magistrate before he can react.

The voice belongs to a corpulent woman with a dress made of fine green silk, a double length of lustrous pearls around her neck. As she barks at me, she shoves her way through the crowd, knocking aside those who impede her. A man—her son, perhaps?—plucks at her sleeve. He knows what dangerous ground she treads upon, but she disregards him with a jerk of her elbow. He wrings his hands, fearful.

One of my guards steps forward, but a soft shake of my head stops her.

"That vagrant is a thief!" The silken sow continues speaking, lecturing me with breathtaking pomposity, as if I am some half-wit.

"What did she steal from you?" I ask.

For a moment she's flummoxed, as if her mere accusation should be sufficient to prove the girl's guilt. Then she announces, "Bread. And a *cloak!*" She proclaims it as if the girl had absconded with those precious pearls. Looking around, she nods, haughty and confident in her unassailable position.

"Tell me then, *why* did she steal?"

My question is met with silence. I allow it to linger until the quiet and the frost from my stare elicit a response.

"Why? That doesn't matter. A thief is a thief. She took what is mine and I will see her punished."

This woman is a fool to interfere with me—or stupid. Perhaps she is both. Her son looks at the ground, his shame plain. Tendrils of fog and indigo darkness stretch out from the hem of my cloak and slither across the ground. Some in the crowd notice and step back, but she continues, oblivious as the tendrils embrace the hem of her fancy gown. They glide upward, unnoticed, along the silk embroidery and lace.

"You are *not* the *law*. The Magistrate may fear you, but I will *not* permit—"

She sputters, her words choked off as one tendril forces itself down her throat while another wraps around her neck, stealing her breath and her voice. It lasts for mere moments, but I know it is eternity to her. Her eyes bulge, brimming with panic and desperation.

But the Goddess does not allow her Sisters to judge the living. We serve as Her shepherds. Her secret-keepers. Her executioners when the need arises. The weight of judgment, however, is Hers. And Hers alone.

"You will be silent and know your place." I pull my hood back to reveal my face.

She blanches before sinking to her knees in the dirt where she belongs. Once there, the tendrils of darkness and fog return to the fabric of my cloak. My gaze rakes across the crowd, and they all see the moons upon my brow: a full moon flanked by a waxing and waning crescent on either side. Every Sister, when she first joins our family, is marked. Those moon sigils are blacker than the deepest abyss of the afterlife, but mine is silver, and I hear the word skim across the gathered throng: *Saudara!*

Indeed.

I am the Saudara. I am the Sister who is above all other Sisters of the Moon. The one who is Handmaiden to the Goddess of Death.

I call out to the crowd. "I have come seeking a new Sister. Go if you wish or stay here and bear witness to her choice. Few are given the opportunity to witness this decision, and fewer still are ever offered it."

Some in the crowd drift away, disturbed by my presence. The others remain, morbid curiosity rooting them where they stand. They can stay or go; I am indifferent so long as they are respectful. I turn my gaze back to the slip of a girl trembling on the edge of life and death. Is the girl a thief? Yes, and I care not. She looks at me—large, dark eyes filled with resignation.

The Magistrate blocks my way, sputtering with consternation. His face has turned an angry, blotchy red. I see temerity in his eyes and hold his gaze. I will not tolerate another challenge. The spark of audacity quails like a whipped dog. He ducks his head and steps aside, glancing at the silken sow still trembling on the ground. One of my sentinels glides forward, taking a discreet position behind him. Sweat dots his brow. He can feel the hand of Death poised behind him.

Wood creaks as I ascend the stairs. The girl's eyes follow me. She doesn't look away, and I know I have chosen rightly. The question now is what she will choose. The executioner remains at his station, his head lowered. Wise man.

"Leave us for now," I tell him. "I will summon you, should your services still be needed."

"Your will, Saudara." He offers a respectful bow before jumping from the platform. There is a muffled thud as his boots find the ground below.

"Why you sendin' him away? Thought you was here to take my soul." The girl's voice is a sorrow-filled whisper.

"Perhaps. Perhaps not. Your soul called to mine, child, and I am here to give you a choice. One that is offered to very few."

"What choice?"

Suspicion and disbelief cloud her face. She lives in a world where obedience is the only choice for someone in her station. I have lived her life. A life where choices offer hope, and hope brings nothing but pain and sorrow. There is a low murmur in the crowd, like the buzz of a gnat in my ear. I ignore it. For now.

"You can choose to free yourself of the noose. To take my hand and become one of my Sisters." I gesture openly, back towards my two guards, who remain silent but as alert as hunting falcons. "You can dedicate the remainder of your days to She Who Is The Darkness and serve Her. But know this: it is not an easy life. The Goddess will demand much from you. More than you can imagine. Yet serving Her is not a command. It must be your choice. If you would prefer the rope, I will not interfere, and I will carry your soul to the Goddess's embrace."

Her brow furrows. "Got no reason to want me. You're a queen...I ain't nothin'." Her voice is small.

"I am a servant."

"Don't no one obey a servant."

I am silent. Her observation is astute. I am a servant, all the Sisters are, but we are not slaves. We are the instruments of She Who Is The Darkness. We shepherd the dying to Her embrace. We conduct the death rites and honor the bones of the ancestors. We are the sharp-tipped blade of death when She commands it—and if you have been marked by the Goddess, a Sister of the Moon *will* find you. And you *will* die. No one is beyond our reach, and we walk with impunity among kings and beggars.

"You look at me, child, and you see the silver moons upon my brow. You see the Saudara: Handmaiden to the Goddess of Death. Yet, above all, you see power because you feel weak. And because you see only the power, you do not understand why some would prefer the Goddess' kiss and not Her notice." I pause. "Power is a terrible burden, and our Goddess can be an unforgiving mistress. I can only do what

She allows—or commands. I am Her servant, and I obey, but it is still possible to serve and be powerful."

I watch as her eyes travel from my face, across my cloak, and to the rings on my fingers. My cloak is woven from the darkness of the afterlife, but to mortal eyes it is richly dyed silk.

She shakes her head. "Got no kin, so I ain't worth nothing. Ain't no one sponsorin' me to some fancy family."

I hear the self-loathing in her voice. She sees herself as an urchin, worthless to those with wealth or power. I understand this more than she knows. "I believed, once, that I was nothing. When the Goddess claimed me, at last I had purpose, a family."

"Then you was lucky. I ain't nobody."

She is so very wrong.

A thin dagger appears in my hand and the girl shudders, waiting for the blade's sting, thinking that I believe her and have judged her lacking. Instead, I cut the bonds around her hands. But I leave the noose around her throat. That she must remove on her own. Free herself from this life so she may embrace a new one. I step back, but she remains still, puzzlement radiating from her.

There is another agitated stir within the crowd. I know they are confused by what they're seeing. They came here to see the girl die. Some are disappointed, some are angry. And despite what I have told them, many whisper to each other about why I am here, talking with a girl who is less than nothing to them. They do not understand that this decision cannot be dictated or rushed. She Who Is The Darkness teaches patience, but I find mine is running thin and I weary of them clucking like hens.

I am about to reprimand them, have my guards drive them away, when a voice shrills, "She is worthless! She steals!"

Ah, the silken sow has once again found her voice and lost her wits. A raging blackness fills me, but as much as I wish to send this fool to the Goddess, it is not her time. Not today. I turn and assess her, my eyes falling again on the ropes of pearls draped over her ample bosom. There is enough wealth there to buy a hundred winter cloaks or more.

Within my mind, I hear the Goddess whisper: *All things in good time.* I smile, and there must be something in it, for the silken sow's son falls to his knees weeping. And he is not the only one.

"Yes, she steals. She steals out of need, out of desperation. But why do you?" My voice rolls over the remaining throng, and I know they all hear me. Their hushed chatter stops.

Her eyes pop. "What? Why do I—? How *dare* you—"

"How dare I?"

I pull darkness and shadow close around me, a thundercloud poised to strike, and a gasp ripples through the mob. Frost appears on the wood around my feet. It scuttles down the timbers seeking the ground and then ripples outward, blanketing the square in frozen diamond dust. Foggy puffs of breath hang in the chill.

"I am the Saudara, and I see much, woman. And I will *tell* you why you steal. For greed. For gluttony. If the Magistrate goes to your mercantile now, what will he find there, tucked under your scales? Enough extra weights to cheat your customers out of a silver or two when they buy barley or corn-flour? You are more a thief than this child."

The murmur in the crowd turns angry. My guard shadowing the Magistrate shoves him forward, and he stumbles. "Do your duty," she orders.

"You!" He points at a sheriff stationed near the gallows stairs. "Go to Madame's mercantile and check."

He looks up at me, his eyes shrewd and calculating. I know that he hopes the sheriff will find nothing, and then he can arrest me for false accusations. That would delight him, but it will not happen, for I speak the truth. The silken sow has made her choices, and she will be judged for them. If her fate is the gallows, I will not spare her.

I do not waste another glance on that foolish woman or the irate crowd now focused on her. My guards will keep the peace. The frost abates, leaving fresh dew in its wake.

There is a phantom smile in the waif's eyes. She holds my gaze for a moment as she starts to tug at the noose—a small step towards a new life, even if she doesn't realize it yet. Then uncertainty stutters in her eyes, and she dips her head. An unruly lock of hair falls across her face. She still thinks herself unworthy, but we are more alike than she knows.

"You and I, we are not so different. I was not much older than you when a Sister found me. I remember the ropes, how they chafed my wrists raw as I waited to burn."

Her mouth drops open as her head snaps back up. The pyre is reserved for murderers, and she knows that.

"You look shocked, child. Yes, I killed a man. A man who believed it was his right to touch me however he liked, no matter my objections. He behaved like a pig and so he died like a pig. Slaughtered. Never once have I mourned him. Never once have I regretted my actions."

"He tried to take you. Like you was a dog."

"Aye, child. He meant to have me whether or not I wanted him."

"And didn't no one care what he'd done, did they? Didn't no one care that you didn't want him back. That you was scared."

"No. No, they did not."

An unexpected wave of anger washes through me. It has been a long time since I thought about that day. It was decades ago but the fear, the anger, it slices as much now as it did then.

A small noise makes me glance at her. The trembling lip, the eyes full of tears. She knows the fear I spoke of exactly, intimately, and I make a silent prayer to the Goddess that whoever had touched her would meet a well-deserved end.

I brush aside those thoughts. While the Goddess is patient, the choice must be made.

"It is time for you to decide—just as I decided all those years ago. Will you become a Sister? Serve She Who Is The Darkness for the remainder of your days and in exchange be pardoned for your crimes? Or do you choose to meet your end here and now, and awake in the Goddess' arms for her judgment? Do not make your choice lightly, for serving is no easy task. The Goddess can be a hard mistress."

Again, she tugs at the rope around her neck, dirty fingers loosening its grip even more. The gathered crowd stills, silence consuming them as if they understand the import of this moment, the balance of life and death that rests on no more than a mote of dust. She hesitates one moment longer before she grips the rope. Her hands tremble as she pulls the noose over her head. She stares at it with loathing, and then flings it to the ground. Tears stream down her cheeks as she reaches out to take my hand.

"What happens now?"

"Now you will receive your sigil, and then you will meet your new Sisters."

"Will it hurt?"

I do not lie to her. "Yes, but it will pass. What is your name, child?"

"Katin."

I turn, my hand on her shoulder, to face the crowd. My voice carries, sharp and clear, across the square. "Katin has made her choice. She will serve She Who Is The Darkness. Her crimes have been forgiven and from this moment on, she is reborn into a new life as a Sister of the Moon."

With a gentle hand, I turn the girl towards me. "For the rest of your days, you will pledge your life to serve She Who Is The Darkness. You will shepherd the dying towards Her embrace. You will tend the bones of the departed. At her command, you will deliver death to Emperors and to beggars, to shoemakers and to priests. To the guilty and the innocent. And you will obey Her without question. It is often a heavy burden to bear—will you accept its weight?"

"If She be willin' to take me, yes."

There it is. The spark in her eye that I knew lay within.

I put my hands on her cheeks as a tiny whimper escapes her. Even after all these years, I remember what it was like when the Sister took my pledge, how her eyes burned into me. There was no secret in my heart she could not see. I had never felt so naked under one person's gaze.

I place one hand on the back of Katin's head and press the other to her forehead. This is the moment where her life changes forever. She can sense the glacial touch of the Goddess and starts to shake. I know she feels this because I have endured, as has every Sister, the Goddess' icy embrace. It settles on her, gentle at first, draping over her shoulders like soft snow. Then her skin begins to prickle with a cold so deep it burns into her lungs, her bones, her very soul. A raging coldness so profound her entire being may shatter at the slightest sound.

I release her and the cold withdraws, allowing warmth to return. Katin reaches up and pauses, looking at her hands in wonder. Her fingernails are now painted with frost and will remain that way forever. She traces her fingers across the new adornment on her brow. I smile at the familiar gesture.

"Come," I say. "Let us begin our journey."

Our descent from the platform is punctuated by the return of the sheriff. His heaving chest and red face say he wasted no time on his quest. He hurries to the Magistrate and whispers in his ear. Apoplectic red rises in the Magistrate's face as we all wait for his pronouncement.

"Arrest Madame," he orders.

My Sisters step back as the silken sow sputters and protests, but her words are thin and lack the conviction of one who has been falsely accused. Two sheriffs take her by the arms and escort her forward, but they only make a few steps before young Katin stands in their way. The sow huffs in horror as she grasps the ropes of luminous pearls and removes them. For a moment she lets the jewels—small, pearlescent moons—roll between her fingers. The Magistrate is about to protest, but I point, and he falls silent. Katin offers the strands to the sow's son, and the reedy man's hands shake so hard he nearly drops them.

"She won't be needin' those no more. Give 'em to the people she cheated."

I know I've chosen wisely.

A SUBTRACTION

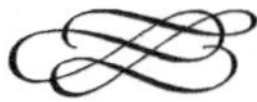

DAVID LEE

"Parting is all we know of heaven and all we need to know of hell."
~Emily Dickinson

I knew why he was leaving.

My brain understood completely and I approved. Better that he get out now, while he was young and had his faculties. He could still make decisions, which might not be the case in a few months. Control would slip away, unnoticed, if he waited too long.

But watching him go was brutal for me.

I don't make friends easily. It's hard for me to let people in. I'm a private person. I'm also an old curmudgeon who's been around the block more than a few times. My view of human beings is not what you'd call "complimentary."

Rip had weaseled his way into my life. Seven or so years ago, a co-worker had asked if I would take her cousin on as an intern. My initial thought was *hell, no,* but I had to work with this woman and wasn't anxious to get on her bad side. Surrendering to the inevitable, but not liking it one little bit, I responded, "Tell me about him."

"His name is Ryan. Ryan Ripley. He's twenty-five years old and just about finished with the master's program at Cal State. All he has left is like six hundred school-site hours. He wants to be a guidance counselor, which is why I thought of you, Will. You two would get along famously. Rip is funny, energetic, reliable, and more than competent. Give him a try. I promise he'll lighten your workload considerably."

Fat chance, I thought. The last intern I'd given a try could have written a book—a book of excuses. She was late almost every day. Her car. Her mom. Her teeth. Then there were the full-day absences. Her aunt's surgery. Final exams. The bachelorette party in Vegas. "I'm so sorry, Will." "You understand, don't you?" "I know I told you I'd take care of those classroom presentations, but this opportunity comes along very rarely. I'll make it up to you. By the way, would you complete this evaluation form for me?"

I wasn't anxious to go there again. Having an intern was *work.* Instead of making my life easier, interns made it harder. You had to plan. You had to supervise. You had to teach. Ultimately, you had to let them spread their wings—but any messes were your fault. Mistakes were your responsibility. You had to explain the fuck-ups to administration. Like the time a few years ago when that former Marine, back from two tours in Afghanistan and then in graduate school to try his hand at counseling, had told Janice, a fragile senior who'd survived a difficult childhood (her father was an abusive SOB), that life was a bitch and she had to toughen up if she wanted to make it in this world. "Stop your whining," he'd told her. That night Janice had gone home and swallowed an entire bottle of her mother's medication. Paramedics managed to save her, barely, but she never came back to school. Neither did Mr. Marine. I saw to that after the principal reamed my ass.

But Rip was just what my co-worker had advertised. He came in at the start of the second semester to discuss his schedule and learn what his duties would be. I was immediately impressed. The guy was on time, dressed nicely but not over the top, and made excellent eye contact when he spoke. (I think what caught my attention that first day was the fact that he seemed *unafraid.* But not in a cocky way.) He wanted to learn, he told me, and would follow my directions. He would ask when he wasn't sure about something. He would take the job seriously. "Okay," I told him. "Three days a week, eight hours a day. You want to be a counselor? You do what I do." There was no turning back. For either of us.

* * *

I *WORKED* THAT POOR KID.

He was my indentured servant. If I told him to do this, he did this. If I told him to go there, he went there. Each morning, when he arrived at 8:00 AM sharp, Rip would find his agenda for the day. Before he left at 3:00 PM, we'd sit down and review the items on the list. We'd debrief. He told me what he saw, what he heard, what he did. I asked him questions and made a point of waiting for him to respond. I listened and so did he. He was good. Amazingly so.

Within three weeks, Rip was running (not simply observing) group counseling sessions with some of our expelled students. He had a natural affinity for the work. The kids could sense that he cared about them, that they mattered. Because their issues were important to them, they were important to him as well. In no time, word got out that the new guy, Mr. Ripley, was *dope*.

He made friends quickly. Staff members took to him right off. Rip's easy smile opened a lot of doors. Even the cynical old vets (the ones who always sat in the back at faculty meetings with their newspapers defiantly open) took a liking to this respectful young buck who actually did what he said he would do. I gave him more and more responsibilities. By the middle of the semester, the teacher/student role had disappeared. Rip and I were equals. The school now had two counselors for the price of one. More importantly, the talented Mr. Ripley and I became buddies. I'll admit it; he won me over. I had not been looking to make friends. But Rip had a way about him. It's like he invited you to let down the walls. It was safe to let him in.

That summer, Rip tied the knot with his long-time love, Fiona. My wife and I were invited but had to send our regrets. Some activity was going on with our kids that made it impossible to attend. We sent a gift. Rip and I lost touch, as he accepted a teaching job in another district. It wasn't until two years later that I rang him up, letting him know some counseling positions were being flown. We—the majority of the faculty and staff—wanted him to come back. And the gods must have been smiling, because he joined the guidance department when school started up again in September.

Now working under the same roof, struggling to serve students, teachers, and parents, Rip became my right-hand man. We faced the same problems and found ways to solve them—or at least finesse our way around them. Sometimes we socialized after work. My wife and I visited his home, and he and Fiona came to ours. My kids started referring to Rip as the "son I never had" (although I *had* three sons). We teased each other mercilessly. I was too fat and needed to get to the gym. On top of that, I was ancient. He was wet behind the ears and had no appreciation for things like newspapers, snail mail, and books that contained words. What can I say? We clicked. When Fiona and Rip's baby girl was born, they asked us to be her godparents.

Around that time, the first symptoms started to appear.

* * *

"I'M HAVING TROUBLE SWALLOWING," he told me one day. "It's been going on for a while now; I suppose I should see a doctor."

"But you never get sick," I responded. "You're a stud, remember? What is it you say? 'Pain is weakness leaving the body.'"

"True. I can't tell you the last time I got sick. But this swallowing thing is annoying. Fiona wants me to go to Kaiser after work today."

The following morning, he gave me the blow-by-blow. "Fucking doctors. I had to wait 80 minutes to get in even though I *made an appointment*. Anyway, the guy did the usual stuff. Checked my heart and ears; looked down my throat; thumped my back and told me to breathe deeply. What surprised me was the checklist of questions he asked. He wanted to know if I exercised regularly, what my family history was, whether or not I was experiencing any spasms or tremors. He had me walk for him and checked my reflexes not once but twice. Then he wanted to know if I was having any 'emotional'

30

difficulties. Go figure. Of course, I didn't leave with a prescription for amoxicillin. That's too easy. He wants to run some tests. When I asked him what he *thought* might be the problem, he just mumbled something about 'wanting to make sure.' I don't know, Will. Maybe I won't go back. I'm certain it's nothing and I wince every time I have to fork over a $30 co-pay. Fucking doctors."

I won't—can't—give you all the details. They're too painful to recall. Rip went in for the tests.

There was blood work and his breathing was checked. Later they did a cervical spine CT and something called "electromyography" (to see if the nerves were working properly). Eventually, a new doctor, a specialist, ordered a head CT, MRI, and spinal tap.

You could see that Rip was getting worse. He was not a clumsy man, but he started acting clumsily. His reflexes weren't the same; he dropped things. The swallowing trouble continued and sometimes he would twitch. The look in his eyes went from annoyance to casual concern to overwhelming fear. My calm, cool, and collected friend was an emotional mess. And watching all this made me one, too.

It turns out the doctor suspected, way back when, that Rip had "amyotrophic lateral sclerosis" or Lou Gehrig's disease. The prognosis was that he would be dead within three years, give or take. Gradually he would lose his ability to walk, hold his head up, eat, or even breathe on his own.

He was thirty-one years old.

* * *

One afternoon, long after the school day had ended, we talked in my office.

"You have to help me, Will. I can't let this thing drag on. It's not fair to Fiona."

"What are you talking about?"

"I want to go out on my own terms. I don't want breathing devices or wheelchairs or voice enhancers. I refuse to be remembered as the guy who prolonged his family's hell by futilely fighting a deadly disease. That's not who I am."

I didn't know what to say.

Religion is something I gave up long ago. To me, it's all a bunch of hooey. If there's a God, and he's up there watching over us, surely he's focused on the big picture. What I do, day in and day out, is probably of little concern to him. No doubt Rip's illness was the same deal . "I've got bigger fish to fry—wars and such," God would say.

Nevertheless, I started to pray.

Belatedly. Reluctantly. Furiously. Angrily. Pleadingly.

"If you're really that benevolent being who loves us, his greatest creation, then prove it. Don't do this to Rip. He's young and good and he's got a family, for Christ's sake. Taking him makes no sense. The world will be a decidedly *worse* place without him. And Fiona will hate you and raise a daughter who hates you. I will hate you and I will make it my mission in life to tell everybody how fucked up you are. Please. Don't do this. Amen."

Mr. "Bigger-Fish-to-Fry" blew me off. Rip steadily declined. He asked me again to help him.

* * *

I SAID before that watching him go was brutal for me. What I didn't say was that I *helped* him go. In the end, regardless of my feelings about the decision, it was Rip's to make. And he was my friend. I couldn't refuse.

Neither could Fiona. She fought him. In the end, she knew her husband would not be swayed. But she couldn't watch. On a Tuesday afternoon she kissed him, said goodbye, and left with their daughter. When Fiona returned to her home five hours later, I met her at the door. She read the look on my face and knew. Rip was gone.

* * *

"YOU READY, BOSS?"

"No, Rip, I'm not ready. Is there anything I can say that will change your mind?"

"It's *time*, my friend. This is for the best. Just hang with me. The muscle relaxants will do the trick. Before you know it, I'll be a ghost—haunting your ass when you least expect it." His smile faded and he grew serious. "Thank you, Will. For being here with me. Don't be troubled. I'll see you again."

The writer Augusten Burroughs said that death, when it comes, "adds nothing to the room, not a light or a spark or a sound…You know it arrives because there is suddenly a subtraction. You will feel it before you know it."

I *felt* it. An emptiness. An absence. A diminution.

Despite my abject sadness, life went on. Fiona and the baby moved back to Chicago, where her parents and siblings surrounded her with love. We talked on the phone occasionally and exchanged Christmas cards, but the years and the distance took their toll and we lost track of each other. I heard that she remarried—an old high school beau—a decade after Rip's death.

I stayed on, counseling high school knuckleheads, for a few more years. I couldn't eat in the back room where Rip and I ate our lunches; they were too excruciating, the memories. I never took on another intern. I couldn't. I just didn't have it in me.

Burroughs also wrote, "Something new is created when a person you love dies. Because they are not the only ones who die: you die, too. The person you were when you were with them is gone just as surely as they are. This is what you should know about losing somebody you love. They do not travel alone. You go with them."

I suppose he is right. I find some comfort in knowing a part of me is still with Rip. We remain friends, together even in death.

ONLY GOD CAN TELL

KAYTALIN PLATT

Paul sat just before Mama's bedroom door as Papa drove the last screw of a metal plate into the foot of it. The steel plate had a hatch door to pass things through and a padlock to keep Paul from peering inside.

When Papa finished, he packed his tools and wordlessly walked away. The burnt smell of whiskey drifted with him.

Tick. Tick. Tick. The constant, predictable ticking of the hall grandfather clock filled Paul's ears.

His eyes locked on the thin crack between the bottom of the door and the brown carpeted floor, where warm amber light glowed from the other side. The light blinked, disturbed by a passing figure.

"Pauly," Mama said, her voice weak and throaty, muffled by the door. "Pauly, are you there?"

Paul swallowed.

Papa had said not to speak to Mama.

She was being punished.

And if he spoke to her, he'd be punished too.

"Pauly, help me. Help me get out."

Paul frowned. He drew his knees up to his chest and covered his ears.

The door rattled. It sounded like kettle drums. Each time Mama's fist struck the door, the wood shook, threatening to snap off the hinges.

Paul closed his eyes.

* * *

EVERY DAY, Papa added a new lock to the door. They varied in type. Some were old and rusted. Others, newly bought.

Papa carried a wad of keys on his belt, held to one of the threadbare belt loops with a scraped and faded red carabiner.

Paul didn't know why he carried them all. Once Papa attached a lock, he never removed it.

* * *

"PAULY," Mama called from behind the door as he passed on his way to dinner. "Pauly, please. I'm so thirsty."

Papa had given her water in a bowl that morning. He'd brought it home from church. He'd said it was blessed and would make her feel better.

Paul wished Papa would drink some of the water. He wished it would make *him* better.

Paul tiptoed by, not wanting her to hear him, and not wanting Papa to punish him.

* * *

PAUL SAT OUTSIDE THE DOOR.

It had been two weeks since he'd seen Mama and he missed her. He didn't get breakfast or lunch. Papa left early in the morning, and he didn't care about those things like Mama did.

Papa was working late, and there wasn't any dinner, either.

Dark shadows clung in the hall around Paul, the only light coming

36

from beneath Mama's door. It occasionally broke with her shadow passing on the other side, a black sweep of a shape.

"Mama," Paul finally said.

The shadow stopped.

"Pauly?"

"Mama, is it true?"

"Pauly, please. Call someone. Get help."

"Is it true, Mama?"

"Is *what* true?"

"Papa said you did something bad. He said you went into the wood at night and fornicated with the devil."

"Pauly... your father's a drunk."

Paul pursed his lips together until they hurt.

"Please, call Aunt Brenda."

"I can't."

"Why?"

"The phones don't work no more." Paul stiffened. A flash of yellow drifted across the walls as Papa's truck pulled in front of the living room windows.

Paul jumped up from where he sat.

"Pauly, please don't leave me! Please get me out of here!"

He ran to his bedroom and slammed the door shut.

* * *

ONE NIGHT, men and women from church gathered in their home. The women wore long-sleeved dresses in colors of pastel pinks and blues, their long hair puffed and bunned at the top of their heads.

They held hands with Papa and walked down the hall to Mama's room. They prayed loudly, speaking in foreign tongues and trembling.

The wind wailed outside, as if it begged them to stop.

Their voices multiplied, their chanting filling Paul with dread.

* * *

THE SCHOOL BUS barreled down the dirt road to the next house, leaving Paul in a cloud of dust. He lifted his hooded, weary eyes towards the farmhouse.

Old, abandoned cars and trucks of various models and years lined their drive. Each of them probably had one very small but expensive thing wrong with it—too expensive to fix—and as such, they left the whole car to rot. The yard itself was a grave of broken machinery, vehicle parts, and tractor equipment. Tall brown grass grew up between them, and weeds strangled a barbed-wire fence surrounding an empty field.

Papa had sold the cows weeks ago to pay for the water he'd brought home from church.

White, peeling paint covered the shiplap walls of Paul's home and front porch. Weathered, gray boards lined Mama's windows, leaving just enough cracks that he knew she could see him coming home. Even still, he tried to be quiet, tried to pretend like he wasn't there so she wouldn't talk to him.

He dared not even glance at her window as he passed it.

The front door wasn't locked.

It never was.

Paul found it odd that Mama's door had so many locks on it, but the front one stayed open. Papa thought the sign hanging on the front door was enough protection: *Nothing in here worth dying for.*

He had to pass Mama's room to get to his. The edges of her door were blackened, as if a fire burned inside and the smoke wafted out to stain the wood.

The locks were rustier than the last time he saw them, but he suspected it was from all the holy water Papa threw on the door each night.

Paul had asked how much longer before Mama was cured of the evil inside her, but Papa said that only God could tell.

Paul had asked God, but God wasn't much of a talker.

* * *

PAUL SAT ALONE at the dinner table with only a single orange lamp dangling overhead to light the kitchen. He ate cereal. He'd asked his father to buy a box since Mama wasn't around to make him breakfast. He ate cereal for breakfast and dinner, since Mama wasn't around to cook dinner either, and Papa always ate something at the bar before heading home.

The house was dark.

Quiet.

Mama had stopped banging on the door. She'd stopped begging him to help her.

She'd been so quiet lately. He tried to remember the last time he'd seen Papa pass food through the door.

* * *

PAPA WAS LATE COMING HOME. Sometimes he had too much to drink at the bar and either fell asleep in his truck or went home with someone else. He'd done that often, even before Mama went into the wood and fornicated with the devil. He'd come home early the next morning, disheveled and smelling of someone else's perfume. Mama would wash the lipstick off his shirt like any other stain—without a word.

Paul used a stool to reach the kitchen sink and wash his bowl so he'd have something to eat out of the next morning.

At night, Paul didn't like the window in front of the sink. Sometimes it was like someone watched him from the other side, so Paul didn't lift his eyes from the soapy water. Not even after he washed his bowl and dried it. He didn't lift his eyes until he was off the stepstool and turning towards the hall.

A brighter-than-usual beam of amber light stretched across the floor in front of Mama's door. The metal latch Papa used to pass food through was open. The lock sat in the center of the light.

Paul froze.

Had Papa forgotten to lock it? If Paul didn't lock it back, Papa would think he tried to talk to Mama and would punish him.

Paul crept down the dark hall towards the door.

A thin, pale hand shot out of the hole, stretched across the brown, matted carpet, fingers bent into claws. Mama's long nails sunk into the carpet. The hand didn't move. It rested, fingers deep in the wool, poised as if to rip the carpet out or her way through.

Mama had always been a thin woman with bony elbows and bony hands. The sharp contrast of the light beneath her door and the dark hall made the already pointed angles of her hand more gnarled and sharp. The tips of her fingers were blackened, like they'd been charred or dipped in ink.

Paul thought she might have injured them from trying to claw her way out of the room.

"Pauly…"

Paul stiffened. He got down on his knees as the hand withdrew back into the room. He pressed his cheek to the carpet and peered through the hole in the door.

He saw part of Mama's face. Just her cheek and eye and part of her forehead. Deep, dark circles hung under her eyes. Her skin was paler than pale. Her cheeks were more hollow than usual.

"Pauly," she said, tears filling her eyes. "Pauly, please. Go out into the shed. Get the bolt cutters. Cut the locks. Let me out. We'll go down the road to Mr. Richards and get help."

"Mama…"

"Please, Pauly. I'm gonna die in here if you don't help me."

Paul's eyes scanned the blackened door, coming to rest on the lock lying next to his head. The metal had rusted to the point that it snapped.

Papa hadn't left it open by accident.

"Papa said he'd punish me…"

"Papa can't punish you if you aren't here. Let's go. Please. Please, Pauly, I don't want to die…" Mama began to sob. He'd seen her cry before, but nothing like this. Tears fell in rivers from her blood-shot eyes. She wailed and thrashed and screamed. She sounded less like his mother and more like a strangled fox.

No, like a *thousand* strangled foxes. Paul didn't want Mama to die.

"Okay," he said. "I'll get the bolt cutters. Hold on."

* * *

PAUL DIDN'T LIKE GOING out at night.

He stood hesitantly at the open front door, staring across the moonlit yard at the gray, weathered, tilting shed.

Paul hated going out at night for the same reason he didn't like looking out the kitchen window. There was something out here. Something watching.

Something he saw on nights when he was forced out of his home for some useless chore, like taking out the garbage.

He'd see it move out of the corner of his eye. A white, tall, four-legged shape, all gangly and faceless. It would poke its head out from behind one of the many cars littering their yard and watch him.

Paul looked for the White Thing before he dashed across the front yard to the shed.

The shed stood in a thicket of tall grass and rogue shrubs. Papa stored rarely used tools in it, and as such, the door was jammed closed by dried mud and tall grass. Paul was small and thin, though. He only had to pry the door open a little to wedge himself into the dank space.

He used a small keychain flashlight to look for the bolt cutters. The shed floor was littered with random nuts and bolts and rusted wrenches. Forgotten toolboxes lay open, their contents half strewn across the floor. Ancient farm equipment—not used since the invention of the modern tractor—hung on hooks along the wall. Sickles and hand saws and other rusted pieces of machinery dangled from the ceiling. At the back of the shed, on an old wooden work bench, lay a pair of bright red bolt cutters.

Paul grabbed them and headed back to the house. He crossed the yard in a dash, keeping his head low and ignoring the blur of white movement out of the corner of his eye.

When he got back inside the house, he closed the front door and locked it.

* * *

Paul dragged the stepstool from the kitchen into the hall. Even with it, he had to stand on his tiptoes to reach. He stretched and stretched, struggling with what little strength his thin arms could muster. He had to cut the locks.

But they were rusted and snapped like brittle plastic.

One-by-one, Paul worked his way down the door until a flash of light beamed across the hall.

Papa was home.

* * *

"Hurry, Pauly!"

Papa's heavy steel-toed boots clanked against the front porch steps.

Paul's heart thundered in his chest, beating so hard and fast that his vision blurred around the edges. He tried to move faster. Even if they were rusted and brittle and snapped like dry rotted ropes, there were so many.

Papa's boots clonked against the porch and to the front door. The brass handle jiggled, but the door didn't swing open.

Paul had locked it to keep the White Thing out and, out of all the keys on Papa's belt, he was sure there wasn't a key for that lock.

Hope swelled in his chest, and he went to work on the last few locks.

Papa beat at the door with his meaty fists.

"Paul! Open this goddamn door!"

BANG BANG BANG!

"Paul! Open the goddamn door or I swear—"

Louder, harsher bangs filled Paul's ears. This wasn't the heavy rapping of fists. This was the sound of a two-hundred-and-fifty-pound body slamming into aged pine.

One thump, hard enough to shake the house.

A second thump.

Paul's hands trembled as he went for the last lock.

On the third thump, the front door splintered off the hinges.

Flakes of paint and wood clattered into the hall from the living room. Paul's hands slipped off the bolt cutters. They thumped into the brown carpet.

Papa rounded the corner, red-faced and breathing heavy. His face was always red, usually from drink, but this time it was almost purple.

"What are you doin'?!"

Papa's gaze scanned the hall and found the bright light spilling out from beneath Mama's door. His eyes widened.

The red in his face drained, like all the blood had been sucked from his body to pool at his feet. He staggered into the wall and stumbled over the stepstool, grabbing hold of the door handle to Mama's room.

He pulled.

Braced his foot against the wall.

But Mama pulled too.

The door opened a crack.

Papa growled and pulled harder.

"Paul! Get my water. Get my water from beside the couch!"

Paul didn't move.

Papa strained. The veins on the side of his head bulged. His arms quivered. "Paul! The wat—"

The knob slipped out of his hand and the door flew open, snapping the last lock at the bottom.

Papa backed into the wall opposite the door. He kept backing, even if he couldn't go anywhere else, as if he hoped the wall would swallow him up.

Paul took a step to the right and peeked into Mama's room. She stood just inside the open doorway, wearing the same silk nightgown she'd worn the night Papa had locked her up.

Her arms and legs were skeletal. Her face gaunt—hollow—with sunken dark circles around her eyes. Everything on her had shriveled except her belly.

Her belly bulged.

Mama had not had such a belly the last time Paul saw her. She'd been thin when she'd headed off into the wood that fateful night.

She'd been thin when Papa dragged her back home, half naked and caked in mud, and locked her in the room.

Paul couldn't stop looking at the bulge of her belly, or the way it rippled beneath the silk gown like water.

The inside of Mama's room had blackened and decayed, like she'd set a fire that had burned itself out.

"Our Father," Papa began, slipping along the wall. "Which art in Heaven! Hallowed be thy name!"

"Thy kingdom come! Thy will be done!" Mama prayed with him. "On Earth as it is in Heaven!"

Papa fell along the wall, stumbled into the living room, and grabbed for the mason jar of holy water by the couch.

His hands trembled as he fumbled with the aluminum lid, twisting it open while Mama waited patiently and finished his prayer. "Give us this day, our daily bread, and forgive us our trespasses, as we forgive those who trespass against us. Lead us not into temptation..."

The lid flipped off the mason jar and rolled across the carpet to Mama's feet. She looked down. "But deliver us from evil."

Papa sloshed the holy water on Mama.

It splashed across her, soaking her hair and gown until the white silk clung to her skin.

In church, they talked about how evil spirits leave the bodies of the possessed. How they bent to the power of God's word and His will.

But Mama only laughed.

She laughed and laughed and laughed.

Paul caught movement out of the corner of his eye and made the mistake of looking into the kitchen, out the window just over the sink.

While Mama laughed at Papa, Paul found the pale, blank face of the White Thing. He'd never looked at one dead-on before. An eyeless sheet of pasty skin pulled over a skull stared back at him.

All the bones and joints in Paul's body locked up. Warmth flooded his pants and ran down his leg into his shoe. He wanted to look away, wanted to scream, but his throat closed around every word and breath.

The White Thing's mouth curved into a gaping wide smile with rows of jagged teeth. A long tongue swept over them, dancing across each point as if counting them one-by-one, back and forth and back and forth and...

Paul tore his gaze away and looked back at Mama. Her mouth was as wide as the White Thing's outside, with rows of shark-like teeth and a tongue sweeping across them.

Paul sobbed. "Mama. Mama... Mama! Please!"

Where was she? Where was the woman who made him pancakes? Who held him when he was sad? Who cleaned his scrapes and sang him songs and stood up to Papa when he was scared? Where was Mama to protect him now? Paul collapsed into the puddle of urine at his feet and brought his knees to his chest.

Mama's jaw popped and cracked and worked its way further from her cheeks, as if she were a snake preparing to gobble them down whole—Papa first.

Papa screamed.

He called to God.

Begged for His salvation.

But Paul had learned over his short years that God wasn't much of a talker.

And, as it turns out, He wasn't much of a doer either.

BITTER FRUIT

S.E. SOLDWEDEL

Below the cloud tops, Jack knows that Nairobi is close enough that the descent should begin any moment. The screen at his seat depicting the flight path confirms as much. He could have taken a suborbital flight directly to Harmon's private landing pad, but going commercial provided an excuse to see Ramya.

Still smarting from the ambush he'd endured during the television interview, it surprised him to get her note after the broadcast. It had prompted her to reach out. An olive branch from estranged daughter to estranged father. His chagrin over his fractured relationship with Ramya is just one of myriad shares of regret. He could buy all the seats on the plane for them, and they would barely accommodate a fraction of the total. At any inkling of regret, Sabine bubbles up too; she's never far from the surface of his consciousness. She comes and goes like a cat, both in real life and in his mind. He wonders whether she'll be home when he returns.

The pilot's voice comes over the comm. He starts with French despite arriving at an anglophone port. Leaving from Saint-Exupery with a francophone crew is apparently reason enough for the *liberté*. It's no bother; Jack's fluent, but he doesn't care anyway. The chatter, in any language, is as superfluous as the seatbelt. If the plane is going to crash, it's going to crash. What's the difference whether he buckles up or puts his head between his legs to kiss his ass goodbye.

The plane descends. His stomach lurches. He's unaccustomed to conventional air travel. It's devoid of suborbital's g-forces, but the absence of extremity is what makes this trip jarring. The turbulence and the sudden lurches are both quaint and tiresome at once. The juddering befits his disquiet, though. He hasn't seen Ramya in nearly a decade, at her behest. She was a teenager then. He's made the overtures, and she's always rebuffed him.

Until now. The olive branch.

* * *

THE PLANE TAXIS to the jetway and there's no fuss to debark. It's just him and a handful of others: an assortment of those well-heeled enough for a semi-private conventional plane but not suborbital, and those wealthy passengers who, like Jack, chose pragmatic over flashy. There's something to be said for hours of captivity. It induces reflection that a 20-minute or hour-long globe hop does not.

The airport is still named after Jomo Kenyatta despite that the family name was long ago sullied by revelations of generational corruption. Jack sympathizes, although his own scandal isn't hidden money from raided public coffers. His plague is what Fatimah Al-Wadi pressed him about on the telly. What elicited Ramya's communiqué. What's been spilling barrels of ink in the British press, which loves to hound expatriate Scots: Jack and Harmon, both. Protégé and mentor.

He approaches the exit. As with the entire journey, his holographic facial camouflage disguises him from prying eyes. He could have been sitting next to someone he knows, but no one with sufficient means wears their real face in public unless they want to be seen. Case in point: Ramya. He sees her before she sees him, her light-brown face hidden behind a ruse of similar complexion. She shared her disguise with him in advance. Jack provided an image of his own ersatz mug—pale like his real one—

so that he, too, could be recognized by his daughter and her retinue.

She's decked in a saffron-hued sari, its trim the color of turmeric. Green pick-stitching accents the ensemble. Jack cuts a dashing figure in his own bespoke threads: charcoal gray linen pants with sapphire blue stitching and a bone-white linen shirt with charcoal stitching. His gray hat matches his pants; its blue band is the same hue as the accent thread. He strides toward his daughter, but her two large bodyguards converge. One of the men is Afro-Indian, the other one Black. They'll reach the European outlander before he reaches her.

She steps forward and calls them off. They remain within striking distance.

Father and child stand a few feet apart, considering each other. He now understands that his access to her is fettered. That, while his skin is *blanche*, his *carte* is not. Despite being an absent parent for most of her life, he'd tried to exert beneficent influence on his first-born—on all of his kids. He attempts to temper his guilt about Ramya, specifically, with having been her chief caretaker during her earliest years. Once Asha had finished breastfeeding, the last thing she'd wanted to do was play mummy. It was Jack who'd taught Ramya three languages, changed her diapers, prepared her meals, and ushered her first steps. After the rift with Asha, he'd tried to preserve the relationship with his child, but her mother refused access to their baby girl.

He says nothing. They communicate tacitly. Ramya doesn't want to put on a show, doesn't want to claim him. He infers that she's annoyed. The posture of her guards screams that he shouldn't attempt to embrace her, nor make any statement of affection.

She raises an eyebrow that says: *Shall we?*

He nods.

Her consular status and their manner of transport means that the 600-kilometer trip to Bukima won't take as long as it would for any ordinary citizen, but it will still take four hours. She could have arranged to make it quicker. Jack knows that she didn't need to do this: take time to get to Nairobi, then travel with him to Lake Victoria, only to immediately return to Dar-es-Salaam. Just to spend four hours with him. Yet those four hours are more than she needed to spend, and fewer than she could have. It's the figure she chose.

Tanzanian flags adorn the car's four corners. It's like a parody of historical diplomacy, but really just tradition that refuses to die. In the cool cabin, they slide onto the bench seats, facing each other. Her back is to the driverless cabin. She and Jack drop their holographic disguises. She orders her guards to deafen themselves. They comply. The Virtual Assistants grafted onto their nervous systems shunt the cochlear nerve. The programs keep monitoring to relay any potential threat. Recording ceases, and no information is otherwise conveyed to the two men. Jack and Ramya's VAs both confirm that the help are stone deaf.

"This is as close to a private moment as we're going to have," Ramya says. Her accent is Received Pronunciation by default; it's the only English she learned.

"I appreciate you coming," he responds in his own RP, instead of his Glasgow. "It's not easy to get around these parts without some help."

"I'm sure *you* could manage, even without me. Kenya isn't Uganda. Or you could have just taken a suborbital and skipped all of this shite."

The first lull comes early. She looks out the window.

Sitting next to her, the Afro-Indian bodyguard observes his boss and her sire, now able to compare them in the absence of their masks. His Black colleague gazes at the passing scenery, but he's practiced at seeming nonchalant while remaining attuned. Jack seems too young to have a daughter in her mid-20s. Yet, such things happen when one 18-year-old impregnates another. He's aware of his paleness and its implications. He sighs through his nose.

Ramya returns her attention to him. "Should I resent that you came all this way to see Harmon and not me?"

"Ramya ..." Jack begins, but she keeps talking.

"—that I'm taking nearly a full day out of my life for a brief spell with the man to whom the world must bow, but who bows to no one?"

He raises both eyebrows at her. She raises one. She must have inherited the trait from her mother. Raja Asha Banerjee, who imparted Ramya's brown skin, black hair, and brown irises. Still, the similarities to Jack are plain: her square chin, her nose, the attached earlobes, the shape of her eyes.

"I don't know what to make of you. How to feel about you." She looks right into his blue eyes. "I've really hated you at times."

Jack resists the urge to interrupt. It's the least he can do.

"And then, at others, I've missed you terribly. Desperately. I feel like I'm betraying myself to tell you that."

He inhales.

Shut up! warns the version of Sabine that lives in his head, acting as his conscience. Sabine, who would struggle to find her own if she were ever to look for it. Sabine, who in real life leaves him alone for months at a time. The sheer irony, that her voice is the one that governs his tact. Sabine, who never varnishes anything. Who will probably wander off with him gone for a week. *Let her talk.* Sabine, whom he can't let go even though he should never have held on. He's been grasping for connection ever since Asha's dismissal, yet always undermining it with poor candidates.

He exhales without a word.

Ramya looks away. "It's hard growing up without a father in a deeply patriarchal society. And being *kutcha butcha* among people who value fully baked bread. Not like there aren't a ton of other half-baked loaves around, especially in T-zed, but there's always that feeling of otherness that never goes away." She hits him with a baleful glare. "And being a bastard made that a lot worse."

Jack grimaces, frowning with his eyebrows. He wants to speak but knows he shouldn't. Ramya doesn't want platitudes; she wants to vent.

"Mum never treated me like I was less-than, just because I was white...which is funny because, to people like you, I'm brown. I'll never be enough of either to really belong. I'm sure Harmon can relate to that. *Kutcha butcha.* But I don't mean to complain. People liked me enough to elect me. Twice." She lapses into silence for a moment, looking again out the window before turning back to him. "I want you to know what it's been like without you."

"I'm sorry," Jack says, letting his Glasgow accent come to the fore. Still, his is not the stuff of jokes about gutter punks. Like her, his education was exceptional. His brogue is distilled. Refined.

She replies with a sharp shake of her head. At the same time, she cuts the air with her left hand, its dominance another trait from him.

"Clearly, I didn't need you," she says, her gaze unflinching.

Jack absorbs the blow.

Silence falls over them again and they sit in it, each watching a different vista of the Serengeti flit by the windows. She looks north, he south.

"What was your childhood like?" she asks, not looking away from the window.

A short pause precedes his reply. "Didn't really have one."

She shrugs. "Mum never talks about you. She never told me how you guys got together. But you hurt her. Your little fuck-and-run left its mark."

Jack doesn't retort. He could say it wasn't a "fuck-and-run" but knows there's no point in protesting. Few people remember their lives before they were five, and he was gone by the time Ramya was four. He catalogues what he knows, which she doesn't—because Asha never bothered to tell her. His eyes flit, sending ocular commands to his contact-lens HUD. It renders a one-handed keyboard on his left thigh, for his eyes only, in his peripheral vision. He taps out a message:

RAM DOESN'T KNOW WHAT WE DID.
WHY NOT TELL HER?

He can't be explicit because, despite knowing that Asha would never be careless with encryption, specifics would be foolish to ever put into text—even in conversation between two complicit co-conspirators. With all the speculation in the news, any affirmation would be suicide. Social. Political. Literal.

"Well?" Ramya presses. "I want to hear it from you. How did you become the man you are?"

The derisive note on the word *man* isn't lost on him, but he allows her the insult. He feels like he's earned her recrimination, though his ego still bristles. He sends the message to her mother. Asha will never reply.

"I had a fucked-up childhood, Ram."

"I don't doubt it," she replies. She allows him the pet name. It sounds like the abbreviation for read-only memory, not a male goat.

"What do you want to know?" He turns his hands palms up and spreads them, shaking his head. "I don't see the value in hashing it all out. Nothing I went through gave me the right to be a walking disaster." He puts his hand to his mouth and rubs the stubble on his chin. "I've tried at every turn to fix what I can that's wrong with me. The wrong I've done." He sighs. "You deserved a lot better. I'm not going to defend myself."

"You've been all over the news, lately. Not like you aren't all the time, but it's been different, these past few weeks. Instead of all the fawning, there's talk about you being a eugenicist, a racist ..."

"And a murderer," he finishes.

"And a murderer," she repeats, nodding. "Although, if you killed any of those bluebloods, I'd argue they had it coming."

Jack opens his mouth as if to speak.

"I don't really want to know," she says, and his gob closes. "I don't care if you killed a bunch of fascist plutocrats."

"That's touching," he replies. He realizes that it sounds sarcastic, so he clarifies. "I mean that."

"I didn't intend for it to touch you. I'm just telling you the truth. You're a selfish arsehole, but you're not a bad person. I know that much...Well, maybe."

Jack sighs and shakes his head. He's not as sure. He looks at the floor, at his and Ramya's feet. Her shoes complement her sari.

"But then you're selfless, too," she adds. "You're complicated."

He looks at her.

"You've been really generous to T-zed. I'm guessing because of mum and me. But we need more from you. The continent, I mean. Africa as a whole is so fucked up from all the European meddling. Sure, Kenya's doing great—even with the embezzlement—but it's hoarding its wealth. Taking after the whites, as usual. The rest of us are trying to get our shit together as a commonwealth. But—after how many hundreds of years of slave-driving, colonization, and imperialism—how quickly are we supposed to turn it around? You helped Egypt build that massive seawall, but what about the loss of arable land? What about the water crisis? For centuries you've extracted wealth from here and spent it elsewhere.

"You love to invest in yourselves. You didn't do it for Egypt; you did it for Egyptology. All that money to preserve a fetish for impressive graves. All that money terraforming Earth and Mars. The lunar cities, the Venus cloud settlements. Fucking Mars! How did that work out, hmm? You sent a generation ship like shooting a giant load into the galaxy. How many brown people were part of that mission? And here, we can barely grow anything. We're dying of thirst. Backwards arseholes are still cutting off girls' clits. All that space money should have been invested in fixing shit, here. Reparations for Africa. For India. For all the places you've gone and fucked up and raped and pillaged."

"Me?"

"Your people. Rapists and pillagers."

"My people? Scots?"

"White people."

"They're not my fucking people, Ramya."

"They look like you," she replies.

"They are not. My people."

"So that's why all your women are brown? Not because you're another Viking spreading whiteness around, but because you're trying to erase yourself? Is that it?"

"I can't even imagine how much therapy I'd need to get to the bottom of why I do what I do...or have done what I've done."

"I doubt much," she answers. "I think it's pretty obvious that you're either a white-supremacist imperialist eugenicist conquering brown women's wombs or you're a self-hating paleface who wants to absolve your guilt by eradicating your heritage."

"Wow," he replies.

"Wow?"

"It's just…I'm speechless."

"Mark this date in the calendar. John Hamish fucking Mason finally doesn't know what to say."

"Am I not allowed just to appreciate difference? Am I not allowed to *not* want to fuck someone who looks like they could be my relative? Why does it have to be something ugly? Why are there only two explanations, both of which indict me in pretty horrible ways?"

"Maybe it's because I'm angry at you. Or maybe there's some truth to it."

"To which?"

"Either. Maybe you *are* a white-supremacist imperialist eugenicist who *also* feels guilty and is trying to erase himself. Amazingly, you can accomplish both the same way. Your kids just need to learn to hate their father and want to erase him, too. The eugenics takes care of itself because, of course, a diverse pool of genetic material makes for stronger progeny."

Jack rubs his sweaty palms on his thighs. The linen is soft and coarse at once. He sighs and looks again out the window. He wishes for another glimpse of the space elevator, but there's no way now that he could see from west of Nairobi all the way to Mwingi no matter how he twisted himself. He spied it from the plane, sticking up from the clouds like the proverbial beanstalk, but tethered to an asteroid instead of a giant's castle. The rich vein of the astro-lift pumps the lifeblood of Kenya's juggernaut economy; it's humanity's lifeline to the solar system. To other stars. It's another middle finger to the Occident from Harmon—the self-appointed savior of humanity's cradle. The West pays handsomely to use it.

"Harmon doesn't have any kids, does he?"

"What?" Jack replies, caught off guard. He turns to face her. "No." He shakes his head. "No, he doesn't."

"Just you," she adds. She's not talking about Jack's own fatherhood, but about his being orphaned—and Harmon's de facto adoption of him.

Jack looks back out the window, thinking of Project Daedalus—

the mission to 40 Eridani A, which Ramya already brought to the fore. He remembers the launch: he'd been an exuberant ten-year-old celebrating the advent of a new age, the creation of a new calendar. As vividly, he remembers being beaten by his actual father for daring to joyfully blaspheme with the wider world at abandoning *anno domini*. So many beatings, for nearly anything. For nothing.

"Just me," he repeats, catching her implication. His breath fogs the metalliglass.

"But he's not your dad."

"Nope," he replies, despite that the question was rhetorical.

"It's almost sweet… that you found each other."

Jack whips his head toward her. Even though the guards can't hear the conversation, they see his face change, his body tense. They tense in response. Their hands go instinctively to their weapons. Ramya holds up her hand to allay them, and the men relax.

"We didn't *find* each other," Jack says. His face is tight with rageful resentment that he's learned to contain, yet only barely. "Harmon found *me*. He *groomed* me. I was a *project* for him. He had an agenda and I fit into it."

"Intriguing, but I'm afraid to pry. Grooming? I don't want to know what digging would reveal, but it's interesting that your relationship with him isn't…wholesome. It's nothing sexual, right?"

"Jesus, Ramya," Jack replies. The disgust on his face says that she's either way off base or too close to the mark. "He's not some homosexual pedophile."

She plays off her relief that Jack's mentor didn't molest him, or worse. "You're clearly conflicted about him, but I doubt you'd defend him if he'd done something *that* fucked-up to you. You seem like a man who believes in revenge…who wouldn't stand to be abused."

"You're right about that."

His vehemence conjures the blood-soaked carpet in the House of Lords. He hears it squish beneath the tread of his boots. The submachine gun is heavy in his hands. A subtle tremor runs through his body. He clenches his teeth so hard it hurts his jaw. He looks down at his light brown loafers and returns to the present. The carpeting of the cabin is gray and dry. His hands are empty.

"I don't stand for abuse. Of anyone. Not me. Not you. *No one.* Where I see abuse, I act. Harmon didn't abuse me ..." Jack again looks out the window. He grimaces. After a spell, he adds: "Not sexually, anyway."

Ramya frowns, but Jack doesn't notice. She realizes that she's arrived where she'd wanted, but unearthing the crown of her father's pain doesn't please her.

"Your mum was supposed to be there," he says, his gaze five thousand miles away, in London, reliving the coup. It was five months before Ramya was born.

"Where?"

He looks at her. "You'll have to ask her. It's not my place to betray her secrets. If she hasn't told you, then she didn't want you to know."

"So you're selling her out," Ramya replies. "Charming."

"She's already poisoned you to me," he scoffs and turns away. A long pause stretches like a big cat. "It wasn't a fuck-and-run, Ram. A man can't stay with a woman who doesn't want him around."

"You couldn't have changed?"

His lips disappear into a dash across his face. He turns back to her. "What change should I have made?" Again, he scoffs. "I was a 21-year-old housewife, and she thought my caring for you and supporting her ambition made me less of a man."

He reflexively clenches his left fist, newly aware of the artificial muscle, sinew, and bone beneath his skin. Over twenty years of being an amputee with no one but Harmon the wiser. He thinks about how much less of a man he'll yet be, once Harmon replaces the rest of his limbs—to gird him for another fight he'd rather avoid.

The silence returns, and neither of them feel compelled to break it. Ramya studies her father, still a young man, but much older than the image she has in her mind. She does have snatches of memory from when she was three. He exists in her consciousness as someone other than the unflattering portrayals from her mother and the international press, none of which encapsulate the whole man. She knows that no one version of any story is the truth, and she can't ignore the burr he's planted in her mind: her mother lied to her—both actively and by omission.

Of course, Ramya isn't so naïve as to think that parents never lie. She understands the utility of misrepresentation; she's a politician. She's practiced in detecting mendacity, and in camouflaging it. So it stings to learn that she's been so blindly in awe of Asha Banerjee that she let the slick woman play her.

"You know," she says, drawing Jack's gaze from the scenery.

It strikes her that his face is so kind. She's never before noticed it in the media she's seen. Handsome, yes. Forbidding, sure. Charming, definitely. But kind? This is a look he doesn't wear in public. Her default image is of him scowling, which may well be his default expression. It's the one that candid public photographs often depict when he's captured out in the world and not hiding behind a hologram. But then she thinks of the gregarious man giving all those interviews on the telly. He's his own PR firm, burnishing his reputation as a beneficent man of the people to counter the reports he can't control. That and his kind face jibe with the memory of him amusing her into eating peas.

"I do remember you," she continues. "I remember you speaking to me in French, feeding me *petit pois.*"

Jack smiles. It's wan, though. So different from the broad grins and effusion of his media persona. She called him a complicated man but hadn't been sure she meant it. She sees it now: the sadness weighing down the delight attempting to draw up the corners of his mouth.

"We could speak it now. If you want," he offers in the Gallic tongue.

She reflects his wan smile back at him. "Pas maintenant."

He frowns at the denial, and she feels a twinge of guilt at the manipulation, but the broad grin that blooms on his face is worth it when she says: "Mais peut-être plus tarde?"

Not now. But maybe later?

CRAB FEAST

PETER L. HARMON

for Beth Ann Shelton

"**D**id you go pee-pee and brush your teeth?" Beth Ann called to her two grandsons as she walked down the hallway from the kitchen to the guest room where the boys were sleeping during their summer trip. She was holding a tall, light green cup in one hand, where her second mixed drink of the night lapped against the sides of the cup like a wrestler bouncing back and forth between the ropes before clotheslining his opponent. It was vodka, sparkling water, a squeeze of a lime, and just a dash of cranberry juice. At the bars she frequented, the drink was affectionately known as a "Beth Ann." If you made a Beth Ann in a short glass instead of a tall one, you better believe she would send it back. In her other hand was a book about Lego superheroes of some sort, the kind of thing her grandsons were totally into.

"Yes, Grandmama," she heard her younger grandson, Calvin, respond. She shot a look over her left shoulder to see if there was toothpaste spit in the sink (there was, bright blue with a halo of white bubbles) because you could never be too sure if the little one was telling the whole truth.

Beth Ann entered the guest room and saw that her older grandson, Christian, was already zonked out, Minecraft sleep mask over his eyes, mouth agape, iPad fallen over on his lap. He had swum and talked and played with the neighbor kid all day; it made sense that he was exhausted. The little one should have been exhausted too, but oh well, Grandmama could spare a few minutes to read about whatever havoc the brick-based bad guys were stirring up in Legoland.

Beth Ann was elated to have her daughter's family in town, and for two whole weeks! Usually her son-in-law had to work and her daughter, who had summers off from teaching, didn't really want to travel alone with their two kids. So they'd blow in like the Santa Ana winds for a long weekend, cause a big fun fuss, then breeze back to California leaving crumbs and popped pool toys and wonderful memories in their wake. Beth Ann was happy to play babysitter for a night or two or three whenever they were in town; she knew how hard it was to raise kids without the help of family in driving distance, to be on separate coasts from your loved ones. She knew all too well...

So Beth Ann had practically pushed Pete and Ash out the door with a slap on the rump for her daughter and a lipstick-staining kiss on the cheek for her son-in-law and told them to go have some fun. She and the boys had watched a movie and eaten popcorn and candy. And their Popple had fallen asleep on the upstairs sofa watching a Nationals game. Now it was bedtime for the boys, time to finish drink number two (eh, and maybe have a third, who's counting), then a little TV before bed on the couch with her doggies and her grand-pug: a perfect night.

When she entered the room, Calvin was sitting upright in his blow-up bed with his pajamas and glasses on. He was absentmindedly playing with his feet, finding little bits of translucent skin to pull off the area by his toenails. He looked like he had something on his mind.

"You ready to read, Cal?" she asked.

Calvin nodded vigorously and hopped under his Spider-Man

blanket in one swift motion. She began reading, but Calvin inter-rupted her a couple of pages in.

"Grandmama," he said. "Did you know that you have a *cwab* gwowing in your pool?"

Beth Ann could usually speak "Calvin-ese," but she was initially befuddled by that statement.

"A *cwab*?" she repeated.

"Not a *cwab*!" Calvin said, beginning to get riled up "A *CWAB*!"

"Oh," Beth Ann smiled; she loved his silly little voice. "A crab? By the pool? We're going to eat crabs by the pool with your cousins tomorrow. Popple is going to get a whole bushel from Abner's. Is that what you're thinking of?"

Calvin was still firm, but calmed, "No. There's a *cwab* gwowing in your pool. Bro and his fwiend found a weird *cwab* and they put it in the pool and it started *gwowing*."

"OK, Cal. You can show it to me tomorrow." And she began the next page in the story.

"When I just looked out the window before I bwushed my teeth I could see its claw. It was bigger than Lily."

Beth Ann wondered for just a moment if Calvin meant that the crab was bigger than Lily, the pretty white dog with the crazy hairdo that was asleep in the blankets on the couch downstairs, or if just the claw was bigger than her. Then she caught herself and figured that wondering that was like wondering if the "Pokemons" went to the bathroom in those little red and white balls that she saw in her grand-sons' video games. It was make-believe, so it didn't really matter.

"OK, honey. Grandmama wants to watch her show before it gets too late, so let's finish the book and go to bed." But as the word *bed* left her mouth, she did hear a strange sound coming from the side yard where the pool was. A sound she hadn't ever heard before, and she had lived in that house for a long time and heard all sorts of strange forest noises coming from the property beyond her back gate. It was like a shovel scraping on concrete, but more… organic.

Her eyes met Calvin's baby browns, obscured by the blue frames and thick lenses that were always smudged with dirt and tears and fingerprints.

"What was that, Cal?" she asked.

Calvin was almost impatient. "The *cwab*!"

As if sleepwalking, Beth Ann stood and walked slowly down the hallway, back the way she had just come. Only instead of hanging a right into the kitchen, she kept on straight to the upstairs sitting room, where the TV was playing highlights from the Nationals game but Popple was nowhere to be seen. She used her left hand to brush aside the thin curtain that covered the window and looked down into the pool area.

The sun had set, but string lights danced around the wooden fence surrounding the pool, casting an eerie glow on the dark blue water. Christian must have left the pool noodles in the water, because there were several cylindrical masses bobbing near the deep end. She was transfixed, seeing some sort of movement beneath the surface. Calvin pushed the stool, the one he used to stand on to brush his teeth and put his feetsies on while he sat on the potty, over to the window and stood tall on it.

Calvin gestured to the pool. "See, I told you the cwab was gwowing. It's really big now."

And at once it snapped into focus. The dark green and bright blue pool noodles were not pool noodles at all. They were crab legs, and they lifted out of the water and planted their spiny points on the deck on either side of the pool. Two claws the size of crocodile jaws also burst forth from the pool and began snapping open and shut. The legs strained, decorative rocks and shells around the perimeter of the pool hopped and danced and skittered. Concrete split where the beast's weight pushed down in full force. The thorax of the crab rose out of the pool, displacing some of the water; Beth Ann estimated that its body looked to be about the size of her younger son's pickup truck.

With a swipe of its left claw, the giant crab took the roof off the gazebo next to the pool. The splintered wood disappeared into the trees. The other claw sliced a pool umbrella in half and the top fell to the ground.

"That's cwazy, right?" Calvin asked his grandmama.

His words broke her trance, and she sprang into action. She ran to the kitchen, unsure of how to proceed, then grabbed a crab knocker and a sharp knife from the drawer .

"Mark!" she called as she carefully made her way down the steps. "Mark, we have a problem!"

All of the dogs were standing near the couch, barking. The scent of danger was in the air. Thankfully their dog gate was closed, or who knew what might have happened.

Calvin was quick behind Beth Ann, but she turned and told him to watch the dogs, to make sure they didn't get out.

"And go find your Popple," she said. She opened the sliding glass back door and ran along the stone path to the pool area.

One of the crab's big black bug eyes turned toward her as she reached the pool gate. Its antennae twitched. It raised both claws high into the air, preparing to attack. The left claw swung down towards Beth Ann, and she ducked down close to the fence. The interior teeth of the claw sliced through the wire fence like a saw blade cutting into butter. The claw slammed down onto the ground next to Beth Ann, so she thrust her knife into it and began hammering at the claw with the crab knocker. "Get out of my pool!" she yelled.

But she only succeeded in making the crab mad. It squealed in the way that its smaller brethren screamed when being boiled alive in beer and seasoning. Beth Ann crawled away and grabbed the top half of the umbrella that the crab had sliced; the umbrella pole was now a jagged spear.

The crab held its injured claw up to its inky spherical eye, examining the damage. Beth Ann opened the pool gate and snuck closer and closer to the monster, hoisting the makeshift weapon, ready to attack the underside of the crab. She closed her eyes and was bracing herself for the strike when she heard a voice.

"Grandmama, I can't find Popple!" Calvin stood in the backyard in his PJs, flip-flops now on his feet.

The crab turned its body towards the young boy.

"Calvin," Beth Ann tried to scream-whisper. "Go back in the house."

"What?" he said. "I can't hear you."

"Go back in the house!"

The crab rose on its back legs and tilted forward, trying to locate the sound underneath its torso. It couldn't decide whether to go after the little thing in the yard or the troublesome organism under it who had hurt its claw. Beth Ann made the choice for it as she stabbed upwards into its belly with all her strength. The sharp end of the umbrella pole cracked through the armor-like shell. Thick salt water and fish-gut-smelling fluid poured out of the wound onto Beth Ann.

The crab was now blind with rage, swinging its claw arms around wildly. One claw took out the rest of the gazebo while the other scraped a gash on the siding of the house like a scorned lover keying an old sedan.

Beth Ann deftly dodged the flailing crustacean limbs and ran to the yard, hugging Calvin close. The crab in the backyard swimming pool hoisted itself up to its full height, almost taller than the two-story house before it. Its claws snipped together menacingly. Beth Ann wished she had her tall green cup in that moment.

She was about to grab Calvin and run towards the garage when she heard a more familiar noise than the strange scraping she hadn't been able to identify earlier. This sound took her back to more pleasant times, like folding laundry and hearing the sound in the background on a lazy Sunday afternoon. A polite putter that started in the driveway in front of the house but revved up as it got closer.

All of a sudden, a hole opened up in the wooden fence that surrounded the backyard. The gate blew off its hinges and Popple appeared, mounted on his riding lawnmower with Christian riding behind him, holding on for dear life with his arms around Popple's neck.

They both had on bike helmets. Beth Ann recognized that Christian was donning her cute purple one. They were also both wearing safety glasses from Popple's workbench, and Christian was even sporting an old catcher's chest protector that Popple must have dug out of the attic (no wonder it had taken him so long!). Popple slowed the lawnmower and gestured to Christian, who hopped off and ran around the port side of the pool. Popple revved the mower back up, drawing the crab's attention, and slammed along the starboard. Christian was wielding a long machete, longer than his arm, the one Popple used to clear brush behind the fence. Beth Ann had the brief thought that it was a good thing that Christian had earned his pocketknife belt loop in Cub Scouts earlier that year.

Christian ran around hacking at the crab's legs, slicing off big chunks of organic matter. Popple pulled a cord on his chainsaw (the good one that he used to trim the overgrown trees) and also began chopping into the crab's spider-like crawlers.

Beth Ann had an idea. She first ran to the pool's heat pump and turned the dial from 'off' all the way to the red 'danger' zone. She heard the mechanism roar to life and begin cranking. Then she snatched up Calvin and ran into the house. The dogs were still barking furiously.

She ran to the laundry room and grabbed a container, then bounded up the stairs. Calvin was quick on her heels. She flung open the upstairs window and looked down on the carnage.

Popple and Christian had done a good job of de-legging the beast, but its claws were still intact, snapping dangerously close to Christian as he hid under one of the deck tables. Popple didn't have a good angle on the crab. It looked like they were stuck.

Beth Ann held out the container to Calvin, who took a handful of red, grainy crystals. Then she took her own handful of the local crab seasoning.

"Cover your eyes," she said to Calvin. Then to the crab, "Hey! Look up here!" The crab's torso tilted towards the second story window, both of its foreclaws extending towards Grandmama and her grandson. As Calvin and Beth Ann tossed handfuls of red, salty seasoning into the crab's angry, black pits of eyes, Beth Ann smirked and said, "Go to *shell*."

The powder blinded the beast, and Christian rushed to Popple's side. Popple slashed off the crab's front claws, leaving the crab as nothing more than a body with withering limb stumps waving about like one of those wavy balloon air machine guys. The pool's pump had done its best to heat the water to a bubbling broth (the seasoning hadn't hurt the process). The crab sank down into the pool, boiling alive and squealing as it was cooked from its original dark green and black and blue to a bright, delicious red.

The cul-de-sac began to smell like a crab feast.

* * *

THE NEXT DAY, since the gazebo had been demolished, the whole family was set up at folding tables with brown paper taped down, dip cups of butter and vinegar every couple of inches, corn piled up, crushed beer cans intermingling with used paper towels.

The kids were down on one end of the table, Christian and Calvin talking too fast, explaining what their cousins assumed was some sort of shared nightmare/dream fantasy from the night before. Pete and Ash were at the other end with Beth Ann and Popple and a couple other adults. Beth Ann had made her famous crab dip as well as crab soup, crab cakes, and crab nachos. Unbeknownst to her daughter and son-in-law, Beth Ann also had an abundance of lump crab meat in both freezers. They were discussing the freak tornado that had apparently only blown through exclusively *their* backyard, specifically the night before only, while Pete and Ash had been out at the bar. Ash couldn't remember any tornado activity in that area from when she had grown up there, but she guessed she could research it on the Internet later. Besides she was a little hungover, and the crab-based foods were hitting the spot at the moment.

"Oh well," Ash said. "Just another project for you and Dad to do around the house."

Pete and Ash had picked up a couple dozen crabs from Abner's earlier that morning but soon realized it was overkill when they saw the crab feast Beth Ann had already set up.

Beth Ann wasn't feeling especially excited about interacting with crabs after the events of the night before, but she was hungry, and there was no sense in letting perfectly good seafood go to waste. She selected a particularly large and heavy steamed crab from the pile.

"This is a big one," she remarked, looking over to Popple, who had popped a bright red tomato into his mouth.

"Yeah," he said, smirking, chewing on the juicy fruit, a tomato seed dancing on the tip of his mustache. "I've seen bigger though."

And with that, Beth Ann and Popple burst out laughing while Ash looked on in bewilderment at her weirdo parents and Pete politely smiled, not really knowing what his in-laws were up to, but just happy to be there, at a crab feast in Maryland with people he loved.

THE VICTORIAN

DEBORAH MUNRO

*B*eth fidgeted with the tassels on her purse. "I had that dream again."

"The one where you're renovating the house?" Dr. Reynolds sat back in her chair and made a note on her tablet. "Has it continued to progress?"

Beth nodded. "This time, I was laying a parquet floor, a lovely pattern of dark and light wood. It was for the foyer, leading to the staircase. You remember the one? It has marble steps with ornate spindles and banister railing." She trailed off and looked down at her hands again.

Dr. Reynolds seemed exasperated. "I know you're an architect, but remember, these sessions aren't about the renovations. They're about you. In dreams, a house is a representation of self, your body. So, tell me, why do you feel you need to improve yourself?"

Sighing, Beth stared out the window. She was thirty-two, and the dreams of the house had been plaguing her for five years. Every time the house appeared, she would wander through it and note how it had changed. At first, it had been fun—a derelict old Victorian coming to life, transforming before her sleeping eyes. She had wanted to be an architect for as long as she could remember, building her first dollhouse at just nine years old, and she had loved her studies **in** college. She landed her dream job at twenty-one, and until the dreams had begun, she'd been a rising star, dazzling her firm and clients alike. But after the Victorian appeared, it was like a vampire that sucked every bit of her creative energy, draining her of the ability to think of modern ideas beyond the early 1900s. All her designs ended up looking antique, Baroque, heavily envisioned in wood.

Dr. Reynolds was tapping her digital pen against the tablet. "Have you tried going on a date since we last spoke?"

"I've been really busy at work—" Beth stopped herself from making excuses. "Actually, no, but I did sign up for a dating app, and I swiped right on a couple of men."

"That's great! Now, I want you to message them and arrange coffee, okay?"

A soft chime signaled the end of their session. Dr. Reynolds got to her feet and opened the door for Beth to exit. "I feel you're going to make a breakthrough soon. Keep trying. Next time, I expect to hear that you sat in front of a man, sipped on a hot beverage, and made small talk."

Beth stepped out into the autumn sun, admiring how the light filtered through the orange and yellow leaves. This was her favorite season in San Francisco. The brownstones with their rust-hued blocks, the dark-cobbled pathways through gardens going dormant for winter, the smells of fireplaces and barbecues still wafting in the air. As an architect, she had always felt as if she belonged to this city famous for its Victorian townhouses. Soon, it would be cold, windy, and wet, and she'd be forced to take the bus instead of walking. With the price of parking in the city, a car was never an option.

She kept a steady clip along the sidewalk, enjoying the light breeze as she made her way home. Her dream always seemed to come back at this time of year, and it was something she'd wanted to talk to Dr. Reynolds about, but they'd run out of time. The architectural firm had fired her two years ago, which was when she'd begun her counseling sessions. Not a single client had wanted to use her for their designs anymore. The only projects she'd been able to do were for historic buildings, museums, and government offices, of which there weren't many. She had won an award for her reimagining of the John and Jessie Fremont estate at Black Point, now Fort Mason. People loved her exhibit and said she had perfectly captured the look and feel of the original house. But those kinds of projects were few and far between.

Her apartment was in the kind of old Victorian townhouse for which San Francisco was famous. She had the third floor flat, but she reasoned it kept her fit climbing those stairs every day. She never tired of her view over Golden Gate Park, although she would admit it was a glancing view from too far away. But if she opened her bedroom window and leaned, it was actually quite nice.

The phone was ringing as she entered. She knew people thought she was old-fashioned with her landline, but she didn't care. She owned a cell phone; she just never gave anyone the number. She grabbed for the handset before the caller hung up.

"Hello?"

Tommy, her cat, leapt up onto the table beside her and mewed softly.

"How did it go today?" came the voice on the line.

"Hi, Mom. It's nice to hear from you, too. Couldn't we start with normal chit-chat before you dive right in?"

Her mother huffed in annoyance. "Don't get cheeky with me. What did Dr. Reynolds have to say?"

This was their routine. Beth's mother would call every day, wanting to know if Beth was "getting better"—which meant everything from applying for jobs to meeting up with friends to having some miraculous breakthrough with her therapist. The latter was her mother's latest hope. This year, she believed psychotherapy was the answer. Last year, it was hypnosis, and the year before that, acupuncture and herbs. Beth's role was to rattle off a list of "accomplishments" for the day, some a little exaggerated, and leave the call feeling like a failure.

"She said the same thing as always, that the house is my body I'm trying to fix, and that I need to go on some dates." Beth twirled the tassels on her purse again.

"So, are you going to go on some dates? You're not getting any younger. If you want to have kids, you're going to have to find a man and marry him, although at this point, I'd settle for a one-night stand."

"Mom! That's outrageous, and I'm not you. Besides, if I get desperate, I'll just freeze some eggs and use a sperm donor. It's a modern world, after all." Beth glanced around her apartment. *Perhaps not in here.*

"You live in a different century," her mother grumbled, mirroring Beth's thoughts. "You'll only have kids the old-fashioned way." Beth herself had been the product of a one-night stand, her mother not even getting the guy's name. These days, however, all her mother seemed to think about was Beth's marriage and some future grandkids.

"Okay, well, I have to go. I have homework from Dr. Reynolds—to ask some guys out for coffee."

Beth hung up and plunked into the chair Tommy had vacated. He changed course and climbed into her lap, purring loudly as she contemplated her cell phone where it sat in the pen cup. She pulled it out and opened the dating app. Seven more men had liked her profile, although she couldn't see why. She'd picked a photo her mother had taken of her sitting in the bay window, hugging her knees to her chest. It was the only recent one she had. She was wearing gray sweats, her sandy hair pulled into a messy bun. Her byline said, "I draw houses for a living."

Setting up the app had been her mother's idea, and she couldn't think of another way to meet people. Bars? No way, and she didn't even drink. Meetup groups? Forget that. She wasn't into hiking, biking, or anime. Her mother had met Chad through this app, and they'd been dating for over a year. Chad was a nice guy, too, so Beth figured this was her best bet to meet a man.

The two men she'd swiped right on had messaged her. *Hey, cutie, want to meet up for a drink?* the first one had said. His confident smile and perfect teeth suddenly nauseated her, so she deleted him, then deleted the other reply without reading it.

She got up to make some tea, taking her cell phone with her. It beeped, a smile emoji appearing on the screen. Curious, she opened the sender's profile. A man with the whitest blond hair and blue eyes smiled back at her, his mouth curved in a shy grin. She could tell it was a selfie and he'd hated taking his own picture. Somehow, he seemed familiar, like they'd met, but she couldn't place where. She searched around the app and found the emojis, and before she could chicken out, she sent him a smile back.

Seconds later, another emoji beeped, this time a smiley face with hearts in its eyes. She replied with a contemplative-look emoji. He responded with, "Hi, I'm Rob." His profile name was "A Guy." (Beth's was "Just Me.") It seemed like they had something in common, so she replied, *I'm Beth, and before I run away screaming, want to meet me for coffee sometime?*

There was a momentary pause in which Beth felt the floor open to swallow her, and then: *How about now?*

Beth looked at Tommy, who seemed to be encouraging her. *Okay, I'll meet you at Haight & Ashbury in an hour.*

A traditionalist. I like that. See you soon.

Beth grabbed a windbreaker and hailed the next bus going her way. Her heart thudded in her chest, threatening to choke her the entire ride into downtown. Ground Zero of the hippie movement seemed a worthy place to meet a man, considering how she'd been conceived. He was already there when she arrived, his height and platinum hair making him stand out, and he smiled broadly as she got off the bus. Beth tucked her hands into her pockets and nodded in acknowledgment.

"Want to walk a bit or head into a café right away?" he asked, his voice deep and resonant.

"Either is fine with me. I don't know the protocol for this."

"I don't think there is one. Let's grab a coffee, then. You'll be cold in no time in that jacket once the fog rolls in."

He pulled out her chair in the coffee shop and turned the paper menu in its clip so they could both read it. When she leaned in, he smelled good, like clean air and soap.

The server came by. "Just coffees, or would you like to see the menu?"

Rob arched an eyebrow at Beth, letting her answer. "I'll have a black tea with milk, please."

"I'll try the same." The server left, and Rob smiled again. "I thought you'd be a tea girl."

Beth returned his smile. "What made you think that?"

"Your profile pic is so simple, just you exactly as you are. That said tea to me." Rob shrugged. "Usually, I go for black coffee. Mmm, extra caffeine. So, you're an architect?"

"Uh, yes. I mean, I was. I'm not doing that right now." The tea arrived, saving her from expanding further. How could she explain that a perfectly healthy woman in the prime of her career was unable to work—that every time she tried to draw a building, she had a panic attack? The Victorian would appear in her mind and obscure the paper.

"Sorry, I didn't mean to pry," Rob said, bringing her back to the present. He didn't seem put off by her zoning out for a moment. "I'm a shop owner. We make souvenirs to sell to the tourists, like screen-printed T-shirts, figurines of Alcatraz, postcards—although those are fast going out of fashion. But that sort of thing. I'm also an amateur photographer, in case that's more appealing to you."

"That's…interesting. How did you get into that line of work?" Beth sipped her tea. She was feeling judgmental of his profession. He was a businessman who owned his own shop, she reminded herself.

"Oh, after law school, I worked as a lawyer for a bit, but I hated it. When my grandparents wanted to retire, they asked if I wanted to take over the shop, and I jumped at the chance. Now, I just meet happy people who want a memento to remind them of their vacation."

Beth took a too-big slurp of tea; it scorched her throat, and she set her cup down with a bang. "Ouch!"

Rob jumped up and poured water into a glass from a decanter. "Here."

She dutifully swallowed some, then placed the glass on the table. "So, what does one say after an awkward moment like that?"

"Next time I'm ordering an iced tea?" He winked, and she laughed.

They chatted after that and whiled away the time. She was surprised with how comfortable it was. She stared at him a bit, admiring his ice-blue eyes, then looked down when he flushed.

They sat silently for a while longer. He seemed to be waiting for her to speak again, but she had no idea what to say. "Well, um, thanks for meeting me for tea."

"Sure, my pleasure. I rarely see someone online I want to meet. How about you?"

"I never do." She glanced at the time on her phone. "This has been nice. Do we go to the counter to pay, do you think?"

"Yeah, okay, um…" Rob glanced around and signaled the server he wanted the check. The server brought it over. "My treat," Rob said.

They walked back to the bus stop. Rob stuffed his hands into his coat and cocked his head. "Did I do something wrong?"

"What? No." Beth felt choked again. "I'm just very new at this. In fact, you're my first date ever."

"Really? I'm honored." Rob smiled again, his slightly crooked teeth making Beth's heart beat a little faster. "Could I text you for another date?"

The bus door opened, and Beth stepped up. "Okay, sure," she mumbled over her shoulder, but he'd heard her. She could see it in his eyes as her bus pulled away.

Lost in thought, Beth realized too late that she was on the wrong bus. She was miles from where she needed to be. She pulled the cord and pushed her way through the throng of people to get off.

And there it was: the Victorian house from her dreams.

Incredulous, Beth crossed the street and stared. The trees had matured and were now stately columns framing the stained-glass front door. She frowned, as the colors were wrong. The house was meant to be dove gray with white trim, but it was a purplish mauve with gray trim. She walked to the front door, intending to knock, but it was slightly ajar, so she pushed it open and entered.

A weathered and scarred parquet floor filled the foyer. Off to the left, the grand staircase curved upwards, the treads of marble covered by a tapestry rug runner held in place by brass bars. Beth continued forward, knowing the formal parlor was to her right through the double doors, the kitchen beyond the wall in front. She turned left beyond the stairs and entered the den, except it wasn't the wood-paneled library from her den. It was a brightly painted space with a massive glass-topped desk.

"May I help you?"

Beth jumped at the sound and turned. A woman about her age stood there, her blonde hair swept up into a sleek chignon.

"I'm so sorry. The door was open, and I just walked right in. This is too weird."

"Okay…" the woman said, evaluating her with wariness. "Oh, I recognize you now. You're the architectural historian who did the Fremont House exhibit. I'm a huge fan of your work."

Beth felt the blood rush from her head and pool at her feet. "I really need to sit down before I faint."

The woman briskly stepped forward and guided Beth to the desk chair. "You look like you've seen a ghost. Can I get you some water?"

Beth shook her head. "Is this your house? I've been seeing it in my dreams for years, except it was new. It was under construction, or brand new, or something. I was renovating it." She tucked her trembling hands under her thighs while the woman continued to stare at her with concern.

"My husband and I bought this house about two years ago. It was quite run-down and neglected, as no one had lived here for years. People said it was haunted, but we haven't seen or heard anything from the beyond." The woman laughed a little. "Legend has it that the original owner built this for his new bride. He was from Holland, but she was American."

"Lars. His name was Lars Andersen." Beth could see him, a tall blonde man with blue eyes, so similar in appearance to Rob, with that same shy grin.

"That's right!" The woman walked over to a coffee table, gathered up a portfolio, and brought it over to the desk. "Here, I'm sure you'll find this interesting."

The portfolio contained mostly photographs of the house as it was being built, but the woman pulled out a grainy photo of a woman seated in a wheelchair, wearing a lace dress. She was on the balcony of this house, gazing off into the distance. Beth took the photo and scrutinized the face. The woman held out another photo, this one of Lars in a business suit outside of a nondescript downtown building.

"Lars was a journalist who also loved photography, such as it was back in the day. I forget which newspaper he worked for. That's his wife in the wheelchair. She took ill at twenty-seven, consumption I believe, and soon couldn't help at all with the build. According to the accounts I've read, she was the inspiration for the design of this house, and when she became too weak to view the work in person, Lars took photographs to share with her. He also documented all her suggestions and advice for what she wanted the finished house to look like. It created this amazing treasure trove for me to work from. I want to restore this house to its former glory and finish it the way they had intended."

Beth's hand began to shake, so she passed the pictures back and opened the portfolio to gaze at the construction of the house. She saw the stairwell go in, the marble steps being laid, then the parquet flooring. It was exactly as she had envisioned. "Whatever happened to them?" she asked.

"She lingered on for five years, which is why there's so much documentation of the house, but it definitely slowed down over time. The last thing Lars photographed before she died was the parquet floor. I hope to polish it back to a high sheen. I'm sure you noticed how damaged it was over the years."

"And Lars?"

"Oh, he completely stopped working on the house when she died. I believe he went back to Holland. He sold the house and never remarried. It's such a tragic love story, don't you think?"

"Indeed." Beth closed the portfolio and stood. "I ought to get going, and I apologize again for barging in the way I did. Thanks for sharing the photos with me."

"It was my pleasure, and I'm so happy you stopped by. I went to your firm to ask if you'd be interested in taking on the renovations, but they said you'd moved on. I'm assuming they told you to contact me?"

Beth nodded noncommittally. "I was in the neighborhood."

"Well, I'll give you a chance to think about it. I don't have a card, but could I give you my contact information? Here, I'll put it in your phone."

The woman reached out and took the cell phone still in Beth's hand. "Call me anytime to ask more questions. I'm open to whatever you feel this house needs to become its best self. Who's this? Your husband? Isn't it uncanny how much he looks like the builder of the house!" She handed the phone back to Beth, Rob's face on the screen. He'd sent another emoji, this time a heart.

"He's...my friend," Beth said. Somehow, that didn't feel true. Was he more than a friend to her? She'd have to find out. "Thanks for the contact info. I'll be in touch."

Once outside, Beth pushed the call button. A deep voice answered, "Hello?"

"Hi, Rob! When can we meet up again?"

THE PATRIARCH

ALY WELCH

Some people are haunted by ghosts. I'm haunted by words. And, yes, I suppose, ghosts too.

* * *

I DIDN'T KNOW what to expect as I walked to the front door of the Monroe home on a cool, overcast day in April. From the line of cars parked in front of the house and the sound of music and laughter inside, I presumed a party to be underway. I hadn't figured Sheriff Monroe for a Beatles fan. Puzzled, I retrieved a notepad from the inside of my coat. I felt certain that he and I had agreed to meet at 6 PM on this day, but perhaps he'd arranged our meeting in a moment of confusion.

After all, he'd buried one of his children a few weeks ago. A twenty-five-year-old woman by the name of Anna Monroe Davis. She drowned near the Santa Monica Pier in California, or so law enforcement initially assumed. Suspicious bruising on her neck and face left the medical examiner with questions, so the FBI was brought in, and I was assigned to the case. After conferring with the medical examiner and investigators with the Santa Monica PD, the case led me to her childhood home in Paradise Valley, Arizona. Her own home was nearby, but her husband had proven elusive.

"Deputy Davis," I said with surprise as the front door opened.

"C'mon in." Deputy Jonathon Davis clapped me on the back and ushered me into the dimly lit parlor. "Agent Hudson, right? Jack Sr. said you'd be joining us. And you can call me Jonathon—no need to be all formal."

I removed my coat and almost draped it over a shaggy dark brown arm. With a growing sense of unreality, I found myself staring into the gaping maw of an angry grizzly mid-roar. Its yellow incisors were as long as my index fingers. Longer, even.

"Beauty, ain't he?" Jonathon grinned, taking my coat and hanging it from a hook beside the door. "Jack Jr. did a great job mounting him."

As my eyes adjusted to the dim lighting, I took in Jonathon's appearance. He was shorter than me - and I'm only five nine - with dark hair and eyes, muscular arms, a stout belly, and that exaggerated broad-shouldered stance of a man compensating for size. For a grieving widower, he appeared almost jovial, though his ruddy complexion and bloodshot eyes provided a hint as to his high spirits.

"Most everyone else is already in the game room. We was just about to toast the Monroes on their thirtieth anniversary."

I followed him into a larger room, the walls lined with the mounted heads of all manner of wildlife: elk, wild boars, wolves, even another bear. A portly man with a balding head and a booming voice stood in the center of a large group of people with his glass raised. He grinned at Sheriff Monroe, who sat at the far end of the room. Even in a sweater and a pair of slacks, the sheriff cut an imposing figure. At his side sat his wife, Eva Monroe, wearing a silky green shift. Only the shadows under her otherwise lovely brown eyes hinted at any pain as she offered a polite smile. Her sleek blond hair, pulled back into an elegant chignon, showed very little gray at the roots. A younger woman with the same brown eyes and longer blond hair, styled just like First Lady Jackie O.'s, stood behind Eva with a hand on her shoulder.

Jonathon offered me a glass of champagne, but I declined as I listened to the toast. "That's the Maricopa County Constable," he whispered as the man spoke.

"Now when Eva first met Jack Senior, she didn't like him much. But you see, Jack Senior here, he liked to hunt. And this was big game."

The women politely chuckled as the men around the room, some still dressed for police duty, guffawed. I found my eyes drawn to the glassy eyes of a dead elk. I glanced at Eva Monroe and saw her own doe-like eyes were drawn to the same, her lips set in a stiff smile. She met my eyes, and I quickly glanced away as the man continued his toast. When he finished, Sheriff Monroe strode to me and gave my hand a hearty shake.

"Gentlemen, this here is Agent Frank Hudson with the Federal Bureau of Investigations."

"FBI?" The constable looked at me with interest. "What brings you out here?"

"The boys and I were already talking about it earlier," a police officer interrupted before I could answer, "but what's the FBI's take on the esteemed Martin Luther King Jr.?" His tone suggested a certain lack of reverence.

"That's not my division."

"A natural diplomat." The constable gave me a wolfish grin. "We're all friends here. Some might even call us family. You can speak candidly."

"It's not really a social engagement."

His grin faded. "We can speak in my study."

Sheriff Monroe started to lead me away as conversation resumed between other guests.

"I'd like to talk to Agent Hudson first, if it's all right with you, sir."

"Suit yourself."

Jonathon exchanged a meaningful glance with Sheriff Monroe as he strode ahead. I followed him out of the room, down the hall, and into the study. He nodded at the leather chair behind a sturdy mahogany desk. "You're the one taking notes, ain't ya?"

I sat and pulled out my notepad and a pen.

Jonathon stood with his hands in his pockets, stance wide.

"I just have some routine follow-up questions, Deputy Da... Jonathon. Now, my records show you told the Santa Monica PD you were in Alaska on a hunting trip with Sheriff Monroe when your wife's body was found, is that correct?"

"Yessir."

"Apart from Sheriff Monroe, can anyone confirm your whereabouts?"

"Does anybody need to?"

"I suppose not. Do you have any idea why Anna left your children with her sister to go out of town while you were away?"

Jonathon shifted uncomfortably. "Look, Agent Hudson, Frank... may I call you Frank?"

I nodded.

"It's no secret Anna 'n I were having problems. She's a headstrong thing, and sometimes these women, they need to be reminded of their place, ya know?"

I hid my distaste. "Was she planning to leave you?"

"Dunno, the Church frowns on that sorta thing, but I'd been suspecting there was another man for quite some time. After another buddy of mine on the force did some diggin', I think I know who it is."

I leaned forward. This was new information.

"I'm not a gamblin' man, but I'm bettin' she planned a little rendezvous with a man by the name of Richard Hanks. Some dowdy ol' college professor, can you believe that? Glasses, cardigans, the whole works. Now he don't look so tough, but Anna, she wasn't a big girl. Taller than me, but skinny. Maybe he got tired of waitin' around for her. Sometimes it's the quiet ones you gotta look out for. You people at the FBI probably know that better than—"

The door burst open before he could finish his sentence.

"Daddy!"

A little girl with curly brown hair ran into the room and wrapped her arms around his leg. The woman I'd seen behind Eva walked in a moment later, clutching an infant with wisps of blond hair and the most unusual stormy eyes I'd ever seen.

"God dammit, Maria!"

Jonathon disentangled himself from the little girl, who stared up at him, pouting.

"Sorry, Jonathon. Sara's barely seen you, and the baby's fussin'. Kristina doesn't know any lullabies. Instead, she's been taking a sad song and making it worse, hasn't she, Sofia? Yes, she has!" Maria cooed at the baby in her arms. "Now give your other daughter some attention. I imagine our FBI agent here wants to speak with me, too."

I rose, offering the eldest Monroe daughter my seat. Maria sat, smoothing her pale blue skirt with one hand as she cradled the infant against her cream-colored sweater with the other. Jonathon grudgingly took the little girl's hand and left the study.

"Kristina's your youngest sister?" I turned to a fresh page in my notepad.

"Yes, but unless your name is John, Paul, Ringo, or George, I doubt she has any interest in speaking to you." Maria smirked. "She doesn't know anything, anyway. Sometimes I think she still expects Anna to waltz in like nothing happened."

"And what did happen, do you think?"

"Not a lot of women like to go for a late-night swim in the Pacific mid-March."

"Not fully clothed in a dress and heels, no."

Sofia cooed and grasped a strand of Maria's blond hair in one tiny hand. Once again, I found myself captivated by the infant's strange gray eyes.

"Beautiful, aren't they?" Maria gazed down at Sofia, stroking her cheek.

"Did Anna have gray eyes?"

"No. Brown, like mine."

"Did she tell you anything, the night she left her daughters with you?"

"Only that she had a fight with Jonathon, and she wasn't going back home until she could pack and leave for good."

"Jonathon thinks she was meeting someone else, a man she'd been seeing."

"Wouldn't be surprised. Do you see any of Jonathon in Sofia's face?"

I shrugged. "But she never told you about anyone?"

"In this family, sometimes the less anyone knows about anyone else, the better."

"Not to pry, but I don't think I noticed your husband in attendance?"

"Peter had to stay late at the office. And he isn't really comfortable around the family." Maria gave me a wry grin. "Do you have family, Agent Hudson? Is there a Mrs. Hudson? Not to pry, of course."

"No, of course not." I allowed myself to return her grin. Maria wasn't a fount of information, but at least I didn't have the sense she was being deliberately deceitful or evasive. "Spent most of my childhood in and out of foster care, was lucky to find work at a law office. Worked my way through school and into the academy. Hasn't left a lot of time for relationships."

"On the bright side, I guess you don't have to worry about conflicting loyalties."

"My only loyalty is to my oath and to my country," I confirmed.

Someone knocked on the door. I stepped to the side as Sheriff Monroe entered the room. "Your mother needs your help in the kitchen," he told Maria. A blonde in a minidress met Maria in the hall and took Sofia from her arms.

"I thought I told you to change into something respectable before you came downstairs," Sheriff Monroe admonished the younger blonde before closing the door. With a heavy sigh, he sat behind the desk. "Learn anything interesting?"

I cleared my throat. "Ah, yes, I do have another lead to look into. But in the meantime, I still have some questions for you. Now Jonathon maintains you traveled to Alaska together for a hunting trip. Here's the thing. I contacted the motels you said you booked between here and Anchorage, and while they have record of you, by all appearances, you traveled alone."

"I'm sure you've stayed in your fair share of motels, Frank. They're not known for their charming front lobbies."

"All the doors are on the outside, yes, I know. Fair point." I tried to ignore the weight of Sheriff Monroe's stare as I continued. "However, one night clerk in Idaho Falls thinks they saw someone enter your room, but it wasn't a man." I chose not to elaborate as I gauged Sheriff Monroe's reaction.

He frowned. "And this has what to do with my daughter's death?"

"Though nobody saw Jonathon with you during your, uhm, hunting trip, a witness did place him at a gas station just outside of Santa Monica the night Anna died. Your stories aren't holding up. Yours in particular leads to more questions."

"You really did your homework, didn't you, Frank?" Sheriff Monroe's frown deepened as he leaned forward. "Next you'll be telling me you had all my motel rooms tapped."

"You weren't even on the FBI's radar back then, to my knowledge."

"And I don't anticipate being on the FBI's radar going forward. We're a family, Frank. We protect our own. I would've thought you'd learned that by now."

I was about to argue that all evidence pointed to the contrary until I realized what he was really saying. My blood ran cold. "Your own daughter." I shook my head. "Who sells out their own daughter for an alibi?"

Sheriff Monroe rose. "I think it's time you leave."

I stood my ground. "I haven't spoken with Mrs. Monroe yet."

"She's been through enough as it is. Between Anna's extramarital affairs and presumed suicide, and our youngest beginning to test boundaries, well, you know how people can talk. It doesn't look good for us, Frank." Sheriff Monroe pushed past me to open the door. "I only invited you here tonight because I thought the appearance of transparency might help to assuage anyone's misgivings."

"And nothing matters more to you than appearances." I walked out of the room and down the hall to the front door, reaching for my coat. "Not even family."

"Men like you, Frank, you never let yourself get tied down to any one person or place. You don't know what it's like to be a pillar of your community. And what it can do to a community if they lose faith in their leadership."

"Then leaders should take greater care not to abuse the community's trust," I told him as I put on my coat. "Enjoy the rest of your party, Sheriff. I'll let myself out."

* * *

I wish I could say the FBI shared my suspicions, but they saw no reason not to take the Sheriff at his words despite conflicting witness statements. He was, after all, a pillar of his community. After Deputy Davis was no longer considered a suspect in the death of Anna Davis, they had me track down a young professor at the local university, but he had an airtight alibi himself - and little interest in the existence of his probable offspring. The case was closed, but I had greater success from then on.

A couple decades have gone by. I'm pursuing my biggest case yet. A few decades of unsolved murders stretching from the desert south-west to the Pacific northwest had finally been linked to a suspected serial killer growing sloppy in his old age. I'd received a tip from a strange woman in a faded Rolling Stones tee. I hadn't recognized her name, but I knew those stormy gray eyes anywhere.

Now I sit outside a dusty motel near the Canadian border. I open my wallet to admire a photo of my wife and children. My loyalty to them has never wavered. A porch light turns on over one of the motel room doors. I return my wallet to my coat pocket and watch as another federal agent knocks on the door. She's small and looks maybe fifteen in her undercover attire, but she's older, and she's tough. I ready my weapon to provide backup.

I like to hunt, and this is big game.

BIRDS OF A FEATHER

DANIEL LEE

*J*ackdaw caw in the apple blossom, binoculars to my eyes. Black mask over gray body. Black wings. Rare in this region, but seen increasingly in recent years. Blue irises. Rictal bristles upon its beak, which held a severed human penis.

Noted time (6:25) and weather (sunny, cloudless blue). Noted a second bird, source of the sound. A female? She tried for the penis, which male surrendered, naturally. Made note of their wingspans as they departed. Female: approximately 27 inches. Male: 30.

Thrilled at the sighting, turned my attention to the scene of the murder at my left. Six crows atop a barbed wire fence, bowed by their weight. All with black mandibles like snub-nosed revolvers. Joined now by a seventh. Larger than the others, yellow stripe along length of hooked beak holding a man's eyeball.

Held in my hands the heavy Nikon Roof Prism Compact, weathered and worn. My first binoculars, given to me by Father when I was still just a little girl.

The memory was still raw. Tires had blown driving north. On the shoulder Father saw my fear. Road stretched on. Gnarled fingers of arthritic trees on either side would bring on dark long before night.

"President Nixon today arrived in China to begin what will be—"
Radio cut off as Father pulled keys from ignition.

"Don't be afraid," he said, affectionately moving my ponytail back behind my shoulder. "This is an adventure."

Nodded my trust with eyes wide and teeth clenched.

From beneath blanket in back seat he produced a gift-wrapped box, handed it to me. "Happy birthday, sweetie."

I hesitated.

"Your mother won't mind," he assured me.

I tore at the wrapping, ripped Spock's face in half. Revealed the binoculars.

Always had a knack for birding. Seemed I could make them appear from thin air, Father would tell me. Little did he know. Several times I had nearly shared my suspicions with him, but keeping them secret kept at least something of my life unchanged.

"Who knows?" he said, opening his door. "We may see something while we walk. Got your field journal?"

Patted my pocket and nodded. Field journal, diary, the small book was both. My observations, thoughts, voice, constant companion.

Stepped from car and Father directed me forward, unaware that I had already seen the caltrops constellated across the road behind us, without a doubt deliberately laid. Our tires never stood a chance.

Noted in journal the time (5:37, nearly dusk) and weather (warm and cloudless, end of summer). Noted chirping of crickets unseen in surrounding grasses, the overgrowth nearly my height.

We walked, keys in Father's left hand, my left hand in his right, Nikons swinging from my neck, hitting my chest with each step.

"Father?"

"Yes, my love?"

"Are we still a family?"

"Of course we are!"

"Mother says you're a monster."

He sighed. Stopped and knelt before me. "What is a family?"

"I don't know. Parents, children, cousins."

"Family are the people you never give up on. The ones who are always there for you."

"Like a flock."

"That's right, like a flock. And I will always be there for you and for your mother. Even if she thinks I'm a monster. Because that's what a flock does. We look out for one another."

"But you didn't tell her when you took me."

"Would you like me to take you back to her?"

I considered that. Considered her new boyfriend telling me I talked like a caveman. "No."

"Atta girl, my little science officer. What say we keep walking?"

I nodded. "Aye, Captain."

5:39 when man stepped from overgrowth. Short red beard, blue Chevron cap, overalls. Knife in hand. Spat tar through his teeth onto asphalt.

Behind us another. Red sideburns to his chin. Skin white but black with coal. Camouflaged.

Ptarmigan camouflage by molting with the seasons. Read so in *The Peterson Field Guide.* Chameleons of the avian world, ptarmigan.

Second man drew a knife as well, whistled as he considered me. Father stood between us.

"Step aside, Mister."

"I recognize you," Father said. "From the Dairy Queen at the last exit."

"We takin' the girl."

"Touch her and you're dead."

"Give 'er here, Mister."

Father whispered. "Run as fast as you can. Go!"

Did as instructed. Sprinted into grass, nearly hidden by its height. Heard behind me sounds of struggle, a loud pop, a gasp. Father's gasp.

Then: "Go ahead an' die, Mister. We gonna have our way with yer daughter."

Dropped to the dirt. Said nothing as Father's final breaths were drowned out by voices of his killers.

"Come out, little chicken."

"Come out so we can see you."

Heard the men walking toward me. Knew my movements would be seen by their effect upon the grass. Had to remain still, hope they passed me by.

"Listen here, little chicken. We gonna chop yer daddy's body into little pieces and feed 'em to the crows. You like that? Come on out and we forget the whole thing."

Felt my heart against the Nikons. Saw scavenger birds already congregating above the road. Above Father.

Get away from him, I thought.

Scavengers dispersed as crunching of boots drew near. Realized I was shaking. It had worked, undeniably. My suspicions were correct.

Saw the man's Chevron cap over the high grass. Shut my eyes and held my breath. Heard honking of a horn. Squealing of tires. Opening of a truck door.

An older voice. "You shitheads gonna leave this asshole's body on the road for anyone to see?"

"Shit."

"Getcher asses back 'ere and clean this shit up."

"Yes, Paw." The men withdrew. Heard them grunting, then heard a heavy object thrown in the bed of a truck.

"Pick up the crow's feet, too."

"Yes, Paw." Their boots kicked loose gravel from shoulder onto road as they collected caltrops which had blown our tires and dumped them into bed of truck on top of Father. "What about the girl?"

"You boys fucked thissun up. Find the girl and bring 'er back to the house."

Heard car peel away and moments later boots on gravel, followed by crunching of dirt again.

"We s'posed to *carry* her back now? Shit."

"Quitcher griping. You heard Paw. Here chicky chicky chicky chicky…"

Needed to run. They would find me either way. And I would be no match unless their effort was reduced.

A thought occurred. Injury feigning was a common distraction display among mourning doves and Charadriiformes. But no, wouldn't stand a chance against these men. Better to keep hidden.

"I can't see shit," one of them said. "She could be anywhere."

Noted time (6:10). Heard their movement through the tall grass, but didn't dare peek to see where they were.

"I know you hear me, girl! You can't hide forever! Whatcha gonna do? Sleep out here all night?"

Fact was, dusk had settled in. Sun had fallen behind the trees and I could see the first star. Made a wish. Saw no flashlight beam and knew the men would have to give up at some point.

Crunching of boots came now from a distance, so I permitted myself a glimpse. They had stopped, stood conversing beneath a large tree. Before long they resumed search, but their path led them away from me.

Considered returning to car, but its current state would only leave me trapped. Zipped up my sweatshirt, preventing Nikons from dancing across my chest as I kept men on horizon and followed them across grass to a frontage road paved black ages ago, now cracked as if by slow lightning across a long horizontal night.

Together they trudged up road toward sunset, their shadows so stretched by red light that they nearly reached me.

Sky went black as we walked, and beneath Milky Way our path curved into an indecipherable knot.

After some time a structure appeared that resembled a condemned farmhouse, third man's truck parked on lawn outside.

Air stank of petroleum. Recognized it as DDT. Clearly these people had chosen to ignore National Audubon Society's recent victory in having the insecticide banned.

Rotted wooden steps led to dilapidated deck where rooster sat perched on rail. Wounds and scars on bird's body suggested he had once been, and perhaps still was, a fighting cock.

It was dark, and a flickering porch lamp gave off the only light, intermittently obscured by a dozen moths.

Back door slammed shut behind the men and voices came from inside house. Words were unclear, but tone was elevated and angry.

Began to approach house when bearded man reappeared on deck. I ducked down and watched him snatch up rooster.

Bite him! I thought.

Cock nipped at man, who cussed and snapped its neck.

Bit my tongue as man went back inside. Now felt like my chance. Stood slowly and, heart like a hummingbird, inched my way across yard. Peered in bed of truck to find it empty, then moved to bottom of steps.

Started up stairs. Five total, on third my foot broke through rotting wood with loud CRACK that echoed into the night.

Almost as I pulled leg from broken step and dove into shadow of deck, back door burst open and there stood bearded man.

Watched through railing as he surveyed darkness with eyes squinted, then saw broken step. Hid myself in shadow of deck as bootsteps thunked upon boards.

View was obscured by shadow and fist closed upon my hair, pulled me up so that I stood now crying out at open fields miles from nearest road.

I was hauled over railing and dragged inside, door latched behind us. House smelled of incense masking odor of chicken coop and formaldehyde.

Chickens roamed freely throughout house, their sounds cacophonous. Through this noise a hacking wet cough could be heard from up a long narrow staircase, but I was forced past those steps down a dark hallway to a kitchen that had once been tiled white but was now stained public toilet yellow.

Three dead chickens were strung by their feet, their blood allowed to drip into a sink stacked with unwashed dishes.

A small door opened and I was thrown in so that I stumbled and fell down several stairs to land on concrete floor. Nikons stabbed my chest beneath sweatshirt and I hoped the lenses were intact.

From the top of the steps:

"You sure 'bout this?"

"What choice we got?"

Door slammed shut.

I rose in pain to find myself in cellar made amber by single bare bulb in ceiling. Along walls flimsy metal shelving units held paint cans, boxes, and bug spray. In center of room a cross had been drawn on floor with what looked like white spray paint.

From beyond door at top of stairs came muffled voices raised in argument.

"I don't know 'bout this, Paw. A little girl?"

"She's perfect. No way she's had 'er blood yet."

"I guess."

"You boys 'member when we took you in? Weren't many woulda taken in the *two*'a ya, more mouths and all, but I knew and Momma knew, right as red-handed, you was what we'd been promised. Delivered by the Lord. Now we's a family."

"Yes, Paw."

"You do as you're told now, the both'a ya."

"Yes, Paw."

"Put these on now, and let's do what our family do."

Door opened at top of stairs to reveal cloaked figure silhouetted against the kitchen light. He descended the steps, followed by two more figures. As they drew nearer I smelled incense, saw a gold censer swinging from leader's hands.

"Judge us, oh Lord," I recognized the leader's voice, "and distinguish our cause from the unholy nation."

Looked around. Grabbed aerosol bottle labeled FLY JINX from shelf. "Where did you put my father?"

"Let our sacrifice please Thee, oh Lord." They stepped onto concrete floor three feet from me. "Come, oh sanctifier, almighty and eternal, and bless this sacrifice for Thy holy name."

"Tell me where my father is!"

They came closer, swinging of the censer hypnotic. Second man in procession carried long curved knife, third held dead rooster from front porch by its snapped neck. "May the Lord accept the sacrifice we are about to bestow."

Sprayed insecticide as they stepped into amber light and saw their faces covered by birdlike plague masks, long beaks extending from beneath hoods of maroon cloaks. I coughed at petroleum stench of spray and backed away from light, up against far wall of cellar.

Smell of incense blended now with insecticide, smoke and mist spiraling together in cone of warm light from bulb overhead.

Grabbed hold of metal shelf to my right and pulled it down upon them. They shouted and ducked as shelf fell. Paint cans and boxes rained down and those boxes exploded to spill rusty tools everywhere.

Took up hammer that tumbled to my feet. Brought it down on head of nearest man, the leader. Felt his skull cave in.

Second man crawled out from beneath shelf and limped toward me, knife still gripped in fist, stepping over third man, who struggled to escape.

Again I swung hammer but man with rooster caught my wrist and twisted, forcing me to floor while still muttering.

"Deign to accept this," he recited, "as You accepted the gift of Your servant Abel, and the sacrifice of Abraham our Father, and that which Your high priest Melch… Melchis…"

"Melchizedek!" cried man with knife, taking position over me.

"Melchizedek offered to Thee," continued man with rooster, his knees pinning my arms to floor, his hands holding dead bird just in front of other man's knife approximately 18 inches above my face. "A holy sacrifice, an unspotted victim."

Through golden smoke emerged bobbing silhouettes of hens clucking curiously as man with knife brought it down at me.

"Help!" I cried, and at once chickens obeyed, their beaks and claws nipping and tearing at my captors, wings flapping, casting motes of feather dust to swirl within golden smoke.

Third man shrieked, releasing my arm, and both men fled through amber cloud.

"That's it!" one of them yelled. "I'm done with this weird-ass shit!"

Followed them up stairs from cellar into kitchen, where free-range hens bit at them, cornering them against sink, over which still hung three dead chickens.

Saw reflected in their oily black eyes my own face. Filthy, bruised, without expression. My eyes tethered to theirs. And so my rage.

"Join the party," I said, and back to life these dead birds sprang, swinging by their feet with each crazed flap, each vengeful bite.

"You too." And so too did rooster clutched still in man's hand awake, taking from its dark master a new taste.

Ears hit floor, followed by chunks of torn flesh. Screaming filled room. Through anarchic beating of wings and screeching of avian voices I strode, lifting hammer into air and with it transforming two men into bags of broken bones.

Yet on they ran despite precariously balanced scaffolding inside them, staggering for front door and night air beyond, leaving trail of plague masks, robes, and items of ritual.

Easy enough path to follow in the moonlight for both myself and my army, eager themselves to draw upon ancient instinct for aggression bred into them long ago but long thought outgrown.

As we tracked our prey among fields of apple blossoms, we accumulated all manner of additional sparrows, jays, and scavengers to our cause, each with its own grievance, perhaps not against these men themselves but certainly against that for which they stood. An evil older than man, known best to creatures born of prehistory.

Against wooden post of barbed wire fence at last the men had collapsed, unclothed, their strength extinguished, fingers black with soil of shallow grave at their feet.

"There he is," gasped red-bearded man, dragging man with red sideburns to his side, boney finger extended at upturned ground. "Wasn't us that buried 'im! Take 'im and leave my brother and me alone!"

Stepped forward and looked down to see half-revealed in the dirt the face of my own father, buried with open eyes open caked blind with earth.

As from when, as a child, I first influenced the will of the specimens outside my window to taunt our neighbor's cat, so now did I extend my fury into the feathered mass gathered about me.

Have at them, I thought, and they did, every chicken, rooster, sparrow, jay, and crow descending upon the two screaming men who had killed Father. True monsters.

Eyes were plucked out, throats pierced, bellies disemboweled. Entrails pulled skyward like kite strings.

Noted the coming dawn and considered stories Father used to tell dinner guests of sky burials of Tibet, fragments of the holy disassembled and served to scavenger birds. Recalled Mother yawning.

Considered the Balinese, who believed the soul was a bird. Upon a person's death a pyre was built for the body. This flaming structure toppled within moments, the corpse crashing through fire to earth. But impact of body on ground was believed to shake free the soul and send it on its way, flying off into next world.

Spied in hole of wooden fencepost a small nest, three tiny nestlings within all peeping for mother, who now appeared. Female robin: 5 inches. Typical diet: invertebrates, berries, and seeds. Watched her regurgitate into beaks of her little family the human flesh just eaten.

Saw now more birds flocking to the banquet, some exotic, likely diverted by opportunity from migratory paths. Unzipped my sweatshirt to withdraw Nikons, fortunately undamaged. The morning was alive with sound.

Jackdaw caw in the apple blossom, binoculars to my eyes. Black mask over gray body. Black wings. Rare in this region, but seen increasingly in recent years. Blue irises. Rictal bristles upon its beak, which held a severed human penis.

Noted time (6:25) and weather (sunny, cloudless blue). Noted a second bird, source of the sound. A female? She tried for the penis, which male surrendered, naturally. Made note of their wingspans as they departed. Female: approximately 27 inches. Male: 30.

Thrilled at the sighting, turned my attention to the scene of the murder at my left. Six crows atop a barbed wire fence, bowed by their weight. All with black mandibles like snub-nosed revolvers. Joined now by a seventh. Larger than the others, yellow stripe along length of hooked beak holding a man's eyeball.

Held in my hands the heavy Nikon Roof Prism Compact, weathered and worn. My first binoculars, given to me by Father when I was still just a little girl.

That was yesterday. I am not a little girl anymore.

Walk with me, I think, and lead my staggering father now by his cold, earth-stained hand down the highway toward a twilit motel whose neon sign boasts free cable. *It has been a long day. Maybe we'll stay there tonight.*

THE SECRET

JASON POMERANCE

It snowed the morning Hannah Green died. Oh, it wasn't one of those storms with light-as-air flakes you tried to catch on your tongue as you danced in circles, head tipped back toward the sky. It wasn't the kind where you might lie flat on your back, waving arms up and down, making angels. It was a heavy dumping cyclone that left a dense white blanket paralyzing the region — tree limbs groaned and sagged precipitously, power lines snapped, throwing everything into darkness, and the thick coating made everything seem hushed, muffled, and somehow unearthly.

Becky Green lay in her bed that morning unaware of what had happened just down the hall. Once, during the night, she had stirred awake. She climbed from the bed and peered out the window; in the dark, she could see flakes swirling in a fury. The glass was beginning to frost over, but she could still make out her reflection — chestnut hair hanging straight below her shoulders, with its off-center part, and that bridge of freckles covering her nose. Then white frost was all she could see, so she turned away.

She heard conversation and cracked open the bedroom door. Her father was slumped in a chair at the top of the stairs, talking into his phone. Becky caught a muffled wail coming from the person on the other end. She considered stepping into the hall or padding down to her brother's room to see if he was awake. But she softly closed the door and slipped back into bed.

She had recently taken ill, her mother, and suddenly the fun, pretty, mischievous woman she was accustomed to had been replaced by something different altogether. This new mom was almost unrecognizable. Yet when her father appeared at her door shortly after dawn and sat on the bed — perched on the edge, facing away, but still she could sense he was wound up tight — and delivered the news that she had passed, it was a shock. "We'll be fine, honey. I promise," her dad had said. "We'll figure it out, and all will be okay." His voice wavered, though, with a little catch in his throat, and Becky felt unsure.

In fact, Becky didn't believe her mother was really gone. She was convinced she had secretly traveled somewhere to heal — some exotic tropical island maybe — and would reappear, whole again, as if the last few weeks had been some disturbing dream. All that soon unfolded at the house — the arrival of relatives and friends, for instance, or the removal of the body (Dad ordered Becky and her brother to their rooms and told them not to come out until he said so. But Becky peeked. What they removed was covered, wasn't it? So who knew what was underneath that sheet?) — all of this could be some elaborate ruse, Becky figured. She was twelve, and often young minds worked in ways that were far from logical. Rob was even younger — almost nine — and just seemed shell-shocked, taking everything in silently, with an eerie wide-eyed stony gaze. He followed Becky everywhere, like a shadow.

"Can you stop doing this?" she said to him at one point when she turned and nearly ran him down.

"Doing what?" Robby asked.

His voice came out in a painful whine; it set her on edge, made her grit her teeth. "You're always there. Everywhere I go. It's getting on my nerves."

She expected him to say something mean back. That was the way with them as a rule, a push-pull back and forth of pranks and spiteful words, even if often this was through smiles and laughter. But his eyes widened and then pooled with tears. His PJs were rumpled and his hair a tangled mess. Becky suddenly regretted even opening her mouth. She considered hugging him but decided against it.

* * *

OVER THE NEXT couple of days, Becky continued to sense that her mother might not really be gone. For instance, there was the time she was in the bathroom after a shower, and she could swear she saw a shadow behind her in the mirror. When she turned to look, nothing was there. But wasn't it just like Mom to play some sort of trick like that, like when they'd play hide and seek when Becky was small? Or sometimes, when they were driving somewhere, Hannah would pretend she had lost her way, and Becky would have to help steer them home.

At one point, she overheard a voice on the phone in the kitchen. "This is Mrs. Green. Yes, I can hold." Becky, heading for the stairs, stopped in her tracks. She dashed into the kitchen, her heart thudding in her chest, sure she would find her mom. Instead, it was the wife of her father's brother. Mrs. Green, yes, just like her mother, but the wrong Mrs. Green, the wrong voice, she realized too late. Still, was this again some sort of signal? Or the time she heard a familiar jangling of bracelets. Another disappointment, though, as it turned out to be Mom's best friend from across town; they had bought matching bracelets on a lark, the friend was telling her father. Of course, all sorts of doubts about her theory began to creep into her head, and Becky began to feel unsure. If Mom was coming back, when exactly would that happen?

And then a funeral unfolded.

This could very well be part of the trick, Becky mused, although if she really thought about it, wouldn't that be taking things too far?

Wouldn't it be, well, cruel? She pushed these thoughts out of her mind. "Put on your best dress, sweetheart, and comb your hair nicely like mom showed you, okay?" her father had said. "And I'll see to your brother."

"Okay. Sure," Becky had answered.

She thought about asking Dad, voicing her thoughts about what had really happened, where her mother had truly gone, and when she would return. But she noticed Rob poking his face out from his room — still wearing that lost look of utter bewilderment — and she kept quiet, deciding that, for now, going through the motions was the right plan.

She headed into her room. She opened her closet. She only had one or two dresses that she hadn't outgrown ("You simply must stop shooting up," Mom would shout, "like a beanpole with those gangly legs!"). The last one had been purchased on a jaunt to the mall taken at the spur of the moment, because they needed some mother-daughter time, Mom had said in a lowered voice almost like a secret pact, as she grabbed her car keys with a sly grin. Becky savored the rare times when it was just the two of them, when her brother wasn't making some sort of fuss, or spilling juice all over himself, or yelling at his video game, or mom's attention wasn't directed at dad. Her mother was usually so much fun to be around (oh, of course there was the occasional flare-up of temper, often when Becky did or said something stupid), unlike the moms of some of Becky's friends, who were strict, or too busy with this or that, or even mean.

Becky pulled both dresses from the closet, laid them on the bed, and scrutinized each. One, frilly and a reddish shade of pink, was clearly for some kind of party. She chose the other because it seemed more somber, a serious dress, as if Mom knew something and wasn't telling? She brushed and combed her hair, attempting but failing to center the part. She always loved watching Mom put on her face, a routine that included first brushing on foundation and blush, then turning to her eyes, adding liner and mascara. She'd cap the process with a coat of lipstick, which was blotted onto a tissue, leaving an almost comic version of bright red lips. Becky considered raiding Mom's make-up drawer. But this was all a big fake, she still insisted to herself, so it didn't really matter what her hair or her face looked like.

They drove in silence to a church they rarely visited. Although it hadn't snowed since that morning, the air was still frigid, the roads slick, icy tree limbs overhead forming a perilous canopy. The ride felt almost dangerous. Dad gripped the wheel so tightly his knuckles turned white, cursing under his breath as the tires spun recklessly, and the car slid this way and that.

Inside the church, though, it was stiflingly hot. There was a casket covered in flowers. It certainly could be empty, Becky reasoned. Relatives and family friends were present. Becky's best friend Sara sat next to her. She'd been calling for days — ever since that morning — and Becky had been ignoring her calls because Sara was sort of depressing, really, always going on about the calamities of the world, and how could they possibly even consider getting married and having children when they grew up. As the service got underway, Sara reached out to grasp Becky's hand. Becky glared at her.

"I'm here for you," Sara whispered. "I just want you to know that even though you may feel the world has come to an end, possibly the future will be brighter. Although there are no guarantees, to be honest."

"Thanks, I guess," Becky said, wondering if she should confide the secret. Wasn't that what friends were for? But she was sure Sara's reaction would be negative, and so she kept quiet.

Sara frowned and stared at her shoes. She looked dour and serious, as if this were about her own mother. Inappropriately, Becky felt the urge to laugh. In fact, a few giggles burped up from deep within, despite her attempts to quash them by swallowing hard or squeezing her eyes shut. Now people turned to look, including Rob, who seemed horror-stricken, as if his sister had gone insane. It suddenly struck Becky that giggles might also pass for sobs, so she covered her eyes, shook her shoulders, and pretended she was crying. Her father reached over and gave her arm a squeeze. Becky dabbed at her eyes.

This seemed to appease the gathered. "Everything is fine," she murmured when she could control her voice again. "All is good!"

The service proceeded. Becky didn't recognize the stooped, frail, old bald man who slipped silently to the podium and said a few words about Hannah Green in a hushed, halting voice. Becky had to strain to actually hear what he was saying. And then when she could hear the words, it didn't sound remotely like her mother, the woman he was describing, but some strange person who had nothing to do with her life. This man was, she thought, more like an actor playing a part, which only further convinced her that this was all just a play up on a stage.

There would be no graveside service. The ground was too frozen to dig the deep hole, Becky gathered from her father's stammering explanation, but she suspected the real reason was there was nothing to bury, so a gathering would only complicate this ruse. Everybody returned to the house. While they were gone, somebody — Becky couldn't be sure who — had come in and set another scene: on the dining room table were platters and platters of food, and in the living room a bar had been set up in the corner. Already there was a crowd and the sound of ice clinking in glasses, as if this was just another party. Certainly there wouldn't be such lighthearted chatter if her mother was really gone.

ALL THOSE WHO gathered returned to their lives. The house seemed too silent, except for the TV in the living room, which seemed to be on all the time, the noise it provided a kind of salve you might apply to a wound. On the news, the weatherman kept predicting a thaw, and a few days later, a warm front blew through. It brought rain, torrential downpours that turned all the snow into thick gray slush and then washed it completely away.

Becky watched the landscape change from the living room window, her nose pressed to the glass. The winter holidays were approaching, and school had shut down until the New Year. For a few days she was alone in the house with Rob, and she did her best to entertain him but wasn't having much luck. Most of the time, she was bringing him snacks or nagging at him to wipe his nose. Also, nobody was doing the chores Mom would normally see to. Laundry, for instance, was piling up, and Becky figured maybe she should pitch in and help. So she gathered up all the discarded and tossed-aside dirty things and separated them into piles. She carried them into the basement. She stared at the washing machine, at all its complicated gauges and buttons, and gave up. Mom would fix it when she came back.

And then, over a dinner of a casserole that had been left in the refrigerator by a neighbor and reheated — what was this unfamiliar thick and gloppy mess? — their father made an announcement: they'd be spending the holiday, just like always, at the mountain place.

Rob gave dad a weak, watery smile. Becky sat for a moment digesting this unexpected sliver of information. She looked at the space where her mom should have been sitting. It was screamingly empty. She looked back at her dad and found it difficult to swallow the hunk of chicken she still had in her mouth.

The mountain place was special to this family, an enormous old sprawling hotel built in a Tyrolean style, as if it had been snatched off a Swiss Alp and dropped back down in the crevice of a jagged peak in the northern part of the state. There was a lake for skating in winter and boating in the warmer months, and just across the lake a twin craggy peak, at the top of which an old stone tower was perched. The owners went over-the-top for the winter holidays, with decorated trees everywhere and fires roaring in fireplaces and massive buffets of delicious-looking sweets. The idea of going there now struck Becky as absurd. She wondered if her father had lost his mind. She felt a sudden surge of anger. She was holding her milk glass, and without even thinking, she launched it in her dad's direction. It missed — he ducked, a bewildered look on his face while a gasp came from Rob — and crashed against the wall, creating one more mess to clean up.

"It won't be the same," she spat. "Nothing will ever be the same."

She leapt from her chair, stormed up to her room, and flung herself on the bed. She expected tears to come, but still they hadn't. Or had they? Suddenly, Becky couldn't remember if she had cried at all. Had she? Had she dreamed about tears? Rob had cried, she knew. She could hear him at night, alone in his room. She had passed her father's room once and caught a glimpse of him sitting on his bed, wracked with sobs. Even if she tried to make tears come, they wouldn't. But then she'd think *why exactly should I cry? She's coming back!*

Later, her dad appeared at her door and hovered at the threshold. Becky lay on her side facing the wall, pretending to be asleep. She stayed that way until she could hear his footsteps retreat down the hall; they seemed to have a meek, defeated sound. She felt a small tug around her heart and almost went after him. She didn't, though.

That night, it hit her — every year at the mountain place, they'd bundle up and hike to the tower. Every year, Mom would pull a special gift from her pocket or have something hidden up there for Becky and Rob to discover, like a treasure hunt. Her surprise return was surely the reason they were making the trip. Mom's reappearance would be the gift.

Suddenly, Becky could barely contain her excitement, couldn't wait to leave, but their departure was still a day away. And so she busied herself with little tasks. She scrubbed the bathrooms upstairs and down. She tidied up her closet, which was something Mom was always after her to do. She considered going into Dad's room but had been avoiding it since that morning. She could see disorder in there but decided to let it be. She went into Rob's room. It too was chaos, dirty clothes scattered willy-nilly, a plate with a half-eaten sandwich on the desk, Rob still in bed staring vacantly at something on TV. When he saw her, his lower lip began to quiver. "Now what?" Becky said.

"Do you think she misses us?"

"What? Who?"

"Doh. Hello? Mom. Don't you sort of wonder what it's like where she is?"

Becky regarded her brother for a moment. "You want to know a secret?" she finally asked. "Because I know something that you don't."

He stared at her. He looked sort of pathetic, it struck her, with his front teeth still not filled in, his hair all matted and spiky, and his nose running yet again, as if he'd had the sniffles for days, and should she have noticed that because Dad had sort of left her in charge?

"Tell me the secret," Rob said, urgency in his voice.

Becky paused, her mouth half-open, as if she might reveal all. But Rob was suddenly on her nerves again, which was often the case, from just the way he was gazing at her, as if she had all the answers.

"Never mind," said Becky as she scooted out of the room.

* * *

THEN CAME the morning they would drive up to the mountain place. All over the TV news, anchors issued dire warnings about a change in weather patterns. Temperatures were predicted to plummet, and a storm was brewing somewhere to the south, but their father didn't seem to mind. He was up early and in the kitchen fixing breakfast, which he was not good at. Becky could smell something acrid even before she went downstairs.

"Eggs à la dad!" he said, aiming for bright and chipper but his expression dubious as he brought the skillet to the table. The eggs had stuck to the bottom, and it took him a minute, wedging the spatula underneath, to extricate them. Also, the toast was burnt, even though he had tried to scrape off the really gross parts.

"Maybe we should stop at that diner on the highway," Becky suggested.

"What?! This breakfast is perfectly fine."

It wasn't though. And it was different. Mom would have made pancakes with chocolate chips for eyes, nose and a smile. There would have been warm syrup to pour on top, crisp bacon, and chilled orange juice. This food was barely edible, Becky thought, imagining the hotel breakfast they'd all enjoy once Mom returned and the world was set to right again. But both she and Rob made attempts to get some of the food down to please Dad.

Soon they were on their way. They didn't take Mom's car — it sat in the driveway looking abandoned and forlorn — and as they left, the sky was changing, first just puffy white clouds passing and occasionally blocking the sun, and then darker ones. After a couple of hours on wide open highway, most of it in stiff, awkward silence, the car exited onto a road that took them first through a small town, then past farms with barns and silos and pick-up trucks parked out front, smoke curling lazily out of chimneys. Once they were up the mountain, the road twisted and turned, and occasionally Becky would catch a glimpse of that tower, and she could barely contain her excitement because she was sure of what was waiting there.

As they pulled into the parking lot of the hotel, snow began to fall in light, airy flakes. Becky emerged from the car and tipped her head back to catch a few of them on her tongue. "Can we go, Dad? Can we hike up to the tower now?" she pleaded.

"Yes," Rob echoed. "Can we?"

Dad tilted his head up to the sky. All the blue was gone. The flint gray that had replaced it appeared threatening. "Later, guys. Okay?"

Rob nodded. Becky frowned. They gathered their baggage and trudged toward the lobby.

IT KEPT SNOWING, and Dad continued to nix the idea of a hike to the tower. So they played checkers and backgammon in the game room. After the sun went down, and fires were lit in hearths all through the hotel, they moved to the dining hall for their traditional dinner. This consisted of rosy pink roast beef carved at a gleaming silver cart rolled table-side, served with a flourish alongside an individual Yorkshire pudding, brown and crisped at the edges, fluffy mashed potatoes, and the richest creamed spinach Becky had ever tasted.

All around them families were celebrating. But the good cheer didn't seem to be contagious — the Green table was eerily hushed.

Rob shoveled food in his mouth. Dad wasn't eating much. Occasionally he would pass a hand through his hair or let out what sounded like an anguished sigh. But Becky felt certain all this would change when they got to the tower. "You know what might be neat? We could do a night hike," she offered while a dessert of floating island — cloud-like meringues in a rich caramel sauce with golden spun sugar woven all over the top — was served.

"Oh, honey, no," Dad said. "Maybe in the morning if the weather clears, but even then the path may be treacherous."

Becky held her tongue. All through dinner she had been formulating a plan, and she didn't want Dad to suspect that she was up to anything. It was exciting to keep this to herself, and she smiled a little tucked-in smile as they left the dining room. She even caught a glimpse of the tower as they were heading back to the rooms. A beacon sat at the top and was flashing on and off, a signal Becky was sure, like a code, speaking only to her.

She was quiet during an after-dinner game of War upstairs. This took place in the same two adjoining rooms they'd stayed in on past visits; Mom and Dad would take the bigger, Rob and Becky the smaller one, with its single beds on opposite walls, flowery wallpaper, and a strong cedar smell that wafted from the closet.

"I guess we aren't not getting no special gift this year," Rob said from his bed after Dad had told them it was time for sleep.

"Aren't not getting no...? I think you want to say 'are not getting any,'" Becky corrected him.

"Whatever."

"Let's just wait and see."

"Okay."

He said this in a tiny voice, the covers pulled up to his neck, so Becky could barely see the top of his head.

She waited until he began to softly snore.

* * *

Dad had the TV blasting in his room, so Becky eased herself out of bed, careful not to wake Rob. She was still in the clothes she had been wearing, blue jeans and a sweater. In the dark, she pushed her feet into sneakers, grabbed her coat, a scarf, and mittens.

She slipped out of the room, scurried through a door marked exit at the end of the hall, and bounded down the stairs.

Outside, the frigid air hit her face like icicles, and the snow was picking up in intensity. This didn't stop Becky as she made her way to the entrance of the trail that would take her up to the tower.

She paused at the trailhead. Signs warned of all sorts of peril and she fought a sense of trepidation, even dread. Also, it was pitch dark, and the storm was turning fiercer. She looked back at the hotel. It was illuminated festively, and fragrant smoke from the hearths was in the air. But then she stepped onto the trail, her feet making crunching noises in deepening snow, her breath coming out in ragged visible puffs. She suddenly wished she'd worn boots, but kept moving forward, the way ahead turning steeper. Every now and then there would be a point where she'd glimpse the tower. Still the beacon flashed, propelling Becky further, even though now her feet were hurting and her mittened hands were so cold she thrust them deep into her pockets.

Higher up the mountain, it was snowing even harder. Becky could barely make out where she was or where she needed to go. She slid on an icy patch and took a tumble, skidding into a jagged boulder and careening off it, ripping a hole in her jeans. And then there was grazed skin, blood on her knee. Tears almost came, but there was that beacon — flashing light and dark like a pulse — and she hauled herself up and soldiered on, occasionally groping for a stick or a rock to grasp.

She reached her destination and stopped to marvel at it. The tower was just as she remembered, solidly constructed of dark gray weathered stone, soaring up into the sky, pointed like a pyramid at the top. There was no door at the base, just an open passageway, and then a narrow set of stairs came into view. Wind whistled through the space, sounding like an eerie moan. But Becky was undaunted. She took the steps two at a time, so eager was she to reach the pinnacle. Here would be Mom, smiling and laughing, throwing open her arms for a hug.

But…

Nothing.

Here was just a small empty space, alternately lit from the beacon, almost blindingly because it was so close, and then pitch inky darkness.

Becky, panting heavily, stood stock still, mouth agape, almost unable to catch her breath.

* * *

A SHORT TIME LATER, Becky emerged from the tower. Finally, she had allowed tears to come, and the sobs came like a wave that washed over her, a big ugly cry that left her feeling totally spent but strangely renewed.

So much snow had fallen that the path back down the mountain was obscured. She pushed forward anyway but soon became disoriented, unsure which way to turn. And then, one more time, she lost her footing, stumbled and wound up on her back, sliding head-first, precipitously and dizzyingly, down an icy section until she became lodged in a small bank of snow. For a moment, she lay there thinking she could be lost, buried until they found just bones. Her mother's voice came back to her — "Make angels, honey!"—she'd always said when they played outside after a fresh snow. A day like that now seemed like ancient history, gone forever except for the memory of a voice, and even that was already starting to fade.

Becky waved her arms up and down and stood to look at her work. There indeed was an angel. She knew it would be temporary, that the wind would carry it away, but that seemed right.

She brushed stray flakes off her jeans and clapped her hands together to remove icy crystals from her mittens.

Still, she was confused about the way forward.

She heard a noise echoing off the mountain. It was faint at first, so that she couldn't be sure if she was hearing it at all, or if it was some trick of the mind. But it grew louder and closer.

Voices.

It was her name they were calling, and then, through swirling flakes, she could make out Dad, so solid and dependable it struck her, and trailing behind him Rob, his mittens dangling from the clips at his wrists, and she would fix that. She called out their names. "I'm here," she shouted, and she began to move toward them. And even though the path was slippery, Becky began to run.

MILDRED

JANE-HOLLY MEISSNER

A gentle rain fell upon a neighborhood that had once bustled with young families. Babies had grown to adulthood, parents became grandparents, and the neighborhood decayed as the generations moved on. Some moved away to live with their grown children, others had been put into long term care facilities, and some had simply passed away. Such was the way of things. Once- proud yards were thick with dandelions, and few remained who remembered the children and their bikes riding up and down the streets.

In one quaint bungalow Mildred O'Rourke sat in an overstuffed armchair, crocheting a scarf. On rainy days like this she couldn't help but think about her late husband, Robert. He would have brought the ointment for his arthritis and had her rub it into his hands when the barometer was this low.

He'd had rough, callused hands from long days and long years working construction. Even when he became a contractor and then managed his own construction company, he still couldn't resist getting his hands dirty. The long hours of work had led to painful joints in his later years, but he'd never complained.

They'd never been blessed with children, but Mildred and her husband had been involved with the neighborhood kids—she'd been the local elementary school secretary and had known each child by name. Robert had coached sports for under-10s, and they had many happy memories celebrating wins and losses with the kids and their parents. Auntie Millie and Uncle Rob, they called them. And then Mildred retired, and Robert couldn't keep up with the children anymore. Life became quiet.

She chuckled, pausing her crochet as she recalled the loudest fight they'd had as newlyweds. Barely a year after they'd been married, she had ended up in the hospital with kidney stones. When she finally came home, exhausted and ready for her own bed, she discovered that Robert had left all the housework for her to finish when she recovered. He'd seen the error of his ways (after a few nights without dinner) and made an effort from then on to pitch in around the house when he got home from work. As an apology he brought her flowers for a week straight—inexpensive bunches, but fragrant and beautiful nonetheless.

Years later they'd taken a road trip to see the Grand Canyon. It was what people did when they retired: rent an RV and see the country. They'd ended up wrestling with an RV that was much too big for them, and Robert had insisted he could back it into the camping spot without help. He had to attempt it four times and took out a sapling in the process but got it done. They laughed about it by the campfire over roasted marshmallows.

A few years after that, Robert came down with a bad cough. At times he seemed better, but the cough never fully went away. By the time he agreed to see a doctor, the cancer had spread from his lungs to other vital organs. Mildred held his hands and tried not to weep as he stoically received news of the shortening of his life to the next few months.

So many moments in a life together full of love. Not a romance for the ages, but respect and affection were written clearly between the lines of a quietly ordinary life.

When he died, she was at his side, her wrinkled and age-spotted hand patting his, assuring him it was all right for him to go. He'd passed with a small smile on his face, his eyes on hers, and her heart broke. Of *course* she had told him he could go; she didn't want to see him suffering any longer. Still, she struggled with loneliness. The house was… empty. She felt the pang of Robert's loss keenly and even wept over the children they never had, despite having made her peace with their infertility decades ago .

Mildred was alone for the first time in her life, facing her golden years in an empty house in a neighborhood that didn't remember her anymore.

* * *

MILDRED TIED OFF THE YARN, completing the work. She set it aside as she got up to light candles, brightening up a rapidly darkening room as the sun dipped toward the horizon. She'd always been sensitive to the supernatural, and her husband had good-naturedly put up with her collection of crystals and little rituals.

"I know I said you could go," she said to the room, "but it's been a year and I just can't go on without you." Mildred retrieved the crochet work and spread it out on the hardwood floor, an unbroken circle of white wool.

The candles around the circle flickered as she added keepsakes from their lives together to strategic spots: a rock from the Grand Canyon, a handful of dried flower petals, a hospital wristband.

Casting the summoning spell, she pulled on all her memories of her husband, and a swirling white mist began to grow in the middle of the circle. Surely, she was about to be reunited with him and they could be a family again: a little family of two.

A sliver of doubt leaked into her intention. Maybe she shouldn't meddle with life after death. Didn't he deserve to rest in peace? What if he only came back as a spirit or couldn't return to a peaceful after-life once she ripped him out of it?

It had been a year and a day since he'd died, and Mildred panicked, all the surety of the last few weeks of preparations flying away. When he was summoned, he would be bound to her will and intention—and what sort of life would that be?

But it was too late: the summoning ritual had begun and would not stop until it was complete. She pushed away the memories of her husband and kicked away the closest memento from the circle. Her uncertainty of the last moments was in itself a new certainty.

What she had pulled of Robert's essence drained from the circle, creating a vacuum in her spell. The mist turned gray and then to a thick black smoke. Through the crack she had opened, something filled the void. A monstrous dark form loomed in the midst of the woolen circle, jagged horns outlined against the ceiling.

"What do you wish from me, mortal?" it boomed, leaning over her, an even blacker gash appearing where its mouth might be.

Mildred completed the ritual with shaking hands, binding the dark creature to this plane and to her commands.

At least she wouldn't be alone anymore.

EMPIRE OF SALT

EVAN GRAHAM

I sit with my back straight, each movement made with poise and purpose, in pristine form for every protocol of this moment. I hold complete control over every muscle in my face, sure to show no emotions that do not give advantage in the conversation. This is how it is done.

My hair is silver and thinning but styled and professional. My hands are wrinkled and age-gnarled but steady and strong. I am seen as I choose to be seen. The face, the body, the voice: they are tools for the mind, and mine are honed to perfection.

My attire serves me the same. I wear a $120,000 Ligotti suit with cufflinks and a tie pin worth nearly as much. My Miloroan blue diamond ring is fourteen carats and worth forty-five million; the other ring is Samrati vaidurite and worth nearly twice that. The number of vaidurite gemstones in the galaxy equal to its value could be worn on one hand. I wear the greatest wealth multiple worlds have produced, and the man across from me knows this.

Carl Vogelweide. I do not normally need to remind myself of people's names, but I do not normally speak to people like Vogelweide. He slouches in his chair with one arm draped over the back, his retail suit unbuttoned, his shirt partially untucked. His big, pale,

"

American face flaps its too-wide, too-thin lips in endless chatter. A fraction of my mind listens to his babbling. The rest retreats into itself, refusing to be so ill-used.

"...Have to say, your hospitality is second to none, Kosawa-san," he tells me, as if I do not know. "Honestly, if nothing else ever comes of this colony, your home should be enough to put it on the map."

The corners of my mouth raise two degrees, acknowledging the flattery without encouraging it. "Thank you, Mr. Vogelweide. Hayden is not a kind world, but I am quite comfortable with the piece I've carved off for myself."

Allston, my chef, places a two-hundred-year-old earthenware tea set on the glass table, pouring two steaming cups of glittering amber liquid. I give him a nod. He gives a silent bow and returns to the kitchen.

"Baihao Yinzhen," I say, raising my cup. "Silver Needle tea, from China's Fujian province. My wife's favorite. We drink to honor her memory."

I watch in still, silent disgust as the American heaps three heavy spoonfuls of sugar into his tea, loudly clanking the sides of his cup as he stirs the grainy, ruined sludge. He raises his cup of vegetative syrup with an imbecilic smile on his fat face. "To your wife."

"To Jinyin." We drink. I savor the smooth, floral flavor as I always do. Memories rise from the steam, pulling my presence to the past.

I recall the conference in Hong Kong nearly sixty years ago. Thousands were there, but even in my untested youth, I knew we were not all created equal. Most attended for the catered meals and elegant hotel suites paid for by company shareholders. A few came to network but stumbled blindly, shaking hands indiscriminately, forgetting and remembering the wrong names, wasting time trying to strike deals with those who were not looking for them.

Not I, though. I stalked those halls as an apex predator. Even as a young man, barely out of university and fresh on the board of my father's company, I knew the taste of blood in the water. I knew the naïve smile of someone who has not earned his confidence, who will hand his marionette strings to the first flatterer. I knew the smirks of bravado from the obscenely wealthy, who could be convinced to invest immense wealth if your request amused them enough. I knew the hopeless eyes of a man who has suffered losses so great he will take a disadvantageous deal simply to keep from losing all he has.

I knew it when I met my future wife.

I knew, we both knew, from the moment our eyes locked. Such eyes they were: cunning, intelligent, ruthless. The eyes of a mako shark. I took her measure and she took mine, and in that instant, we knew we would have each other.

Her story was much like mine: the child of a powerful corporate mogul, every bit as ambitious as her father. Through pure indomitable willpower and cold-blooded pragmatism, she'd ascended to Ming Construction Corp's board of directors. Few understood this at the time, but she was one of the most powerful women in all of China.

"Never had the privilege, myself." Vogelweide's oleaginous voice intrudes on my thoughts. "But several of my colleagues knew your wife, and they still talk about her from time to time. She must have been quite a woman."

Quite a woman. An insulting understatement. I would look down on him for it if my opinion could be lowered further. "What exactly do your colleagues say about my late wife, Mr. Vogelweide?"

"Ah, well." He takes a nervous sip of tea, buying his mind the generous time it requires to form less foolish words. "Only that she made quite a name for herself, even before the Corsica Event, and how she was one of the few who really managed to keep her head during and right after. Hell, you're both legends for that. You know your crisis management strategies are required reading in every business school in the colonies?"

An amused smirk creases my lips. "And what, exactly, do they teach about that? That you should wait until a technological singularity causes a rogue AI to self-evolve into a wrathful god that devastates half the Earth?"

"No, sir. I didn't mean it like that. I meant the way you and your wife handled yourselves and your companies during that catastrophe. I understand it was quite chaotic during that time."

He is too young to understand. Humanity had never seen a catastrophe like the Corsica Event, a night of sirens, screams, and shattered skies. Billions died in its wake. Nations fell. Economies collapsed. After fifty years, the memories are as sharp and terrible as ever. The burning waves, the cracking streets, the demon storms that raged and ravaged with monstrous purpose...

I was at our Tokyo office. Half the board was there, the rest held up in traffic. The urgent sounds of several cell phones heralded the Corsica Event's arrival. The building shuddered and groaned under typhoon winds and rocked on its foundations when the first tsunami hit. The boardroom fell to chaos. I alone kept calm. I alone understood the stakes.

I beat the old men to the door and drew the pistol I carried for protection. I informed them in certain terms I would allow none of them to abandon my father's company during this crisis. We would hold Kosawa Global Communications above the water or we would sink beneath the waves. I was not bluffing, and they could tell. They came to their senses, and we began the task.

Our Yokohama, Osaka, and Nagoya offices were completely gone, as were our international offices in Honolulu, Miami, Sydney, São Paulo, Madrid, and Shanghai. This confirmed the worst of our fears: the event was global. We could not contact the absent members of the board, including my father. We assumed the worst, but I allowed no grieving. Tracking the damages, we learned storms were the least of our concerns: satellite networks were failing, and global communication was breaking down.

We did not know then that the Corsica Event was the growing pains of a machine god, but we knew something catastrophic was happening to the network. A technological cascade collapse a hundred times worse than anything in history. The Kosawa communications empire had met its nemesis, and it fell to me to save our family legacy.

So I shut it down. On my order, every office, network hub, cell tower, server, and satellite shut down and disconnected from the grid. Just a few minutes into the grim cataclysm, Kosawa Global Communications went silent.

I do not know how much that choice truly cost the global community. I have been told by some who hold me in low regard that Kosawa's sudden communications blackout caused as many as 12 million preventable deaths. It does not matter. What matters is that a few hours later, as suddenly and mysteriously as it began, the Corsica Event ceased. And by the end of the day, our network was online again.

For my quick thinking and decisive action, the board I had just held hostage unanimously named me to replace my father at the head of our company. I took the position with pride. The world remained in chaos for many years to come, but not Kosawa Global Communications. We grew only stronger, as I put my predator's gaze to the same use I had at that conference in Hong Kong. An upturned world is a treasure trove for one with an eye for opportunity.

I was not the only one with such an eye. Ming Jinyin's experience during the Corsica Event was a perfect mirror for mine. She too lost her father on that day of carnage but saved his company with ruthless efficiency. Quick acting and quicker thinking let her save most of Ming Construction Corp's assets, and she wasted no time capitalizing on the devastation left in the Corsica Event's wake.

We stood alone amongst the rubble, she with her international construction firm, and I with my global communications company. We saw one another through the smoke, and the same silent exchange happened between us.

I must have you.

And we did. The most powerful people in the post-Corsica world united: king and queen brought together in matrimony to unite two kingdoms. She was no tame housewife. It was clear that ours would be a true partnership of equals. I'd have had it no other way. Her power attracted me above all. Legends alone, our union made us gods.

In a few years, we rebuilt ravaged cities that should have taken decades to recover. Ming-Kosawa pulled humanity from the clutches of a true dystopia. Almost every major achievement and innovation at the turn of the twenty-second century bore the Ming-Kosawa trademark.

Almost…

"And here we are, in a mansion on a planet you practically own. Quite the rags to riches story, sir."

Vogelweide's sycophantic mewlings once again dredge me from the depths of memory. I sip my tea and notice a faint white line along the length of my sleeve. I glance at the table and frown at the thin dusting of faint white powder on its clear surface. My scowl reflects back at me through an elbow-shaped smear. I will chastise the cleaners later.

"My father instilled a value in me at a very young age," I say. "'Masuyo,' he said, 'prosperity can always be found. There is no situation that cannot be turned to one's favor, no matter how grim, if you have the wits for it.' That is our family bond. That is the mindset that brought the Kosawas from the fish markets to the apex of interstellar commerce in just five generations. My wife held the same values. Her great-grandparents were rice farmers, but their children aspired to greater things."

"I like the way you put that," Vogelweide says. "Optimistic, but active about it. You can do anything, but only if you work hard enough to get it. My employer seems to have a similar philosophy."

I smile thinly and nod. He is right. He is all too right.

For five blissful years, the Ming-Kosawa corporate empire saw success in every endeavor. We became the wealthiest couple in history, expanding our influence beyond the wildest dreams of history's greatest industrialists. Our influence exceeded that of most governments. We had four healthy children to carry our legacy to even greater heights. We were feared, loved, hated, worshiped.

And then, in the summer of 2099, I made the gravest mistake of my life.

That year, a gangly German-American, with a miniscule private research and development company barely large enough to fill a rental warehouse, did the unimaginable: Vaughn Oberwelt successfully reverse-engineered a piece of tech created by the hyperintelligent AI responsible for the Corsica Event.

Through means still not truly understood, this technology allowed for a seemingly impossible phenomenon: a circumvention of physics dubbed "mass de-simulation." This mass de-simulation technology allowed physical objects to behave as if they lacked mass.

Much of what occurred during the Corsica Event defied the understanding of conventional science. Cracking its secrets had been the scientific holy grail since the dust had settled on the Event itself. Ming-Kosawa's own R&D department had hundreds of scientists studying a dozen Corsica relics day and night, yet this underwhelming upstart with his underfunded startup beat us to the prize.

The day after he announced his discovery to the public, I landed my private helicopter at Oberwelt's doorstep and made him an offer: nine billion US dollars in exchange for his research. To my shock, he refused.

I doubled the offer. Tripled it. I offered him more money than my own company had once been worth for just a few exabytes of data. I offered to buy his company, recruit him and his entire staff into Ming-Kosawa's R&D department, give him all but unlimited resources, total access to the Corsica relics we possessed. He politely declined every offer.

My only regret in my long life is that I did not offer him yet more money. Every man has a price; I would have found his eventually. But I did not. I walked away.

I thought he would come crawling to me once he realized no one on Earth could outbid me. I thought he would take his company public, and I could simply buy a controlling interest. I thought my massive R&D team would soon duplicate his success on their own. How...oh, how did I not notice it when I met him? How did I miss them?

Those predator's eyes of his...

Allston brings a bottle of daiginjo sake to the table. The meal will begin soon, but not soon enough. I want to conduct our business and send Vogelweide back to his master without delay, but I must honor decorum. I must treat this as I would any other business dinner. He must not know how much pain this meeting causes me.

As Allston pours, my glance catches Vogelweide's eyes, and I take their measure. They are the eyes of a scavenger, not a predator. Vogelweide is a pilot fish, swimming in the shark's dark shadow, content to feed on the shreds of meat his master leaves in his wake. He is nothing to be feared in himself, merely a harbinger of the true threat.

I had once thought Oberwelt would look back on his refusal of my offer as a grave mistake, given time. In truth, he simply had a better understanding of what he possessed. After just three years, his tiny company developed a practical application for mass de-simulation technology that would change the course of history: the superluminal drive.

He'd created a drive system that could transport a starship beyond the lightspeed barrier, and he had done it entirely in-house. The superluminal drive was the key to humanity's future among the stars. Oberwelt and his tiny tech startup held total, exclusive ownership of every secret in its design.

Every country that still had a space program ran to Oberwelt's door. Every company that hoped to capitalize on the vast resources of space, including Ming-Kosawa, had to do the same. In just a few years, Oberwelt's little R&D company evolved into a corporate titan: a rise to power that felt all too familiar. One company's name was on everyone's lips, and it wasn't Ming-Kosawa.

It was Exotech.

Oberwelt was smart with his money, reinvesting it in Exotech's own space program. Five years after inventing the superluminal drive, Exotech was exploiting the vast mineral wealth of the asteroid belt. Four years later, they had permanent colonies on every Jovian moon. By the end of the decade, every rock in the solar system with a gravity well had an Exotech presence.

Ming-Kosawa competed as best we could. Eventually, my scientists did reverse-engineer Exotech's mass de-simulation technology, finally breaking their monopoly and letting us create our own superluminal ships, but by then Exotech had an eighteen-year head start. Shortly after we cracked it, Solios Intersystems had their own superluminal drive as well, and the Nakshatra Group developed one the following year. The corporate space race was on, and we had plenty of competition. Exotech did not.

Allston returns, bringing me back to the now. He sets a plank of Hinoki cypress before us, adorned with an elegant spread of sushi. "Gentlemen, we have here tuna tataki with ponzu sauce, fluke sashimi, toro tamari, salmon avocado maki, and tiger shrimp nigiri. I hope you both enjoy."

"Ooh," Vogelweide coos. "Looks delicious, thanks." Allston gives an appreciative bow and departs the room once more. Vogelweide seizes one of the shrimp nigiri in both hands and slurps it down messily.

"Itadakimasu," I mutter, gingerly plucking a salmon roll for myself.

"Mmm...Kosawa-san," he mutters around dual cheekfuls of food, each syllable punctuated by the launch of an errant grain of rice from his lips. "Delicious. Compliments to the chef. And the host."

I give the smallest bow protocol allows. "Thank you."

I take a salmon maki and consume it. Vogelweide is not cultured enough to understand how little praise this meal deserves. My tongue detects every imperfection in the striations of the meat. This salmon is synthetic: cultivated stem cells 3D-printed into a familiar meat shape. This far from Earth, it is impossible to get live fish. We must settle for frozen food or imperfect simulacra like this. Once I had hoped to have a salmon farm built here, but that, as with many plans of mine, fell through.

I force the false fish down my throat, masking my disgust at its aberrant flavor. As with everything I have eaten on this godless planet, it tastes oversalted.

Here I sit, the king of an ocean world that harbors no fish.

Nobody in Ming-Kosawa ever held the keen vision that I did, save my wife. My board of executives were all toadies and fools, useful as tools, but worthless for ideas and insight. Jinyin and I bore the burden of guiding Ming-Kosawa's every action. Every project we touched prospered, but two people could not oversee every operation on every planet. We needed a different strategy. Rather than spreading our resources thin across the stars, we committed to maximizing our potential on one world. This world. Hayden.

Freshly discovered and barely explored, Hayden brimmed with potential. Its gravity was nearly the same as Earth's, and it had vast oceans of liquid water. True, it was imperfect: its atmosphere was thick with toxic chlorine gas, and its oceans had such high salt content that no Earth lifeform could survive in it without extensive filtration. But these problems could be solved with time and ambition.

There never was a project as ambitious as the colonization of Hayden. Freighters flew in daily with hundreds of tons of steel, aluminum, and titanium, as thousands of robots and human laborers worked to erect the monumental bones of the Hayden colony. Several governments watched our progress with renewed interest. They were curious to see if we could do it. I knew we could.

Then it fell apart.

Two years into our project, Jinyin boarded a luxury cruiser called the *Gran Largesse* departing from Luna. It made a standard superluminal jump and never arrived at its destination. The *Gran Largesse* was never seen again, and it remains one of the worst and most mysterious tragedies of modern spaceflight.

It is no mystery to me. I will not be convinced this was anything less than an act of sabotage against Ming-Kosawa. The loss of my wife crippled me. How was I to run this business alone? I had no one to share the burden of power.

My thankless, worthless children refused to carry our family tradition. Not one of them assumed their expected roles in the hierarchy of Ming-Kosawa's leadership, not that any of them had the wits for it. Jinyin and I put them through the most expensive schools in the colonies and did all we could to train them for the destinies we had planned. They could have each sat enthroned on my new world, but the ungrateful fools refused to help build it, even after their mother was stolen from me.

Construction on Hayden began to accumulate complications. The saltwater, caustic atmosphere, and the local microbial life proved far more corrosive than predicted. Our machinery broke down with alarming speed, and the supports and walls of many of our buildings had become structurally unsound. Half-completed buildings were demolished and rebuilt, only for the steady creep of Hayden's encroaching salt to ruin the materials again.

No matter what materials we used, no matter what weather-proofing techniques we employed, salt found a way into everything we built. I never could have known it would cost so much more than our most alarmist predictions or that my family would abandon me to solve these problems alone. I toiled tirelessly to make this world a home for humanity.

It is not my fault Exotech found a better one.

Who could have known that, after I had spent eleven years and most of Ming-Kosawa's wealth laboring to make Hayden inhabitable, Exotech's probes would discover a planet better suited to human life in every way? Showalter was practically perfect: Earthlike gravity, temperate weather, breathable atmosphere, potable water. If my best efforts had prevailed, it would still take centuries to make Hayden half as livable as Showalter already was. Within the year, the first homesteaders from Earth had already migrated there. Hayden's viability as a colony was obsolete. My options decreased by the day until I was left with just one. The last choice I ever thought I would make...

Allston returns, for the last time, clearing the table. Vogelweide sits back in his chair, patting his distended belly in satisfaction. His undiscriminating palate has allowed him to consume most of the food while I sat in silent reflection. He compliments Allston, who accepts the praise with undue pride before taking the empty dishes away. Vogelweide and I now sit alone.

"To our business, then," I say, erecting a cordial lie of a smile.

He stifles a belch. "Yes, I suppose there's no sense putting it off. Captain Batra would like to take off sooner than later." He sets his briefcase on the table and draws a handful of documents from it. Far fewer than I had expected. "Most of the process is already done. This is really just a formality. We needed an official Exotech representative to watch you sign the final few documents in person. You understand."

A sneer twitches the corner of my mouth despite my best efforts to hide it. "And Oberwelt was too preoccupied to make the trip himself, I assume."

"Mr. Oberwelt is a very busy man, I'm afraid. He can't directly oversee every company acquisition in person, as much as I'm sure he'd like to."

I fight the urge to strike the man. This is no common "company acquisition." Ming-Kosawa is more than a feather in Oberwelt's cap, a curio for his mantelpiece. I know exactly what this is to him. Forty years ago I came to him with a generous offer to buy his company. Now, he sends a lackey to buy mine for a fraction of its worth. This is a personal insult to me, four decades in the making.

And I have no recourse but to take it.

I take Vogelweide's papers. I study them with a practiced yet weary eye, and one by one, I sign them. With each page, a chunk of my family's legacy slips from my fingers into the gluttonous maw of Exotech Industries. Within the hour, I am done. Ming-Kosawa is no more.

"Well, Kosawa-san, it has been a pleasure to experience your hospitality," Vogelweide says, barely waiting for the latch on his briefcase to click before he stands.

I give the falsest smile I've ever crafted as I rise. "Allow me to escort you to your ship."

His smile is too broad and stupid to be anything but earnest. "You're too kind, Kosawa-san."

I lead him down a hall with floors of polished pelagic obsidian from Miloro, and I notice its glimmering black and deep blue whorls are marred with intermittent white footprints. We pass a set of five-hundred-year-old Gusoku samurai armor, and I see it too is tarnished with patches of white crust. As we reach my manor's airlock, I look at the towering portrait of Jinyin and me that overlooks all who enter this domain, and I spy a white handprint on the corner of its golden frame.

How? How does it get *everywhere?*

We enter the airlock and don our suits, he in a standard baggy gray Exotech Magellan IV, and I in a custom-fitted black Ravier Castellan with twenty-four carat gold trim. Once we are suited, breathable air cycles out as Hayden's noxious atmosphere spills in, and the outer door hisses open with a belligerent groan.

A cloud of salt flakes billows and glitters in the evening sun as we step outside. The airlock closes, and behind us we see the towering dome of my manor. Vast, convex panels of interlocking ceramic plates protect it from Hayden's serrated winds. Several crab-like cleaning drones scuttle across its surface, scraping the invasive salt buildup in a ceaseless war with the elements. Their joints squeak from strain as their bodies slowly succumb to the same inexorable foe.

We descend the sloping road to the sea. Knobby stone stromatolites adorn the surrounding terrain, the ancient abodes of the extremophilic bacteria native to this world. I envy their ability to flourish in these conditions even as I despise them. Their respiration is responsible for Hayden's poisonous chlorine atmosphere. I'd had such ambitious plans for driving them to extinction one day.

As we near the beach, billowing halite mounds overtake the terrain. Drifts of hardened sea salt a meter thick pile together like frozen ocean foam. We reach the shoreline, where gentle frothing waves glint golden under Hayden's yellow sky. A floating dock connects the shore to Vogelweide's ship: a *Gannet*-class sealander shuttle.

"Thank you again, Kosawa-san." Vogelweide speaks over his suit's comm. "Exotech is deeply honored to inherit Ming-Kosawa's legacy."

"One thing, Mr. Vogelweide," I say softly. "Can you tell me what Exotech intends to do with Hayden?"

"Ah." Vogelweide raises his voice as the *Gannet*'s engines begin to rumble. "Actually, Kosawa-san, I believe Exotech plans to write this colony off as a loss. We'll be diverting your construction resources to Showalter, where they'll be of most value."

I gaze down the western shoreline, where the urban edifices of my unfinished spaceport are silhouetted against the setting sun. Vogelweide speaks again, with feigned compassion. "I know that might come as a disappointment, sir, but look at it this way: this whole planet is, essentially, all yours. God knows I wish I had my own planet." He chuckles until he looks me in the eye. With a nod and no further banter, he follows the dock to his ship's airlock.

From the shore I watch the *Gannet* rise into that sickly, urine-colored sky. I walk the stony beach, hypersaline waves lapping my feet. I think of Jinyin but quickly shove her from my mind. Wherever she is now, she would look upon me with shame.

I would not have blamed her, but the shame is not mine. I am not responsible for Ming-Kosawa's collapse. The fault is our children's. Not one proved worthy of us, of our legacies. Each bore both our proud surnames: Ming-Kosawa, yet none lifted a finger to save the corporation that first held that glorious name.

Akihiko, my firstborn, chooses to languish as a nurse practitioner in an emergency clinic in Sakura. He does not even have the ambition to become a doctor. Xiuying is an agricultural engineer enriching farmland on Showalter. A twenty-second century farmer, regressed to the ignominy of her mother's ancestors. Katsuo is now an environmentalist, wasting his life dredging trash from Earth's ruined oceans. Leiting—I should say *Chen* Leiting, since she has chosen to reject even the gift of the Ming-Kosawa name—is the greatest disappointment of them all. She has become a politician and has actively campaigned for policies that hindered her own father's prosperity on Earth.

None of them speak to me or allow me to see my grandchildren. Jinyin and I pushed them to be strong, to value our legacy, to make our family ever greater. Any of them could have taken their rightful place at Ming-Kosawa and carried the torch as Jinyin and I had done for our parents, but each rejected destiny.

So be it. If they will reject their legacy, their legacy will reject them. When I am gone, the Ming-Kosawa legacy will die with me. My ungrateful spawn will inherit nothing. They have earned nothing.

But Masuyo Kosawa will be a name remembered with awe and reverence for centuries to come. My mark is made on history, but they will be forgotten. I will die a pharaoh's death: entombed in a monument surrounded by wealth befitting my status.

My eyes catch the jagged civic skyline of my incomplete spaceport. I can see the desalination plant from here: the only major building we ever finished, though we never got it running. Its twelve-story bulk is half encased in salt, its broad face bearing the kanji logo of my company. Or half of it. Sandpaper winds have eroded "Kosawa" almost entirely from the concrete wall, and "Ming" has begun to fade.

I stand in ankle-deep seawater, staring at that grave portent. Time eludes me as rivulets pass my creased cheeks.

Hayden's cursed flavor touches my lips, and I turn back to twilight's dark horizon.

THIRTY MINUTES TO LIFE

JENN NEWMAN

Cars passed by, and people bustled in and out of various businesses downtown, doing errands as if it were a normal Saturday morning. For them, it was. Today was not their wedding day, and they were not sitting on a bench outside of Imperial Dry Cleaners with a carefully bagged wedding gown beside them. Of course they weren't—who would be?

Clumsy brides, that's who.

All I could do was hope that the owner would show up soon to prepare for a busy Saturday and take pity on the girl getting married in less than four hours.

The bank's clock tower across the street chimed 8:30. On any other day, I would have found this sound familiar and routine. But today it only increased my anxiety, already pushed to its limits. I knew the sound well, having heard it many times walking through downtown or while inside working as a teller. I had to resign two weeks ago to help Mother prepare for my wedding, honeymoon, and the move to the new house. I missed the familiar sounds of downtown.

The branch manager had hired me right out of high school because my math grades were exceptional, and over the course of my two years there, I'd made some good friends. I even managed to save a decent amount of money. Today the chimes sounded different, as if they were sad that I wasn't going to come back to hear them after the wedding. *You're being silly*, I told myself. *You've got an exciting future ahead of you, so stop reading into things. Everything is going to work out fine.*

This is not how I pictured the day unfolding when Mother woke me at 5:30 after another restless night of sleep. I had been dreaming a lot lately, mostly about the wedding. Sometimes in the dreams I would put on my gown and discover it was too tight and I couldn't breathe, waking up gasping for air. Other times I was swimming in it and couldn't fight my way out. Those mornings, the bedclothes were everywhere.

The dreams weren't always that way. In the peaceful ones, I was wrapped up in the soft silk of the dress from head to toe, and Richard was holding me in his arms. Nothing bad could happen to me; I was completely protected from the world.

My hair and makeup came out just as Mother and I had planned. Well, mostly Mother, but I had to concede that her choices were perfect. The loose brown ringlets that fell around my face and the pastel color palette made me look more beautiful than I thought I ever could, and certainly more mature than 20 years old. Mature enough to be getting married, at least.

My sister and my aunt were just as excited about my wedding as Mother. It was a lot of fun planning all the details, from the lavish floral buntings that would hang from every possible space in the Old South Cathedral to the decadent canapes and signature cocktails that complemented the wedding colors. There was even a catered pre-ceremony breakfast at the house so the family and wedding party could eat before the big event. The caterers arrived by 6:30 with freshly baked croissants, berry compote, omelets, and mimosas. They went right to work making sure everyone had whatever they wanted.

"Charlotte?" Mother called from the living room. "Cut that croissant in half. You don't need an overfull stomach giving anyone the wrong impression." My Aunt Linda tried to hide her face, but I caught her rolling her eyes.

I had my sister to thank for that comment. She was always suggesting within Mother's earshot that I would end up in trouble and have to get married. The lectures from Mother had become a weekly event.

"I know all about those friends of yours, and I'm telling you right now that you need to scrape them off like dog poop on the bottom of your shoe. How do you expect to find a satisfactory husband if he thinks you're one of those free-spirited hippies? You need to build friendships with the kind of people that aspire to an affluent lifestyle."

"Okay." I placed the croissant on a napkin and resigned myself to starving as an alternative to spending the day under her disapproving glare.

Noticing my quiet compliance, Aunt Linda tried to be encouraging. "Don't worry, Charlotte. Once you are officially Mrs. Richard Walmart, you can do whatever you want."

"His last name is Walton, Aunt Linda."

She thought back on her words for a moment and laughed at her mistake. "Ha! Oh yes, I guess it is." And off she went back to the food table in the next room.

I pondered her words for a moment. I could only imagine the feeling of freedom that being married with my own household would provide. But could I really do anything I wanted?

WITH BELL-SHAPED SLEEVES MADE of tulle intertwined with lace that gathered at the wrist, and a heavily laced bodice with a high neck and lace insets in the flowing skirt, my dress was truly a vision. I stared at myself in the mirror, feeling as though I was having an out of body experience and wondering for a moment if I was having one of my dreams. I'd always fantasized about what I would look like on my wedding day, but my musings had not prepared me for the over-whelming sense of awe I felt when I gazed at the very real reflection.

Aunt Linda brought me out of my trance. "Here, Charlotte, you need to stay hydrated," she said, handing me a glass of orange juice wrapped in a white napkin. Expecting the refreshing juice to satisfy my dry mouth, the shock of the champagne bubbles sent me into a choking cough. In an awkward move, I leaned forward and brought the napkin up to my mouth so I wouldn't spew the drink all over myself, but my jerk reaction caused the glass to tip just enough to splash an orange stain the size of a baseball onto my right sleeve. Mother, having watched the entire episode, immediately spiraled into an apocalyptic panic.

"Oh my God, Charlotte! What…what have you done? How in the - do you have to be so damned clumsy ALL of the time?" She sputtered in disbelief and rage.

Somewhere in the back of my mind I knew that this was a rhetorical question, but I couldn't help myself. "I spilled some orange juice, Mother. It's not the end of the world. We'll just rinse it out or use some bleach."

She was not amused. "That's a terrible idea. What do you know about stains like this, anyway? I swear on the Good Book, you will NOT ruin this day for us, Charlotte!"

I decided not to voice an opinion after that.

The photographer arrived moments later to take some pre-wedding shots. Mother had me pose for a few pictures with my sleeve strategically out of the way, covered by my bouquet or placed behind someone else. She did not miss an opportunity in between each pose to stare at the stain with a scowl, always making sure I noticed her before looking away. Once those initial pictures were done, Mother gave me my marching orders. I was to take the dress to the cleaners immediately for either a fast cleaning solution or to have the sleeves altered, whatever it took to make the stain disappear.

"You need to deal directly with the owner. The regular help won't know the best way to take care of this, and I won't risk any further embarrassment." She was on the verge of tears over the idea that this small, unfortunate incident might unravel everything she had accomplished to make today happen.

The clock tower read 8:37. I thought of Richard, my fiancé. Or husband, soon enough. He had been somewhat of an afterthought during the wedding preparation, to be honest. Not that he would be unhappy with anything. His family had made a considerable contribution to the cost, and Mother certainly made sure this would be a newspaper-worthy event. But shouldn't he have been my first thought when I woke up today? My last thought as I fell asleep after the rehearsal dinner celebration? I wondered.

He caught me completely off guard when he proposed; we had only been dating for three months at the time, after being set up by my mother and a mutual family friend. He was such a nice guy, and I was sure he would be a good husband. When I told Mother that we didn't have the best chemistry, she told me that I had read too many romance novels and needed to live in the real world where a faithful husband, a house, and security were what really mattered. Like I said, he was a nice guy. And I guess eight years isn't a huge age difference, but why did he want to marry a twenty-year-old?

Mother was ecstatic when she saw the ring, exclaiming how the years of private schools, dance lessons, and home economics training had finally paid off. She had engineered me to be the perfect choice for a man like Richard Walton of Bentonville, Arkansas, who would provide me and my family with a future without financial worries like she had to deal with after my father left. Richard's family had opened thirty-eight discount stores in addition to the original ones in Rogers and Harrison. They were doing very well, and some people even referred to it as a growing empire.

I wanted to stop worrying about the dress, so I stood up and pondered the posters and flyers that were taped to the store fronts around me. Most were about the Women's Strike for Equality that had taken place on Wednesday. I read about it in the papers and saw news reports on television, and it seemed to me that people couldn't make up their minds about whether or not women were oppressed. I didn't think I was oppressed, but maybe I was. How would I know? President Nixon even seemed to support the efforts by the women involved, but Mother said you couldn't trust his judgment.

"Charlotte, just ignore all of this silliness over what it means to be a woman. History has already shown us the way, and I won't have you ruining your future over a pipe dream of running the world someday."

That was the same day she told me to write my resignation letter to the branch manager.

Most of the articles I'd read this week talked about how women were being left behind to work in the home, expected to do all of the household chores like cooking and cleaning, while men were given business opportunities and public recognition for their accomplishments. Then there was the whole nasty business about abortions, but I couldn't say I had an opinion on that subject. Maybe I should?

I sat back down. Would I be one of those women who felt like she was being kept from doing something exciting with her life because she was responsible for a household and children? That's what was supposed to bring me the most joy, wasn't it? What could be more important than a good family life? I'd always felt I missed out because Father left us to struggle financially, and Mother wasn't exactly the nurturing type. I wasn't sure that meant I was restricted to succeeding in the kind of life she always wanted for herself, though. I wondered, feeling uneasy about what my marriage to Richard could mean.

He already had a successful business, so there was no reason he should expect me to need (or have time for) anything besides taking care of him and raising a family. But it was 1970, and women were doing amazing things with their lives. Doctors, lawyers, business owners...women could become almost anything now. There were opportunities out there, and women could really accomplish special things. But I also read that women weren't being paid as much as men to do the same jobs. I definitely had an opinion about that.

My heart started racing. It was 8:47, so where was the cleaner? If I could just get the dress taken care of, I could move on with my day and stop thinking about any of this. Richard and I would be married, and I knew he would provide a wonderful life for us. I would be fully engaged in the household: cooking, keeping a clean house, and filling it with happy, healthy children. And it wouldn't be necessary for me to consider things like my rights, or lost opportunities, or accomplishments.

The realization hit me like the shock of the champagne. I was allowing myself to be turned into the 1950's housewife that Mother always wanted to be. Did I want that?

More thinking. My head started to spin, so I leaned forward and concentrated on the pebbled surface of the sidewalk, careful not to unfurl the ringlets pinned to my scalp.

I couldn't even imagine the consequences if I didn't go through with the wedding. Mother would disown me, throw me out of the house, and never speak to me again. I would have to see if the bank would take me back as a teller so I could support myself. I was a good employee, so I think they would. One of my bridesmaids, Cheryl, lived nearby in a two-bedroom apartment with her husband. They would probably let me stay there for a little while until I could find my own place.

I did have some money saved up, and it was in that bank. It was there waiting for me in case of an emergency. And my situation was starting to feel more and more like an emergency. Coincidentally, the bank also opened at 9:00.

I looked up again to see the clock tower read 8:52. It struck me as bizarre that I could decide the course of my life in the next eight minutes by choosing either the bank or the dry cleaner. I could choose.

The thought terrified me.

A tall woman with keys in her hand, wearing a beige dress and red hat, approached the building. She stopped when she saw me on the bench with my large white garment bag embellished with a bride's silhouette. I had seen her before when dropping off cleaning, and I knew she worked here. Her face became concerned; I imagine my own looked distraught at this point.

"Good morning," she said. "I'm just opening up now. Sorry for the wait."

"It's okay. Can you tell me if the owner will be here soon? I really need to speak with him."

"I am the owner." She smiled, clasping her hands in front of her. "How can I help?" She spoke with a soothing tone, as if she knew the magnitude of the decision I was facing. And she was the owner. She'd accomplished something amazing. I was embarrassed by my assumption.

"I'm sorry, I didn't realize…"

"Don't give it another thought. It's a common mistake. You look like you might be in a…difficult situation." When I didn't answer, she nodded towards the garment bag. And at that point my emotions had reached their limits, and I started to cry.

"Oh dear, I'm sorry if I've upset you. What do we need to do here?" She sat next to me on the bench and placed her free hand on top of mine. Although I'd just met this woman, she felt like a kindred spirit. I composed myself enough to ask her a question.

"How did you become the owner of a business? Was it hard?"

Her initial look of surprise at my question turned to thoughtfulness before she replied. "Oh, yes, I would have to say it was. A lot of people told me it wouldn't happen."

"But you did it anyway?"

"I didn't listen to them. I listened to the people who had faith in me and wanted me to be successful. There was a lot of hard work involved, but I don't regret it for a second."

I thought carefully before asking my next question. "What if taking that chance prevented you from having a family?" I realized this topic was personal and frankly none of my business, but I had to know.

"Well, it didn't. Though I realize some aren't as fortunate as I am. My husband works third shift at the foundry. The littlest one stays with my mother during the weekdays while the older two are in school and my husband sleeps. We make it work, whatever circumstances turn up."

I looked at this woman in amazement. I wondered how many people had walked in and out of the dry cleaners and met her, not realizing how much she'd accomplished. I felt empowered by her.

"Now," she said. "About that garment bag. Is there something we need to do with the contents?" I thought her wording was very poignant.

"The dress hasn't really been worn yet, but there's a stain on the right sleeve. It needs to be cleaned or altered or something to be fixed enough for a wedding. I was thinking… Could you do me a favor?"

"I'll certainly try." She stood and reached for the garment bag to bring it inside and work her magic to make the dress as good as new. I stood up and looked over at the bank, taking a deep breath as I did. My lips formed into a small smile as my resolve tightened.

"If you can clean it, or fix it in some way, could you please give it to someone who could use it?"

"Of course." She looked thoughtfully at me, taking in my formal hairstyle and carefully applied makeup. "Are you sure?"

I contemplated her question for just a moment as the bank's clock tower chimed 9:00.

"Yes, I'm sure. I've just realized it doesn't fit me."

I gave the woman a genuine smile then, and she nodded her understanding. I turned to walk over to the bank to speak with the manager, and she called out to me.

"If you happen to be looking for a job anytime, please come see me."

OUR LOVE

BYRON GILLAN

~1~

The Goddess Bath did face the vile serpent, Kaya, and from their clash
was born the Sprawl. A thousand kingdoms for a thousand tribes.
    -From "In the House of the Mother"

Everything was burning.
    The air was acrid, the sky blackened by an impenetrable
haze. Flecks of glowing ash fell from the dark heavens to rain down
on the smoldering world below. The young princess, Luwan
Des'Chain, knelt amidst the ruins of her home. Her hair was wild,
stained with soot and dried blood. She gripped her stomach, both
hands glistening and wet as the wound running along her stomach
wept crimson. She barely felt the pain. Her attention remained fixed
upon the daemon-spawn lying dead before her. It was a sprawling,
serpentine thing, hideous to behold, even in death. It, too, was burning. One eye of the great beast remained open and staring emptily at
the world. The eye began to bubble from the heat of the flames that

were engulfing its corpse. White ooze slowly leaked forth from the pallid eye, dripping down the side of the daemon's inert jaws. The nightmare became ever-more grotesque. Still, Luwan could not look away from it.

I have taken everything from you, a voice spoke to her. The daemon? That was impossible. *You will never have any of them back. Your people, your home, your family…*

The daemon's poison, she realized. It was inside of her, coursing through her veins, turning them black and sick. Luwan slid forward, collapsing into the dirt. Her body felt heavy as lead. Her eyes glazed over. Was it becoming darker? She tried to conjure with one hand to heal her wound. A flicker of light, that was all she could manage, no more. The corruption had done something to her. She could not channel Bath's gift.

Everything, the voice whispered, returning to her mind. *Gone, forever...*

"You are not real," Luwan cried. "You are dead and burning!" The truth of that, whether the voice she heard was real or not, it changed nothing. Her family was gone. Her entire world was shattered and broken. She tried to rise but her limbs refused her.

Luwan sighed. All that remained of her will flooded forth, draining from her. What did it even matter? What use was there in prolonging this struggle? She closed her eyes, allowing the darkness to overcome her. The warmth of the fire's heat against her body was oddly soothing. Dying like this, it wasn't so bad. She could just let go, drift away. It would all be over soon enough...

"Luwan!" A lone voice cut through the chaos to reach her. "Luwan!"

It was her sister's voice.

Luwan stirred, pulling herself back from the dark precipice of sleep. Her sister was alive. Chesa was alive.

Desperation rose in her throat. With all the strength she could still muster, Luwan screamed. She cried out her sister's name until her voice went ragged and died. Chesa did not answer her. *She cannot hear me*, Luwan realized.

And now she was afraid.

Luwan's eyes fluttered, she gasped. It was growing difficult to keep herself awake. Her body was shutting down. She no longer had the strength to scream, to move or fight back the exhaustion that was overwhelming her. All she could do was lie there and wait.

The flames drew closer. The fire was already consuming the corpse of the daemon. Its bones were visible where its flesh had already been burned away. Its eyes had melted. Soon enough there would be nothing left.

She could still hear its voice, whispering to her as she drifted into a dark and warm sleep.

~2~

The Ishari were a strange people. A matriarchal society, the women of their culture were uniquely powerful sorceresses; wytches, they called themselves, and the strongest of all were those whom within their veins flowed the blood of nobility.

-From "A Chronicler's Tales"

CHESA TRACED two fingers along the edge of the broken cobblestone road.

The scar stretched for over half a mile, from the shore to the very edge of town. Ten years ago the daemon had come, slithering up from the ocean floor to destroy her home. Ten years later and still this scar remained, a lasting reminder of that awful day.

She released a deep sigh and rose from where she knelt. For a long time afterward, she stared down the length of the sprawling fissure the daemon had left, beyond it, across the vastness of the Argo ocean. Dark clouds were gathering over the sea. She heard the distant rumble of thunder. Chesa could feel it, a wrongness in the world. It was all around her, in the air, the ground, and the water. Bath's gift granted her that insight. Something awful was stirring in the world, she could feel it...why not Luwan?

"She's wrong," Chesa finally said.

"Who?" her friend, Tala, replied. She was still kneeling beside Chesa and staring at the serpent's crater. Tala was three years younger than her. She had been only five when the daemon had come.

"My sister," Chesa clarified.

"Ah," Tala murmured as she nodded her head. "I suppose I should have figured that's who you meant. Which thing is our Queen wrong about *this time*? You not being allowed to leave, or her sticking her head in the sand when it comes to whatever is happening out there?"

"All of the above?" Chesa offered. She sighed as she looked at her friend. "The few merchants we still receive are all saying the same thing - there is something evil in the ocean, something terrible lurking out of sight. Boats are going missing, dead things washing ashore…even the weather has been unnatural as of late. Ill omens, wherever one looks…"

"Merchant's tall tales," Tala responded. "Men of the sea love their stories. Some are grand, others small, but they are only stories.

"Not always," Chesa said. "The daemon was real enough." She was staring at the crater as she spoke.

"That was a long time ago," Tala said. "Besides, the Queen says there is nothing for us to fear. She senses nothing of the corruption."

"My sister says so, yes."

"Are you calling the Queen a liar?"

"No, of course not. It's just…" Chesa threw up her hands. "I have my own gift. I know what I sense. There is something wrong." Tala was staring at her intently. "What?" Chesa asked her.

"You're a worrier," she said. "You always have been."

Chesa frowned. "Do you really believe that's all there is to this?"

Tala offered a simple shrug of her shoulders. "I'm only a simple craftswoman, Chesa. What do I honestly know?"

"Nothing, and less than that, still," Chesa told her.

Tala giggled. "Fair enough. You're the one of royal blood here, gifted by Bath with powers beyond the rest of us. It's your humble job to lead us poor souls who haven't got a clue."

"That's my sister's job, not mine."

"Then why are you unhappy with every decision she makes?"

Why indeed, Chesa thought. "I don't know," she admitted. "I truly don't." She returned to staring out over the ocean. A current of wind rolled inland, ruffling her dress and her hair, the first tidings of the storm to come.

"So…what *are* you going to do?" Tala asked.

"I'll tell you when I know," Chesa replied. She said no more.

~3~

Bath has left us, but her divine gift empowers us. With it, this world can still be saved.

    -Unknown Matriarch's Blessing

EMERALD FLAME LICKED HUNGRILY at her cheeks.

The conjuring was poor. Luwan deflected the spell easily. It died violently, bursting apart in a spray of white-hot ichor which rained down upon the dueling field. The air was soon filled with the putrid odor of magic and burning gravel where the shattered magic had landed. The stench of it all never failed to remind her of that other time, all those years ago when the daemon had come. She hated it.

Luwan pushed through the rising dread she felt, preparing her counterstrike. Raw manna channeled through her veins, bringing flames to life in the palms of her hands. It was harder than it should have been, channeling Bath's gift; it had been for so long now. Her battle with the daemon had changed her, weakened her. Even just this simple practice-bout was draining.

But Luwan was never given the chance to respond to her opponent's attack. Across the practice field her opponent crossed her arms over her chest, signing her acquiescence. The match was at an end.

Luwan relaxed, allowing the power to dissipate from her body. It was an indescribable relief to have that burden lifted, even if she was disappointed at the abrupt finish of her duel.

"Winner - Her Highness," the Seneschal, Danillo, announced from

147

the sidelines of the arena. He was an older man, well into his late sixties by now, with wispy, gray-white hair and a pair of wide-rim spectacles that clung to the bridge of his hooked nose.

"Well done, as always, my Lady," Pia called out to her, her shoulders rising and falling with each breathless gasp. The young girl was only sixteen, yet she was already a rising talent in the magical arts. *And this despite her having not even an ounce of royal blood*, Luwan thought. *If only Chesa could ever show such enthusiasm for her training...*

"You fought well, Pia," Luwan said. She dusted away some of the ash that had begun to accumulate on her uniform's sleeve. "You gave me a run for my coin if I do say so. Once or twice, I thought you might even take the match." That was a little bit of a white lie, but what did that matter? Pia was now beaming with fresh enthusiasm. Her smile was entirely worth it.

"*Really?*" Pia gasped. "I mean...thank you, My Lady - Your Highness! Thank you! Your praise means so much to me."

"There's no need to thank me, you earned every bit of praise."

"But I must! To receive praise from you? It is nothing less than an honor, more so, even than the privilege of having been allowed to face you in practice!"

"Pia, you do yourself too little a service. You are quite talented, even in just these past few months, your gift has grown tremendously-" But her voice was suddenly cut short as a sharp pain sliced through her stomach. Luwan hissed through clenched teeth before she nearly buckled and fell.

Pia saw her struggle. She looked incredibly concerned. "Is...everything alright, my Lady?" she asked quietly.

Luwan grunted, her only admission of the knife twisting itself in her side. "I'm fine," she said. "Just a little sore, that's all." She noticed that Danillo was watching her intently. She waved him towards her with one hand. "Water," she shouted. "A towel, as well."

The Seneschal brought her everything she had asked for. Luwan drained the water first, savoring the cool liquid as it slid down her throat. She spread the towel across her free arm and moved it to hide her side, where a bloody stain had begun to take shape.

"Is it the mark, my Lady?" Danillo whispered to her, his voice filled with concern.

"Not now," Luwan spoke under her breath, hushing him. The last thing she needed now was to make a scene. Without missing a beat, her attention returned to Pia. "Pia, you're no doubt as spent as I am. I believe this shall suffice for our training today. Why don't you go and clean yourself up? And do give my regards to your mother the next time you see her."

Pia regarded her for a moment longer, her face unsure. Luwan could tell the girl knew there was something wrong, but thankfully she did not press the matter. Pia left, though not before offering a final bow and a weak smile to accompany it.

"She's suspicious," Luwan observed. The sound of thunder drew her gaze to the sky. Dark clouds were forming overhead, churning with the first signs of a storm. She hadn't felt it coming, no doubt in thanks to her scar. The daemon's wound had left her connection to the land fraught, even after all this time…

Danillo pulled her arm aside. "Your jacket is soaked. The wound's opened up all over again. I thought I told you to take it easy?"

"You did," Luwan replied, wincing. "I just didn't care enough to listen." She groaned. "Although I'll admit, I'm beginning to regret that choice…"

"I'll bet." Danillo sounded as though he didn't believe her in the slightest. "Always lamenting after the fact, never thinking about the consequences…" He sighed. "That will be needing new stitches. We should get you back to the Keep. Allow me your arm, I'll help you walk."

"I should hardly think so," Luwan replied, aghast. "The last thing anyone should see is their Queen limping her way back to the castle. I can walk just fine on my own."

"You're bleeding."

"I am fine," Luwan reiterated, her tone growing combative. "And that is the final word on the matter."

Danillo shook his head, unhappy but clearly unwilling to argue any further. By now the old man had learned it was easier this way, once she had made up her mind. Overhead the sky churned as dark clouds continued to gather. Luwan heard the rumble of thunder, felt the first drops of rain.

"You worry too much," Luwan told the Seneschal. "It isn't as bad as it looks." But even as she said the words, her legs felt strangely hollow. She heard Danillo speaking to her, but she couldn't understand what he was saying. The next thing she knew, she was falling.

~4~

The daemon has many heads.
    -Old Proverb of the Ishari

It wasn't the first time Luwan had done this. She would push herself beyond what she should, and, inevitably, Chesa would find herself sitting here, waiting in the small living room outside of her sister's bedroom as she was tended to by Danillo and the Menders.

A single, distant moan escaped through the closed doors. Muffled voices followed. Chesa shifted uncomfortably in her seat, wanting nothing more than to go in and be by her sister's side...but no, she knew she would only be in the way. So here she remained.

Another moan.

You're such an idiot, Chesa thought. Almost immediately she regretted it. The daemon's mark was no natural wound, for the spawn of Kaya were not natural creatures. They were abominations of the dark abyss, not natural things of this world.

Chesa shifted once more, trying to refocus her attention on something - *anything* - that might distract her, but all she found were old reminders of why she hated this room. There, by the dining table, was where she'd hidden when the daemon had first come. Over there was where she had wept endlessly once she'd finally understood her parents were not coming back.

She hated this room.

The doors swung open as Danillo strode out of the chamber. The white apron he wore was stained crimson. Voices followed after him,

150

chatter amongst the several women still tending to Luwan. Danillo stopped when he saw Chesa.

She pushed herself up and out of her seat. "How is she?"

"Alive, healing." But he did not sound pleased, only angry. "It needn't have come to this. You know that already, I suspect."

"What happened?"

"The same, as always," was his answer. "Your sister does not listen to reason."

"She rarely has," Luwan said. She hesitated. "Can I see her?"

Danillo looked back towards the bedroom. "She's resting, but I don't see what harm it will do." His eyes returned to focus on Chesa. "I thought the two of you weren't on speaking terms after what happened."

"We aren't," Chesa replied. "But she's my sister."

~5~

Queen Luwan Des'Chain was always beloved by her subjects. Regarded as both wise and fair, her rule was not without conflict. Her choice of isolationism would become a source of conflict in the years after her ascent to rule, following her parents' deaths.

-From "A Chronicle of Queens"

Her dream was always the same.

A burning city, a black-orange sky…and the daemon looming over all. Its eyes emitted a hellish light. Its vision pierced the thick smoke choking the air. It saw her.

She heard her parent's voices. Run, they begged her, their voices desperate. Hide. The daemon roared, shattering the air and drowning out her parent's cries. Luwan couldn't move. She couldn't do anything. Her parents screamed.

Luwan opened her eyes.

She was graced by the sight of serene normality. Bright sun filtered through the curtains of the window beside her bed. A gentle breeze rolled over her. The cool air made her skin bristle.

"It's about time you woke up," Chesa said. She was sitting beside Luwan's bed, a book lying across her lap. "You've been in and out of it for a while. You missed the storm. It rolled in from the bay and raged for hours. I'm surprised it didn't wake you."

Luwan tried to rise. That hurt far too much. She tried to speak, but only a phlegmy cough came forth. That hurt too.

"Take your time, there's no rush," Chesa said.

"I feel like shit," Luwan grunted.

"You look like shit."

Luwan frowned. "What happened?" she asked, though she suspected she already knew the answer.

"The same thing as always. You pushed yourself too far, *again*, and your scar tore itself wide open. *Again*. And will you stop squirming so much? The Menders only just finished closing you back up. Honestly, Luwan, what were you thinking?"

"I was helping Pia with her training." Luwan explained, her tone growing defensive. "I needed the practice, as well. You haven't sparred with me in months, so I needed someone to train with."

"I stopped sparring with you because it wasn't safe."

"That's the only reason?" Chesa scowled at her, saying nothing. Luwan bit back a further response. "I'm surprised to even see you here. I thought you were still mad at me."

"I am still mad at you. That doesn't mean I don't care about you."

Luwan turned her head, staring at the window. Some of the tension seemed to dissipate from the room.

"I remember sitting right here, you know, the first time this happened, after..." Chesa paused, sounding unsure if she should continue. "After the daemon came, after you faced it all on your own. You were lying right here, all bloody and bandaged. I was afraid you would have to look like that forever. I was just a child—what did I know? I sat by your bedside, waiting for you to wake up. I was even desperate enough to pray."

"We both know you don't pray."

"I did then," Chesa told her. "I begged the Goddess, please, let my sister live. Let my heart be tied to hers, forever afterwards, and our love shall be enough to sustain us. And sure enough, you woke up. My prayers had been answered."

Luwan looked back at her sister. "Then why stop?"

"Because that was the first and only time they ever were."

A subtle quiet settled between them, dragging on and on for what felt like an eternity. It was only broken finally by the distant sound of a dog barking.

"Kirin came into port this morning," Chesa said then. "He brought the usual spices, some decent coffee, not much else. He says it's been getting harder to trade, there's less boats moving between the isles… and more talk of something wrong in the waters…" And now Luwan understood what her sister was doing, why she was here.

"Chesa…"

"He also told me another ship has gone missing. Ten people this time, all of them just…*gone.*"

"Chesa." Luwan repeated, growing tenser. Her fingers dug into her bedding. Chesa would not stop, she would not listen.

"This is happening, Luwan. You can't keep ignoring the outside world. That's the third trader this month who has told us exactly the same thing. There is something out there, something dangerous, and if someone doesn't find out what-"

"I said, enough!"

The sharpness of her own voice caught even Luwan by surprise. Pain followed. Her wound echoed fresh pain. Soon she could feel blood seeping through the fresh stitching.

"*Enough,*" Luwan repeated, weaker this time. "I will not do this with you again. Not now, not later - not ever. I have made my decision clear. We do not leave this island. There is nothing out there for us. *For any of us.*"

"Why?" That was all Chesa said. The words came forth as nothing more than a whisper.

"Why what?" Luwan responded bitterly. "Why am I doing this? Why am I keeping us safe? Is that what you want to know?"

"No…why are you so afraid?"

Chesa threw her book aside and rose without another word. She spared a final glance at Luwan, then turned and stormed from the room.

Luwan said nothing, did nothing. She watched her sister go, listening as her footsteps retreated from the chamber. The sound slowly faded, until only silence remained.

Luwan leaned back in her bed, still in pain, still angry and hurt.

A sound.

She glanced hesitantly across the room. It was there, as it always was. A great serpent coiled tightly upon itself. It wore the daemon's burned face, white bone half-revealed beneath singed flesh. It's eyes were gone, but it saw her all the same.

The apparition made no sound. It didn't move. It just watched her, as she, in turn, regarded it. It was always here, always with her. There was no escaping it. Her scar burned.

"Damn you," Luwan muttered, speaking to no one.

~6~

She was always a rebellious child, fire for spirit even before she could conjure the actual thing in the palm of her hand.

   -From "Chesa Des'Chain, A Profile"

"Are you sure about this?"

"Of course not, but it's the only idea I've got."

Tala raised one hand to cup her own neck, as if she feared she might soon be without the head it was attached to. "But the Queen..."

"Is sick and bedridden," Chesa told her. "She'll be that way for a week or longer, with half the castle fretting over her head the whole time. That includes our old and ever-so-loyal Seneschal. That means far less eyes on us."

Tala was positively pale now. She didn't speak.

"Oh, come on, Tala, where's your sense of adventure? Weren't you the one saying only this morning that it was your job to follow what us royals tell you to do?"

154

"But stealing a boat? I've never left the island before. Neither have you! Do you even know how to sail?"

"What need do I have for that? I can simply move the waves around us. Beyond that, we'll get by."

"That doesn't really inspire much confidence in me...besides, it's only the two of us?"

"We can't trust anyone else," Chesa said. "It can only be us."

"I don't like this, Chesa. I don't like any of this..."

"Do you think I do?"

"Maybe. You are getting everything you ever wanted. The chance to finally leave, to go out and see the world."

"That has nothing to do with this," Chesa snapped. "I love my sister, despite everything she's done, and I know that my leaving will tear her apart. That's something I'll have to live with...but we don't have a choice. We need to go out there and make sure our island, our people —our home is safe."

A long moment passed by. At last, Tala acquiesced. She nodded her head weakly. "Alright," she whispered. "I know I'm going to regret this."

Chesa took her friend's hands in her own and squeezed them tightly. She smiled. "Probably, but don't worry, you've got a princess on your side."

~7~

"Forgive yourself for not knowing better."
   -Ishari saying

"That really hurts, you know."

"I'm not surprised," Danillo muttered under his breath. He only seemed to be half-listening, focused as he was on the careful nature of his work. "But if the wound isn't cleaned it will fester. Surely there's no need for me to remind you—your scar only opened back up because you insisted on pushing yourself."

The old man was sitting hunched on a stool beside her, working

155

balms into her exposed side. Luwan winced as another stabbing pain shot through her.

"How did your conversation with your sister go?"

Luwan didn't answer.

"That bad, hm?"

"You know how she can be…"

"I also know how you can be. Don't forget, I brought you into this world, pulled you from your mother's belly. I was there when you opened your eyes and spoke your first words. I have watched you two grow all your life."

"And?" Luwan asked him. "Is there a point to this?"

"Only to say that you are stubborn as a krayt-fish, and you should consider listening to your sister, rather than always choosing battle."

"She talked about leaving again. She says Kirin told her another boat has gone missing."

"Oh? And how did you handle this?"

He had her trapped, but her pride refused to submit. "I said no. That is the law. We stay on the island."

"And how did lady Chesa react?"

"She left."

Danillo sighed. "If I may speak freely?"

"I have never stopped you before," Luwan told him.

The Seneschal cleared his throat. He seemed to be searching for the right words to say. "Perhaps there is wisdom in what your sister seeks." He stopped, as if unsure whether or not he should continue.

"Go on," Luwan said.

"You have always carried scars—some seen, others hidden. Not a single day goes by where I am not reminded of that horrible night when we lost so much…but now I worry that you are allowing your scars to cloud your better judgment."

Luwan began to drum her fingers on one knee as she stared at him. "Why, Danillo, it sounds almost as if you've taken a side."

"I am not on *anyone's* side," he protested. "I am merely fulfilling my role to you and your sister; to serve you both faithfully and fairly until the last days of my life. I counsel you now not on Chesa's behalf but on your own. This conflict between the two of you has dragged on for far too long. If only you would hear my wisdom, then perhaps this rift between you and Chesa might finally be repaired."

"And it would be *heeding wisdom* to send my sister forth into the unknown? To face only the Goddess knows what?"

A sound in the corner. Luwan knew it was there, watching. She refused to look at it. She would not acknowledge it. *You are not there,* she told herself. *You are not real…*

"We cannot remain as we are," Danillo told her. "I have said as much before, and if there is any truth to these tales we have been told, missing boats and—"

There came a knocking at the door.

Danillo paused and turned. "What is it?" he asked, irritated.

"It's Tala, my lord," came the young girl's voice from the other side. "I've come to speak with the Queen."

Tala? Her sister's friend? Luwan didn't understand. Was this some sort of peace offering by Chesa? Or was it Tala trying to intervene, just as Danillo had tried and failed.

"You may enter, Tala," Luwan said before Danillo could speak.

The doors opened, and the craftswoman came forth. The young girl had her hands tucked behind her back and her face was filled with unease. She stopped in the center of the room.

"You may leave us, Danillo," Luwan stated.

Danillo lingered beside her. He seemed to want to say something more, but whatever it was, he held the words back.

"That will be all," Luwan told him.

Danillo rose and bowed for her stiffly. "As you command, my Queen." He shuffled towards the door, striding past the daemon where it waited, watching. It's tongue flickered at Danillo as he passed it.

"Danillo," Luwan called after him. He turned back to her. No doubt he thought her eyes were on him, but she could not look away from the daemon. "Do not lecture me about what is best for my sister ever again," Luwan uttered.

Danillo left. Now it was just the two of them. Tala tittered nervously beneath Luwan's watchful gaze.

"I'm sorry for intruding," Tala said.

"It's alright, if anything, you saved me from having to deal with him any further. We haven't spoken much before, have we?" Luwan patted Danillo's empty seat. "Come sit with me," she said, but Tala remained where she was.

Luwan could sense it now. Something was wrong. "What is it?"

"Forgive me, Your Highness, but I thought you should know. It regards your sister."

Luwan pushed herself up. "What has Chesa done now?"

Tala's frown deepened. "It's not what she's done, Your Highness, but what she's planning to do…"

~8~

"To be merciful is Bath's will, while to act is man's."
  -Ishari Proverb

The ocean wave crashed against the beach. The water rushed up the shore, almost reaching her feet. Chesa watched it recede as she waited beside the small fishing boat.

There was still no sign of Tala. She was supposed to have met her here hours ago. *She'll come*, Chesa promised herself. *She will.*

She looked over the Argo, endless and iridescent. *And somewhere beyond that, only the Goddess knows…*

Another wave crashed against the beach. Still, Tala did not come. Chesa was beginning to worry. She touched the boat beside her, ran her fingers along the fine wood. She could do it, even on her own, if it came to it. She didn't need Tala, she didn't need anyone.

She thought of Luwan, of all that had happened and all that still lay unresolved between them. She didn't want to feel guilty but the feelings came nonetheless. She hadn't wanted things to happen this way. Perhaps that was foolish, perhaps this had been inevitable. Luwan had not left her with much choice.

The day was fading rapidly. The sun had begun to fall into the distant horizon. Chesa knew it must be soon. With or without Tala. *Just a little longer*, she thought. *A little longer...*

~9~

"The unseen and the unsaid often go hand-in-hand."
  -Unknown

Luwan walked along the beach, alone, clutching her side with one hand. The world was metamorphosing from day to night as a blue-white hue washed over all. The twin moons had begun their ascent. The Sister-Moons, they were called; Yara and Evalla were their names. Against a darkening ocean they rose to take their place amongst the heavens. Surrounding them was a sea of stars.

It was then that she came upon her sister. Chesa was sitting beside a small boat with her arms wrapped around her legs and her chin resting on the top of her knees. Even dark as it was, it was obvious Chesa had been crying. She was staring at the ocean, watching the tide as it came and went. She didn't acknowledge Luwan.

"What are you doing out here?" Luwan asked her. Chesa never looked at her.

"Sitting."

The tide came, retreated, returned and went.

"I suppose Tala isn't coming," Chesa said.

Luwan exhaled. "No. She isn't."

"I should have known better than to trust her with this," Chesa first said. "No, it isn't her fault. I never should have tried to force her into this. She didn't want to go. I did, not her."

"Why didn't you leave?" Luwan asked.

"Because it wouldn't have been right," Chesa said to her. "Leaving like that, without saying goodbye." She laughed. The sound of it was pitious. "It's all I've ever wanted, you know. A chance to see the world, to do what I wanted. I was so close. All I had to do was get on that boat and go. I'd have been free...only that isn't true. The guilt of aban-

159

doning you would have torn me apart. I couldn't do that, not to you, not after everything that had happened. So I stayed. I…" Chesa sniffed. She wiped at her face with one sleeve. "I wanted to know that you would still love me when I returned. That we would still be sisters."

Luwan approached Chesa and lowered herself to sit beside her. "We are," she whispered. "We always will be."

"Sometimes it doesn't feel that way," Chesa revealed. She looked down. "Our love feels toxic, like it's destroying us both."

It was like a dagger through her heart to hear those words. Luwan felt the sting of tears in her eyes before too long. "I'm sorry for how I treated you earlier. I didn't mean any of it."

"I know," Chesa said. She still wouldn't look at her. "We can't keep doing this."

Luwan knew it was true. "I know."

Something moved along the beach. A dark shape slithered up the beach towards them. The daemon materialized from the darkness. It rose before Luwan, watching her. *What*, she wanted to scream at it. *What do you still want with me?*

She saw Chesa was staring at her now. "And now?" she asked her. There was a flicker of something behind her eyes. The look was only there for a moment and then it was gone.

"I don't know," Luwan revealed.

"Neither do I."

The daemon hissed.

"Maybe we can just sit here for a while," Chesa offered. "Perhaps something will come to us."

Luwan didn't respond.

"What is it?" her sister asked. "What are you staring at?"

"It's nothing," Luwan told her. She couldn't look away. "Nothing at all."

BEYOND THE FENCE POST

KELSEY RAE BARTHEL

"Thank you for your business." Cecelia smiled as she handed her customer their purchase of modest clothes and saw them off with a polite farewell. With another transaction complete, she meandered about her family's quant tailor shop, straightening stacks of fabrics and dusting the shelves. As she tidied the bay window display, she caught herself gazing out into the street, basking in the warm sunshine as she looked out into her home, the village of Aplor. The cobblestone streets and humble wooden buildings cloistered in the mountain valley gave the small farming community a cozy appeal. The rhythmic clomping of horse hooves on stone and dirt sounded throughout the streets as the residents moved their wares and supplies with wooden carts and wagons.

Cecelia had seen the modern motorized vehicles and new electric lights in her few trips to the larger cities, but she didn't see the hurry to upgrade that others did. With the rise of industry her country of Eprington was experiencing, she knew it would affect her small world eventually, but she hoped those new developments would take their time. She was content with the slow, easy pace of the village.

She was wrenched from the serene moment when she saw her

father standing stern in the backroom doorway. Cecelia yelped with surprise.

"Father, you startled me. Do you have to look so grim?" she asked with a nervous smile.

"What are you doing here, Cecelia?"

"I'm minding the shop."

"I see that. Why are you here? It's Carmen's day. You were supposed to pick up the material order."

"Mother said she would do that for me."

"So if you're doing Carmen's work, and your mother is doing your work, what is Carmen doing?"

Cecelia fidgeted with her apron. "She said it was important."

With an irritated scowl, he stomped away. "Whatever it is, I hope it's worth it."

* * *

"OH NO! IT'S THAT LATE?" Carmen cursed, noting the time by the sun's position. She shoved her journal into her satchel and scrambled down the tree she had climbed. She had to hurry or she would miss closing time.

The sun slipped under the horizon as she made her way back to the shop in the dark, the fire of the street lamplights guiding her way. When she arrived, the windows were shuttered and the door was locked.

He definitely knows now. She let out a frustrated grunt and shuffled her way from the closed shop to her family home.

She thought her strict father would be waiting for her with a lecture, but when she stepped into the house, the entranceway was unoccupied. When she heard Cecelia's voice from the sitting room, Carmen quietly closed the door.

"Are you sure about this?"

"I am. I have thought long and hard about this and I couldn't be more certain. Cecelia, will you marry me?" an unfamiliar male voice asked.

Carmen followed the warm, flickering light from the sitting room and peaked in. Cecelia stood in front of the roaring fireplace. Their parents sat on the couch, smiling as they looked up at their daughter. But Carmen's eyes were locked on the young man, down on one knee before her sister. With his clean, crisp suit and his rat's nest hair combed back, Carmen hardly recognized the rancher's son, Derek. When she saw the golden ring he was offering Cecelia, Carmen scowled.

"So, what is your answer?" Derek stammered.

Cecelia fiddled with her apron. "I'm sorry, but I will need some time to discuss this with my family. Please forgive me."

"Of course. Take all the time you need."

Derek wished her parents well and left through the front door. Carmen flashed him a subtle sneer on his way out. "What was that about?" she demanded.

All eyes snapped to Carmen. Their father returned her scowl with his own. "Where have you been?"

"Don't change the subject! Cecelia's only sixteen. She can't get married."

"Cecelia is of marrying age, and it is her decision. If she does agree to get married, it will be because she is thinking about her future. *Cecelia* doesn't constantly run from her responsibilities like you do."

"Harold! Don't be cruel," their mother protested.

"This is serious, Margaret," Harold snapped at his wife before turning back to Carmen. "You need to start taking your situation seriously. You're eighteen and have no prospects outside the shop. All you do is avoid your work and gallivant around the woods. You don't gain other skills; you don't socialize with others. How are you supposed to start a life of your own when you have nothing to build on? We can't care for you forever!"

"I can take care of myself!"

"And do what, exactly? Wander aimlessly like some vagabond? That's a fleeting fantasy. Do you know how much we worry about you when you run off for days on end? You could've been abducted or killed by enemy soldiers closing in on the border."

"Harold! Don't speak of such things. The border patrol will protect us. No need to alarm the girls.".

"I spent my days with the guard patrolling that same border, Margaret. One thing every patrolman knew was that peace between Eprington and Hetrayle continues to hang on by a thread. Hetrayle have been eyeing up our country's resources for years. We have to stay vigilant."

Carmen rolled her eyes. "Not this again."

"I'm sorry, but I have to account for any threat to our family."

"This isn't about me! This is about Cecelia! Does she even want this, or is she just making you happy?"

"Instead of yelling at me, why don't you ask her." Harold gestured to Cecelia.

Carmen pushed down her bitter emotions and faced Cecelia with a show of support. "What do you want to do?"

Cecelia pulled her gaze to the floor. "I think I ..."

Carmen rushed to her aid. "If you're unsure about this, you don't have to say yes. You're still young—you can take your time to find out what you really want."

Carmen turned to her parents with eyes begging for tenderness and understanding. Margaret moved to her husband's side, and they shared a knowing gaze.

"Cecelia, no matter how we feel, this is your decision. We just want you to be happy," Harold said with nothing but love in his voice.

Cecelia's face lit up with a smile as bright as the morning sun. "Thank you. I love you all. And thank you, Carmen. I know you were just trying to stand up for me."

"Do you know what your answer is, Cecelia?" Margaret asked.

"Yes. I'm going to accept his proposal."

Carmen's jaw dropped. "Are you sure?"

Cecelia nodded. "Derek is a good man with a good family. This is what's best for both of us."

Margaret swelled with joy as she gave her daughter a hug. Harold wrapped his big arms around both women, his gruff face brightening with joy and pride.

It was a happy moment in a family where, despite their disagreements, love was never hard to find. But Carmen couldn't join them. Her already small world was shrinking, and now it was strangling her. She left her family with their happy moment and stepped outside.

Feeling anxious and unsteady, she sauntered through the backyard to the tree swing that carried memories of childhood play. The refreshing night air held the smell of the mountains. The clear, night sky showed her an awe-inspiring vision of the stars that soothed her mind as she swayed, thinking of her future.

So deep in thought, Carmen didn't notice Cecelia's approach until her sister tapped her shoulder. Carmen wiped the moisture from her eyes. "Oh, sorry. I just needed some fresh air."

"What were you looking for today?"

"Huh?"

"Why did you need to go out today? It seemed important."

"It's fine, Cecelia." Carmen forced up a small smile to assure her sister. "This is a happy time for you. You should be celebrating with Mother and Father, not worrying about me."

"I can do that later." Cecelia sat on the grass beside Carmen. "I want to know what you were doing out there. Tell me, please."

Carmen couldn't refuse her sister's sincere request. She retrieved her sketchbook from her satchel to show Cecelia a drawing: a family of birds cuddled in their nest.

"They're adorable."

"I've been drawing them at different parts of their growth. I wanted to get one more picture of them before they migrate." Carmen displayed her sketches of the birds from when they were eggs to the present.

"These are wonderful."

As Cecelia admired the pictures, Carmen built up the courage to ask her the question that was pecking at her mind. "Do you really want to get married?"

Cecelia closed the book and took a steady breath. "I'll admit, I didn't think it would happen so soon, but I am happy with it."

"But do you even know him? Have you talked to him that much?"

"Of course. I wouldn't marry a stranger. Did you think he saw me from a distance and had to have me? We started talking once when I was out doing errands. After that, I think he made an effort to continue to run into me. He's been to the house multiple times."

"I don't remember that!"

Cecelia laughed. "That's because you're always out on your ventures."

Carmen laughed with her. "I guess that's true."

"He's a good man, Carmen. He's kind and good to me. I truly believe this will make me happy. And it's not like I'm leaving. We'll still be in town. I'll probably still work at the shop," Cecelia said, trying to lighten the mood, but Carmen's sullen expression didn't change.

"Maybe that's the problem. You're going to marry Derek; you'll grow roots, have children, and grow old in the same place you were born."

"Is that a bad thing?"

"No. Maybe. I don't know. Don't you ever feel nailed down by all this? Haven't you ever wanted to venture beyond Aplor?" Carmen was struggling to give words to her objections.

"Not really. I love it here. I love our family, the shop, the mountains, and the people of this town. I think if I had a whole life in this place with the people I care about, it would be a good life."

"And that would be enough for you? How can you be sure?"

Cecelia shrugged. "I just am. It's difficult to explain. But I do understand that this kind of life isn't for everyone."

Carmen's lips curled into a bittersweet smirk. "You could always see right through me."

"We're sisters. I've always known that you wanted to leave this place."

"It's not that I hate Aplor. I love it, even when it looks like I don't. I believe you can love something but not want it to be all you are. Do you understand?"

Cecelia nodded. "We had a peaceful upbringing in this town, but it isn't what you would call exciting."

"When I go out there and find something I've never seen or even heard of, I get so excited. It's all I can think about. What if everyday could be like that? A whole world filled with things I've never seen." Thoughts of her explorations lit a fire inside Carmen. But her enthusiasm soon faded. "Like Father said, it's just a fantasy."

"It doesn't have to be. If you just talked to him like you talk to me, he would see the passion you have. He just wants you to be happy."

"Cecelia ..." Carmen's words were cut off by a strange noise in the distance. It was the loudest sound she had ever heard, like a stampede of roaring beasts.

Cecelia's eyes bulged as she pointed up at the sky. "Look!"

Carmen's heart pounded in her chest as she saw a brilliant green light streak across the sky, brighter and closer than any fallen star. Most would've run to shelter, cowering for safety. Carmen stood firm, unable to look away as the unknown object plummeted into the distant mountains.

"What was that?" Cecelia wondered.

"Whatever it was, it didn't land that far from here," Carmen said, flashing a thrilled smile.

Cecelia returned a skeptical grimace. "Carmen, what are you thinking?"

"Let's go find whatever that was! First thing tomorrow. We'll make it there by midday!"

"It might be dangerous! We should tell Father and the town authorities about it."

"If we do that, they won't let us go. Others probably heard it—but we saw it. If we head out early, we can be the first to find it. Just like when we were kids and ventured out together."

"I don't know."

"One more adventure together. After that, you can get married and have babies and I can figure out my own future. What do you say?" Carmen held her breath, hoping for her sister's approval.

"Alright, Carmen," Cecelia conceded. "One more adventure."

* * *

"I think we're getting close," Carmen said, navigating by memory and her experience as they moved up the forested mountain.

"I hope so. Mother insisted that we be home before dark. I think Father's talk of invading soldiers frightened her."

"What do you think it was?" Carmen mused, bounding through the terrain with a practiced step.

Cecelia shrugged. "I saw a picture in the capital newspaper of an object that fell from the sky into a farmer's field. Just looked like a large rock."

Carmen frowned. "That doesn't sound interesting."

"What do you hope we find?" Cecelia asked with a chuckle.

"I don't know, something extraordinary. Something we've never seen before. Something you would imagine came from the ...stars." Carmen's words froze mid-sentence as she stepped up to a ridge.

"Don't let your imagination run away on you. You'll just be disappointed." Cecelia caught up to Carmen and the sisters stared down, stunned at the remarkable sight before them.

Nestled in the small crater created from the crash landing was a strange object the size of a small house. Its symmetrical dimensions differed greatly from the natural formation of a boulder and, even from a distance, they could see the surface glinted in the sunlight like metal. But its hue was unlike any she had seen. The smooth lines of its shape reminded Carmen of an aquatic creature.

"That's no rock," Carmen stuttered.

"Definitely not a rock," Cecelia concurred.

The odd nature of their discovery tugged at Carmen's lust for adventure, and she began to scramble down to the landing site, Cecelia following. But even Carmen's eagerness had its limits. They moved in close and inspected the oddity without physical contact, encircling it like it was a delicate museum piece.

The aerodynamic form suggested it was a vessel of some sort, but it lacked any of the details Carmen associated with other vehicles. It had no wheels like a motorcar, and what could have been wings looked more like fins, not like any plane she knew of. The bottom that wasn't buried under dirt looked smooth like a boat, but she couldn't find any seam or door to get inside.

The feature that grabbed Carmen's imagination and wouldn't let go was the prismatic shimmer of the object's surface. At a glance, it looked like it was black but, when Carmen looked closer, it was like the metal glistened with every color she had ever seen simultaneously. Carmen glanced over to the deep gash in the earth from the landing. Despite the wreckage, she didn't see a scratch on the vessel.

"What in the world is this thing?"

"You think it's some kind of war machine?" Cecelia guessed.

Carmen shook her head. "It doesn't look like any tank I've ever seen. Plus, I don't see any guns or weapons mounted on it. It looks kind of like a boat with a closed top."

Cecelia scoffed. "How would a boat fall from the sky?"

She shrugged, conceding that point to her sister.

Once they had seen all they could, Carmen pulled a piece of cloth from her bag and wrapped it around her hand. With the slight precaution taken, she slowly moved her hand to make the first physical contact.

"Wait!" Cecelia jumped.

Carmen froze. "What?"

"It might be dangerous to touch it."

"It's been sitting here ever since it landed, and it looks like nothing's happened. We won't get anywhere just looking at it all day."

"What if it's a trap? What if it's rigged to blow when you touch it?"

Carmen gave the idea a bemused smirk. "If it was, it would've already blown when it crashed."

Cecelia looked away as she ran through Carmen's logic. "I guess so."

"Do you want to stand back?"

"No, no. I'll stay."

With all objections aside, Carmen squared off with the oddity, took a deep breath to steady herself, and reached out to make first contact.

She started with a quick tap of her wrapped fingertips. Nothing happened. She quickly worked her way up before laying her wrapped hand against the surface of the strange vessel. Still, nothing happened.

"It's not even hot. It looked like a blaze when we saw it." With the uneventful result, the next course of action was clear. She pulled her hand back, removed the cloth, and laid her palm flat on the prismatic metal.

The moment her bare hand touched the object, she felt a gentle vibration ripple out from her palm. That vibration intensified, and the metal began to pulse with a strange glow, reacting to her touch.

The vessel jerked with motion, and Carmen jumped back with a yelp. Her heart pounded with fear and excitement. Appendages sprouted from the vessel's underside, and it rose from the crater, dirt and debris sliding off it.

"What did you do?" Cecelia screamed.

"I don't know, I just touched it!"

The forest erupted in a cacophony of animal distress as the vessel continued to adjust until it stood upright and still. The woods fell silent except for the sisters' panicked breaths. A soft hissing sound drew their attention to the back of the ship, where they saw a ramp leading up into the interior of the mysterious craft.

They both stood at the edge of the ramp, staring into the interior with an awe-struck fascination. Carmen's lust for discovery tugged away at her inhibitions, but the sense of uncertainty in her sister's eyes gave her pause.

She took Cecelia's hand and gave it an assuring squeeze. "Are you alright? You don't have to go in if you're scared."

Cecelia's mouth stiffened, and she steadied herself with a breath. "No, this is our last adventure, and we're going to see it through together." Her lips curled up in a small smile. "Don't think I'm so set in my ways. Believe it or not, I'm curious about this...machine."

Carmen grinned ear to ear, and they made the first steps up the ramp and into the unknown.

The ramp led into an open room placed at the front of the vessel, with large windows that shared the exterior's opalescent shine. The view from the windows depicted the forest, but they hadn't seen any windows from the outside. The interior matched the outside aesthetic, with its smooth curves. The walls, floors, and ceiling all flowed seamlessly into each other. Whatever foreign material that made up the inside pulsed with a soft glow, illuminating the room.

The strangest feature of the ship's interior was its barren nature. There were no visible controls, no pilot seats, no furniture. The only thing standing in the empty vessel was a large sphere in the center, suspended at eye level from the ceiling and floor, as if the vessel itself was reaching out to support it. It emanated a pure white light.

Carmen scrambled around the space, searching and taking in every detail of the area with a childlike giddiness she could hardly contain. While Cecelia slowly stepped closer to the radiant sphere.

"I don't see any controls anywhere. If this is a ship, how do you fly it? It flew to get here," Carmen said.

"It's missing a part of itself," Cecelia said in a shallow tone.

But Carmen didn't notice Cecelia's sudden change. Her own lust for discovery had a stranglehold on her attention. She scurried along the walls, feeling for hidden compartments or mechanisms. "It's missing everything that it should have. The plane at the capital's military parade had buttons and switches and a whole mess of controls to fly them."

"It's empty inside. It needs a pilot. A mind and soul to give it direction."

"The outside didn't look damaged at all. Maybe the pilot survived."

"The pilot is gone," Cecelia said. "It needs a new connection. It wants me."

Those ominous words sent a chill down Carmen's spine. She turned to her sister and saw her standing perfectly still, fixated on the sphere as if in a trance. "Cecelia, are you all right?"

Cecelia stayed put, not reacting to Carmen's question. "It's reaching out to me. It needs me."

Carmen's unbridled joy of discovery was washed away by the horror of the unknown. She clenched her jaw and pushed down her fear. "Cecelia, move away from that thing."

"It needs me to make it whole. It needs me to fly." Cecelia reached for the sphere.

Carmen sprinted to stop her, but it was too late. The moment Cecelia touched the orb, her body started to disappear. Working down from her fingertips, like she was made of shining sand, being blown away and absorbed into the sphere.

Carmen lunged at Cecelia, pushing her from the source of the destruction in a vain attempt to save her sister, but it was useless. Before she could make it two steps, Cecelia's body, the form that had felt solid just a moment ago, was gone.

Carmen fell to her knees, staring helplessly at her empty arms.

"Cecelia." Carmen's soft cry erupted into a mad scream of horror. "CECELIA!" she bellowed over and over as she darted into every corner of the ship, frantically searching. When she found nothing, she ran from the ship, towards home and the people who could help her.

* * *

THE MEAGER FORCES of the town marched through the night with weapons and lanterns, ready for whatever they might face, Carmen's ravings fresh in their minds. But when they arrived at the familiar ridge, all they found was a deep laceration in the ground.

Carmen scoured the site, searching for any sign of the vessel. Her panicked muttering drew the weary eyes of the townspeople until Harold organized them into a wide search of the forest.

They scoured the mountainside, deep into the night and in shifts over the next several days, pulling together the community to find one of the town's beloved daughters. But as the hours passed to days with no sign of Cecelia or the vessel, their optimism began to diminish, replaced with dread, sadness, and suspicion.

Even after the town gave up the search, Carmen and her parents continued to comb the woods. After a month, her parents stopped the search, leaving Carmen to go out on her own. Anxiety and sorrow blanketed Carmen's days. With every failed search, her faith in her own senses began to waver. She would often look back in her memory, trying to discover any clue that what she witnessed wasn't real, but found nothing. Every exciting and terrible moment of that memory felt as real as the crater she kept returning to.

She noticed the distrustful eyes of her neighbors, the rumors that drifted through the town. Words like *unhinged*, *delusional*, and *liar* were spoken in hushed tones they thought Carmen didn't hear. Spiteful rumors gnawed at her mind until she closed herself away from the town she called home.

Little did she know that events outside her control were moving into place. These forces clashed on the day of Cecelia's funeral, which Carmen refused to attend. She couldn't bear watching them bury an empty box to say goodbye to her sister.

She hid away in Cecelia's room, reliving happy memories connected to her old belongings, loitering in bittersweet agony. She didn't notice the sun sink below the horizon. Her parents returned at the tail end of twilight, where she met them at the door with a candle to light the dim room.

"How was the service?" Carmen asked.

Margaret looked away and retreated upstairs to her room.

Carmen frowned but kept silent.

Harold took a deep breath. Carmen could tell that the weight of his crumbling family sat heavy on his shoulders. "It was hard on your mother. Give her some time."

"And you're fine with saying goodbye to Cecelia?"

"It's been months, Carmen. She's not coming back," Harold said, nailing every word into their cold reality.

A thick layer of tension hung like dark smoke between them. Carmen's bitter anger smoldered inside her. She summoned up her courage to ask him the question she'd held onto for a long while. "Do you believe me?"

Harold met Carmen's gaze, his eyes filled with pity and regret. "Carmen, it's been a long day."

"Please tell me! What do you think happened that day?"

"I'm not going over this with you again!" Harold insisted, fleeing away from the question.

Carmen chased after him. "Tell me what you think happened! Do you think she fell off a cliff and I imagined the ship? Do you think she ran off or that I killed her?"

"Carmen! Stop it!"

"Tell me what you think!"

"I don't know, Carmen! I don't know what happened. All I know is that my daughter is gone. I don't want to blame you, Carmen, but I can't keep hope alive. We have to let this ..." Harold's words were cut short by the deafening shock of an explosion that rattled the entire house.

Harold sprinted to retrieve his rifle from the cabinet and loaded it with a practiced ease. "Soldiers from the border. We have to retreat to the woods. Margaret!"

Margaret flew down the stairs. "Harold, what's happening?"

"No time to explain. We need to go to the woods. NOW!"

With Harold leading the way, his rifle at the ready, they left the house and fled for the tree line. The moonless night was illuminated by the raging fires of burning buildings. The usual quiet was replaced with far-off explosions, gunfire, and the screams of frightened people. In her flight, Carmen caught the sight of a couple being gunned down when they fell behind.

"Keep running!" Harold ordered, stopping to take a shot at a soldier.

Carmen grabbed her mother's hand and sprinted while Harold guarded their rear. Her heart fluttered with hope as she spotted the edge of the town.

Margaret suddenly screamed, and Carmen felt her mother's hand slip from her grasp. She leapt to Margaret's aid but froze at the sight of blood oozing from her mother's leg.

Harold caught up with them and crouched to his wife's side, placing pressure on her wound. "Carmen, keep heading to the tree line. We'll catch up."

"I can't leave you!"

"You have to! I can't lose you, too!" Harold commanded, pushing her away.

"I can't!" Whimpering cries bubbled up in her voice.

"GO!"

The fear inside her gained control of her body, forcing her to run for safety, tears blurring her vision. She left behind the raging fires, the sounds of violence, and the last unmistakable cries of her parents. Her heart wanted to scream, wanted to fall to her knees and weep from the very depth of her anguish. It wanted to linger in the deep pain of having her parents ripped from her, but her mind knew that wasn't an option. Her mind knew her continued survival depended on putting one foot in front of the other as fast as she could. All she could do was run to the darkness of the forest, holding her grief inside.

But the shadows of the woods failed to provide the safety for which she had hoped. She could hear the footsteps of a group of soldiers approaching fast. Choking down her sobs, she kept running, her body flinching with every pop of gunfire.

Her arm suddenly erupted in white-hot agony as her body was hit by a force that spun her like a fallen leaf. She tumbled to the forest floor, screaming and clutching at her arm, finding nothing but a bloody stump at the elbow.

She lay on the cold ground, pain and anguish assaulting her every thought, her blood flowing into the earth. She could do nothing but wail in agony as the chaos of the invasion roared around her. She had lost everything. Her parents, her home, her sister, and now she was going to lose her life and there was nothing she could do. As she prepared for her demise, she heard a familiar voice that bestowed a flicker of hope.

Carmen! Keep going, Carmen.

"Cecelia," Carmen whispered.

Just a little closer.

The dream that her sister could still be alive was enough to give her the strength to pull her battered and broken body up and to her feet. "Where are you?"

"Someone's over here," barked a soldier.

Carmen caught a glimpse of a pair of soldiers moving towards her. She held her arm tight to her body to try and slow the bleeding as she stumbled away from the approaching soldiers, her vision blurring from blood loss. She felt her body weaken with each step, but she forced herself to move, even if it was just towards a faraway delusion.

As if plucked from her dreams, the mysterious vessel appeared before Carmen in a flash of brilliant prismatic light. The soldiers cried out and made a hasty retreat.

Get on the ship! Cecelia's voice commanded as the ramp lowered.

"It was real. It was all real," Carmen whimpered, crying tears of joy. With the last of her dwindling strength, she staggered onto the ship, her legs buckling under her as she fell onto the floor. Then everything went dark.

* * *

"Carmen," Cecelia's voice called in the darkness. "Carmen, wake up."

As Carmen's mind returned to consciousness, memories of the invasion came to her in a flash. She woke up in a shot and grabbed at her missing limb but stared in astonishment when she discovered the limb she thought was lost was intact and functional. She thought it must have been a dream until the unforgettable opalescent shimmer of the vessel recaptured her attention.

"Carmen, you're awake. How do you feel?"

Carmen's head swiveled back and forth, searching for the source of her sister's voice. "Where are you?"

"Over here."

Carmen followed Cecelia's voice to the strange sphere, where the radiant white light had changed to a soft lavender. "Cecelia?"

"I know this may be hard to believe, but my mind has merged with the ship. That's why it had no controls. It needed the pilot to merge with it and become part of its body."

"You … you're part of the ship now?"

"And so are you. You lost your arm while running from those men. The ship is made of millions of tiny machines that react to what I want. I was able to make you a new arm with them," Cecelia explained.

"How is this possible?"

"I'm not entirely sure. Something happened to the old pilot when it crashed. That's why it reached out to me."

"But when I brought Father back to the site, the ship was gone. I spent months looking for you, looking for any sign, and found nothing. I thought I was crazy. Everyone did."

"I'm so sorry you went through that. When I joined with the vessel, I didn't know what was happening. It was like I was trapped in a void. I couldn't see, hear, or feel anything. I don't know how much time passed, but one day, I heard your voice calling out for me. I think because you touched the ship first, I was able to connect with you, and that helped me realize how to reach out with the ship's senses, as if it was my new body. But by the time I fully gained control, the army attacked Aplor."

"Aplor! The town is being attacked. We need to help them!"

"Carmen, it's too late."

"What are you talking about? We can help them before the rest of the army moves in."

"Carmen, you've been unconscious for a week."

Her heart sank. "What?"

"The town has been destroyed. I guess what Father was saying all these years was true. Hetrayle finally made their move. They moved in a strike force to crush Aplor, then used our small village to gain a foothold in Eprington's border. They took the capital before our government could react. They must have been planning this invasion for years. Our country is gone, Carmen."

"How do you know this?"

"The ship can remain hidden while reaching out with its sensors. I was able to see without being seen. I kept an eye on the situation while you were healing. I'm sorry, Carmen."

"They're...gone. It's all gone." The full scope of Carmen's reality set in. She stumbled to the wall in a stupor and slumped to the floor.

"You're safe here, Carmen. You're far away from what happened. It will be okay." Cecelia's disembodied voice still carried the sincerity Carmen remembered, and she believed her sister's words. She was safe to let out the grief and sorrow she had bundled inside for the sake of survival. It started with a tiny whimper and built up to a relentless cry and a fountain of tears. She held nothing back in the sanctuary of the mysterious ship.

After what felt like an eternity of emotions, she felt her sobs slow down, and she wiped her eyes between soft sniffles.

"Feel any better?" Cecelia asked.

"This is all my fault," Carmen said in a weak murmur.

"What is?"

"What happened to you. It's all my fault. I had to have one more adventure. Why couldn't I have gone alone? Why didn't the ship take me? I ruined our family."

"Carmen, this isn't your fault. I chose to go with you. And if we didn't, we both would've been killed in the invasion. You can't dwell on it like this," Cecelia assured her in a steady tone.

Her sister's reassuring perspective was comforting, but Carmen remembered how Cecelia used to be. How she would whimper and cry at every lost pet as they grew up. She had always worn her heart on her sleeve. "How are you so calm?"

"I...don't know. Maybe it's because I don't have a body anymore. Maybe it's part of the effect of the ship. I know that my heart is broken over all of it. Over our parents, Derek, the townspeople. I know I miss them and grieve for the loss...I just don't feel it like I should."

Cecelia's words spoke of a desperation her tone couldn't reflect. This may have been new to Carmen, but Cecelia had been part of the ship for months. She acted and sounded like Cecelia because she remembered what it was like to...be human. How long would it be before she forgot?

"Cecelia?"

"Yes?"

"Is there a way to reverse what happened to you?"

"I don't know. I have access to a vast cache of information of what the vessel has seen, but it doesn't have anything on the ship itself or the people who made it. It's like that information was purposely removed."

Carmen rose, a spark of determination glinting in her eyes. "Then we'll find them. We'll find whoever built this thing and make them turn you back. I don't care if we have to go to the other end of the world."

"You'll have to go farther than that," Cecelia said. Suddenly the windows at the front of the vessel shifted and reverted to their translucence. Carmen looked out from them and was met with a dazzling view of stars and a planet, a lovely blue marble in the dark expanse of space.

Carmen's eyes widened and her mouth gaped. "Is that…?"

"Yes, it's our home planet. The information of the ship's makers may have been taken, but I know that they are from another world, far away from here."

Carmen had never left her home country before, and now she was looking down on her entire world. Her small town, in her small country, on her small world was only a speck in that sea of stars, and where they needed to go was just another unknown speck. Despite that, her path was clearer than it had ever been. "It doesn't matter."

"Carmen, the chances of …"

Carmen's weary hands balled into fists, and she turned and marched towards the lavender sphere. "It doesn't matter how far it is. We'll find it. I'll find it. I'll fix this, Cecelia. I'll do everything I can to give you your body…your life back. Even if we have to cross this sea of stars to its edge, I will fix this, I promise."

A long stretch of silence hung between them before Carmen heard what sounded like a tiny chuckle. She couldn't see it, but she could've sworn that Cecelia was smiling.

"One last adventure?" Cecelia proposed.

Carmen smiled back, tears rolling down her cheek as she laid her hand on the sphere. "One last adventure."

THE MEMORY POOL

JASON CHESTNUT

Things get built. Things fall apart.

Paul sat in an empty house, looking through the sliding glass door to the backyard. A large, partially excavated hole was in the center, surrounded by mounds of gray and brown dirt. The wife had taken their two young sons, Ezra and Asher, to visit their grandmother and wouldn't be back for a couple of weeks. This left Paul alone to stare out at the gaping wound in the otherwise meticulously maintained back lawn. As the sun dipped below the suburban rooftops, clouds converged overhead, followed by a distant rumbling. Paul's fingers curled around the neck of a whiskey bottle while his wife's last words reverberated in his head.

"I want a divorce," she had said. "I don't think this is fixable."

Those words skipped in his brain like a broken record, stabbing into his chest every time.

Things break. Things can't be fixed.

She said he'd have to talk to the boys, but he didn't know what to say. In fact, he wasn't sure how he was going to explain to anyone. He hadn't been unfaithful or abusive. He didn't have any addictions or obsessions. That was the hardest part: it wasn't just one thing.

She liked to socialize, to have lots of friends, to keep up appearances. She enjoyed setting up playdates for the kids, going to PTA meetings, and endlessly renovating their house. Paul was an introvert. He had maintained the same close circle of friends since high school and suffered perpetual social anxiety. He was good about maintaining the house but didn't understand why the furniture had to be rearranged every few months, why they needed new floors, or why the cabinets needed to be painted. In retrospect, maybe none of that had been about the house at all.

I don't think this is fixable.

A few months ago, Paul and his wife had taken out a second mortgage to put in a pool, something the boys had always wanted. This was a decision made while the direction of their marriage was still not completely clear. A decision made, like many other renovations, in the spirit of trying to fix something they didn't know was unfixable.

The project kept getting postponed as the gulf between Paul and his wife widened. They'd halted construction for two weeks after Paul moved into the spare bedroom, his wife telling him it was because of his snoring. Delayed again by four weeks after a shouting match over loans and mounting credit card debt. Postponed by another two after couples' therapy devolved into marathon sobbing.

Everything had come to a head a couple of weeks ago. Paul left his solitary confinement in the guest room to lie next to his wife in the master bedroom. Before he even said a word, she told him not to touch her. She didn't even look at him. Even though they had not been intimate for quite some time, hearing those words out loud made everything very real… very *immediate*.

The excavation was complete, but the delay was now indefinite. There were several days of tension-filled silence before she said her piece. Then it was off to Grandma's house. The kids were told Daddy couldn't come because of "work."

Work, Paul thought, his lips curling in mild disgust as he stared at the hole in the yard.

He spent the evening drinking and scouring the internet for a model of the USS *Lexington*. Paul's father, Joe, had been a history buff and built models of World War II era planes and ships—when he wasn't drinking himself into oblivion. When Paul was eight years old —the same age as his eldest son, Ezra—his father had promised him they would build the *Lexington* together. But they never finished the model. Joe walked out on the family not long after, the incomplete aircraft carrier a constant reminder of things left unresolved.

Things fall apart. Things remain in pieces.

Paul still remembered the day his father left. Paul's mother and younger brother had stood in front of their small South Florida apartment, watching the disheveled patriarch pack a few random items into an old, ruddy brown Honda Accord. He wore an old red and white trucker cap that struggled to contain a messy head of curly dark brown hair. A job was waiting for him in Orlando, he said, and he'd be back soon. But Paul took one look at his mother's stony expression and knew that none of it was true. Joe was never coming back.

Paul pinched the bridge of his nose and took another swig of whiskey. He closed an article about black holes and continued his search for the *Lexington*. Something in him burned at finishing that model once and for all. It felt symbolic. There was no way in hell he was going to bullshit his own children into believing he was just "going away" for a while, that everything was going to be okay. Nothing was going to be okay. Things were not fixable. But the model was something he could finish, something he could control... if nothing else.

Thunder rumbled on, and the first few droplets of rain pelted the sliding glass door. Paul pushed the computer chair away from the desk in the living room to look outside. It was dark now, with occasional muted white flashes of lightning and distant rumbling thunder. Something about the storm felt accusatory. A growling admonishment enveloping the house... the house he would soon leave behind. Paul cursed and drank some more of the whiskey, the bottle half full at this point.

Or is it half empty? he thought, his eyes blinking away the dull pull of intoxication.

Paul stood and swiped the bottle from the desk. His search for the *Lexington* had been fruitless. Sold out at every hobby shop online and going for far too much on eBay than he was willing to pay. After all, he still had to figure out where the hell he was going to live and how much rent he could afford. The thunder rumbled again, and Paul grunted back in response. He would not take any more criticism from the sky; his mind was made up. He would find that model aircraft carrier and finish it once and for all. He would not think about the hole in the yard and certainly would not think about talking to the boys. Not yet. Not now.

Thunder roared as rain poured against the windows.

"No!" Paul stomped over to the glass door, sliding it open. "I will do what I want! I don't care!"

He strode out into the backyard in his blue flannel robe, white t-shirt, and boxers. He yelled back at the clouds every time the thunder rumbled, cursing out an argument he wouldn't have with anything with a pulse. Water drenched his thinning hair and clothes as his bare feet slid to a halt at the edge of the hole in the ground. He screeched and poured the rest of the whiskey into the pool of water forming at the bottom of the hole.

"I don't care!" he yelled. "What can I do? Who *am* I?"

He looked down, seeing the whiskey disappear into the darkness of the unfinished excavation. *Pointless*, he thought, *everything is pointless*. Even the *Lexington*—if he had it with him now, he'd push it down beneath the muddy water at the bottom of that hole. He'd bury it and hope the mud would drag him down as well.

Paul tossed the empty bottle aside and turned to grab two sopping handfuls of soil from one of the dirt mounds. He tossed them into the abyss below, watching them disappear just like the whiskey, all obscured by rain and darkness. He grabbed two more handfuls and as he turned to toss them, his feet slid out from under him.

Paul tumbled onto his back and slid over the mouth of the hole and into that same darkness he had been tossing everything into. He yelped, but the sounds of thunder overhead drowned out his cries. He splashed into the water like a sack of potatoes, the whiplash momentarily turning his world to black. He struggled, flailing beneath the surface, water stinging his eyes and nostrils. His limbs felt like they were passing through liquid concrete. He bobbed for a bit, the air leaving his aching lungs, his head going light, the pain of sudden forced sobriety stabbing into his temples. Paul's foot touched something at the bottom of the hole, and he pushed himself up and out of the water.

He gasped and grabbed the edges of… a bathtub? As he coughed up water, his eyes slowly adjusted to his surroundings. He was no longer outside, but how? Where was he? Panic gave way to confusion, his throbbing head on fire. There were white porcelain tiles along the wall beside the clawfoot tub. The water he had regurgitated formed a puddle on a tan linoleum floor. He stared down at the puddle, finding clear water bereft of any sediment. His eyes trailed to a white porcelain toilet that sat against the wall next to a matching sink with a round mirror above. He crawled out of the tub and fell onto his back. Had the entire episode been a dream? Had he fallen asleep in the tub?

As Paul's ragged breathing subsided, he realized this was not his bathroom. He was also no longer in his flannel robe, shirt, and boxers. He was wearing black slacks, a brown short-sleeved button-up shirt, and black work boots. His clothes were not even wet. Hadn't he just climbed out of a bathtub? He rolled onto his stomach and pushed himself to his feet.

I'm dying, he lamented with a heavy sigh, *drowning in that damn unfinished pool. My dying brain is dreaming.*

He looked around, feeling a strange nagging at the back of his head. Something was familiar about the bathroom, something he couldn't quite place. He took a couple of small, cautious steps out into the hallway. He knew this hallway, this stark white corridor with its brown carpeting. At the left end of the hallway was a closed door shrouded in shadow. The right end of the hallway opened to what looked like a living room, a familiar blue sofa partially visible. Directly across from the bathroom was a partially open doorway. Light poured out of that door across the hall, and Paul felt drawn to it like a moth. Some terrible feeling of dread tore at his insides, and he felt frozen for a moment. He wanted to run, but something kept him from turning away. A magnetic force he couldn't resist, a demand to *see*… to *feel*.

With all his willpower, Paul took two hurried steps across the hall with the same urgency one would take to jump into a freezing swimming pool. He exhaled once he was in the room, and all at once he felt himself crumbling apart, the weight of the sight pinning him down from the inside.

It was his bedroom. Not the bedroom in the house that he and his wife had bought. No, it was his childhood bedroom in that same South Florida apartment all those years ago. The bunk beds with their chocolate brown frames set against the wall on the right, the Spider-man and Star Wars posters on the walls, the closet doors open with toys spilling out. Against the far wall under the single window was a desk. Paul's heart sank.

A partially constructed aircraft carrier, half the flight deck unpainted and mostly just a skeleton, sat in the middle. Paul stepped toward the model and looked it over, his eyes hot with tears. Just as he reached out to touch it, his fingers trembling, he heard a voice behind him and froze.

At first, he thought it was the voice of one of his boys. But what he saw when he spun around struck him to his core. Eight-year-old Paul looked back at him with pleading, worried, red eyes, standing among the discarded Transformers and GI Joes.

"Are we going to finish it?" Little Paul asked, his voice cracking.

Grown-up Paul nodded but felt a strange resistance in his muscles. There was pain behind it, an uncertainty that gnawed at his chest.

"We'll finish it when I get back," Grown-up Paul heard himself say. "Just take care of it while I'm gone, OK?"

Paul choked, realizing that he had not willed himself to say those words… they were being said *for him*. He tried to say something else, but nothing came, and he felt his legs moving on their own. He felt his hand ruffle eight-year-old Paul's hair as he walked past him and out of the room.

No, Paul thought, trying to cry but not feeling the tears coming. *I know what this is. Please don't let me do this.*

Paul finally realized what was going on and looked down at himself. He recognized the clothes he was wearing, felt the trucker cap on his head of messy dark brown curls, saw the hastily packed collection of belongings by the front door to the apartment as he exited the hallway.

No no no, he pleaded, but no sound came out of his mouth. This was not his mouth… this was not his decision.

With all his might, he reached out and grabbed the edge of the apartment doorway just as the door swung open. He would not let this happen. Not this time. Never again. But as the door opened, he didn't see the parking lot. He didn't see his mother and brother waiting by that ruddy brown Honda. Instead, he saw a vast, swirling black hole, tinged in purple and blue. The vortex stretched the surrounding stars into thin, futile lines. Paul cried out, grabbing the door frame with both hands as the gravitational field pulled his legs out of from under him. He looked back into the apartment and saw the lights inside slowly flicker away.

He caught one last glimpse of his eight-year-old self in the center of the living room of the darkening apartment. The boy's eyes were closed, and Paul closed his own. In that moment, feeling the gravity threatening to swallow him up, the sheer *weight* of it all, he considered just letting go. Maybe that was what his dying brain was trying to tell him. *Give up and let go.*

But, in that same moment, his eyes still squeezed shut, he saw the face of his younger self replaced with that of his eldest son, Ezra. Saw his own boy with the same pleading, worried, red eyes he had seen on himself just moments earlier. Seeing that ignited something within Paul. Something angry, defiant, and possessed of a strength he didn't think possible just a few seconds earlier. He gritted his teeth and held on. He held on until he felt his fingernails digging into the wood, until he felt his fingers bleeding. No matter what, he was going to *hold on*.

Paul gasped, coughing up wet soil. His arms flailed, trying to find the edge of the door frame, dirty water burning his nostrils. His eyes shot open, blinded by a sudden burst of light as he coughed and shivered. He expected to see that same swirling vortex pulling at him. Instead, he saw the sun blazing overhead like a white-hot pearl.

It took him a moment to realize he was back in the hole in the backyard. It was no longer raining, and morning had arrived. He took a breath and wiped mud and water out of his eyes, trembling all over. A ladder stood against the inside of the hole, and he pushed through the muddy water, his temples pounding. His body felt weak and freezing, and it took what seemed like eons to climb up the ladder and out of the hole. He collapsed to the ground and rolled onto his back. Wispy white clouds parted before a clear blue sky.

After forcing himself to stand, Paul stepped into the house, shaking so badly his teeth rattled. He peeled off his dirty clothes, leaving them in the laundry room next to the kitchen, then lumbered upstairs like an injured beast. The feverish trembling in his limbs threatened to consume him as he reached the top of the stairs, stumbling into the bathroom.

The warm shower was refreshing and almost instantly, Paul felt life returning to his battered body and brain. He stayed in there for a long time, thinking back on what he had seen, what he had experienced. Had it been a dream? What if he had drowned? The weight of that question turned his insides to stone as a slew of painful images darted through his mind. A litany of words left unsaid, promises left unfulfilled… things left *unresolved*. He looked down at his hands, at his fingertips, expecting to see them a bloody mess, but they were only wrinkled from the moisture.

The hot water subsided, and Paul stepped out, dried off, and put on a clean shirt and boxers. He threw back a few aspirins and some water from the bathroom sink before making his way back downstairs. Sunlight poured in from the backyard windows, painting the house's interior a melancholy orange. He walked into the kitchen to brew up some coffee just as his cell phone buzzed, rattling away on the counter. He picked it up, saw the incoming number, and took a breath.

"Hello?"

"Hi, Daddy." It was his eldest.

"Hey, Ezra." Paul smiled. "How's Grandma's house?"

"Good," Ezra answered before falling silent for a tense handful of seconds. "Mommy says you have to talk to us about something."

Paul pinched the bridge of his nose and looked out the windows set over the kitchen sink. He sighed and then said, "Yeah... yeah, we're going to finish the pool, kid."

"Yay!" the boy exclaimed. "Are you sure? Mommy said we might not."

"Look," Paul said, leaning against the counter, staring out at the sun rising higher in the sky above the suburban horizon, "we have a lot to talk about, but we'll wait until you're back home. I want you to know... that sometimes things may seem like they are breaking or can't be fixed. But the truth is not everything has to be fixed. Sometimes they just have to *change*."

The other end of the line went quiet for another moment before Ezra said, "OK, Daddy."

Paul laughed. "It will all make sense in the end, kid. I promise. I have something to show you when you get back."

"What is it, Daddy?"

"Do you know what an aircraft carrier is?"

Things break.

No. Things change.

1989 REDWOOD LANE

ESTELLE WARDRIP

I have a knife in my hand because I am loading the dishwasher. It's still in my hand when I jump and spin around, but I'm not thinking of stabbing anyone. I'm just startled.

"Whoa, watch that knife!" Craig takes a hasty step back.

"What...did you?" I stammer, unsure how to say it, then I blurt, "You grabbed my butt!"

"Relax, I didn't mean anything by it." He smiles. "You're starting to fill out."

"Don't touch my butt!" I remember I have a knife in my hand and should do something with it. I wave it vaguely between us.

"Calm down, killer." His tone of voice is joking. "It was a compliment. You have a nice butt."

"Don't do it again." I know he isn't listening. You can always tell when adults aren't listening.

"Don't try to stab me. That would make me late for work," he says, heading for the door.

I stay where I am, the back of my legs pressing against the metal racks of the dishwasher, knife still in my hand. The only sounds come from the Saturday morning cartoons Lily is watching in the living room. I stand there until I hear his car start up in the driveway and pull away. He didn't scream at me, but it still feels like I have done something wrong. I'm not sure what, but whatever the appropriate response was, that wasn't it.

I search my memories for anything useful. I remember when I was littler, Lily's age. Mom and I had been at a bus stop. Some guy we didn't know had grabbed Mom's butt. She screamed at him and scratched him. I remember him stumbling out of the bus shelter with red lines on his face, and Mom chasing him out into the rain, cursing at him. When she came back, she told me to never let a guy put his hands on me without my permission. I hadn't really understood what that meant. I still didn't. Should I have stabbed Craig? That seems like a bad idea. He's punched the wall a few times when he was mad, and he probably would've punched me if I'd really stabbed him.

I decide I'll tell Mom when she gets up for lunch. Saturday and Sunday are her days off from being a mom, and she likes to sleep in. I take care of Lily and the chores. It's fair since I get those days off school, and I like cooking for everyone.

Once I have a plan, I'm able to unfreeze. I grab Lily's cereal bowl and start the dishwasher. Then I get the laundry going, with the laundry and dishes washing themselves I can watch cartoons for a little while and still be getting chores done. Lily makes room for me in the comfy chair, and I settle in for what's left of a normal morning.

I'm so focused on the cartoons that I manage to forget about what happened. When my mom yells for me from her bedroom, all I'm thinking about is that if I get her what she wants quickly, I might not miss too much of the show. I run down the hall but enter her room quietly; she does not like a lot of loud noises or running around in the mornings. It's dark in her room, and it smells like she's already had her first cigarette, which is good. It means she won't be so cranky.

Her tone of voice immediately proves that assumption wrong. "Your dad just texted me that you threatened him with a knife this morning."

Craig isn't my dad. I don't even like him. This isn't the time for that argument though, and it's always an argument. "He grabbed my butt," I tell her.

"He did not."

"He did!" I'm not sure why she would say he didn't. She wasn't even there.

"Craig wouldn't do that, not to family," Mom insists.

"He did." I say again, because it happened.

"It must have been an accident, so maybe he bumped into you. The kitchen isn't very big." Mom sounds a little uncertain.

That uncertainty feels like an opening. I might be able to convince her if I keep pushing. "He did grab my butt," I say louder than I mean to, but I press on. "I called him on it and he said he did! He didn't deny it. And I didn't threaten him with a knife—I just had one in my hand because I was doing the dishes."

Mom is quiet for a few minutes. It feels like forever, but I let her process. I'm confident that once she's thought about this she'll be on my side.

I'm wrong.

When she finally speaks, her voice is furious. "So what if he did? It's not like he hurt you."

"I didn't like it." I should have known that was a stupid thing to say. Mom hates it when I complain.

"Oh, you didn't like it?" Her voice is mocking, "Well, I didn't like getting kicked out by my parents when I was eighteen for getting pregnant out of wedlock. I didn't like being left by my boyfriend when I wouldn't abort you. I didn't like living on the streets and trying to raise a baby in a car. We don't always like what happens, princess. Your stepdad is the reason we have a roof over our heads and regular meals and you have all those nice clothes and toys in your own room. So you think about all that before you threaten the man who owns the house you live in."

I open my mouth to say that I didn't threaten him, but I'm not so sure anymore. The whole thing is kind of an uncomfortable blur. I remember I had a knife in my hand, and I remember waving it around, but I can't remember exactly what I said. Maybe I said I'd stab him if he did it again? I don't know.

Mom notices that I almost said something, then didn't. "Didn't think of that, did you? You're so immature—do you really think having your butt grabbed is worse than living on the streets? Why don't you go try that for a while and see how much you like scrounging all your meals and not knowing where you'll sleep each night."

I try to get a word in, to defend myself, but she talks over me. She keeps going on and on about how awful and selfish I am and how I'm putting the family at risk. I just stand there and try not to cry, because I know if I cry I'll be insulted for that too. Finally, the washing machine buzzes that it's done.

"I need to put the clothes in the dryer," I tell her, grateful for any excuse to leave.

"You do that. I need another cigarette." Mom glares at me. "You know these things are bad for me, you know I'm trying to quit, but you keep stressing me out, and what am I supposed to do? If I die of lung cancer, it's your fault."

I just nod. I've heard that before many times. Then I make my escape.

As I load our school clothes into the dryer, I think about what Mom said. Specifically the part about if having my butt grabbed was worse than living on the street. The thing is, I remember living in a car. Mom didn't move in with Craig until I was six. It wasn't that bad. It was warm. It was probably cramped for her but there was plenty of room for a little kid. I don't ever remember being hungry. We'd spend a lot of time at the park or the library so I got to play with other kids. I honestly liked it. It was Mom and me together all the time—we were a family, just the two of us. Living on the street had been kind of fun. I'd rather go back to that than get grabbed again, or yelled at, or punched.

But then Craig had come along, then Lily, and our family changed. Some of the changes were good. Lily is a great kid, and having my own room is nice. But some things weren't so great. I have a lot of chores now, and I don't see Mom much. She's always in her room smoking and watching television. It seems like the only time we talk anymore is when I'm in trouble. I miss when it was just Mom and me, and sometimes I feel like she's replaced me with her new family.

Lily interrupts my thoughts. "Iris, I'm hungry. Can I have a cheese stick?"

"One sec," I say, starting the dryer. I realize that Mom hasn't replaced me with Lily. She's replaced me with Craig. That's why she never says anything when Craig makes fun of me, that's why she's not going to do anything now. Maybe she is only able to love one person at a time. When it had been the two of us, it had been me. When Lily was born, Mom had loved Lily, but she and Craig fought a lot. Once Lily got bigger and I started taking care of her more, Mom and Craig made up. Now Lily is my responsibility whenever I'm home.

I realize that I have to take Lily with me when I run away. I can't trust Mom to take care of her when I'm not around. Lily is big enough to help with things sometimes, so living with her might be easier than living alone. I have an idea of a place we could live.

I plan our escape while I fix lunch. When our clothes come out of the dryer, our bags are ready for them to go in. Mom emerges from her room, and we both act normal at lunch. I haven't told Lily anything, and Mom always likes to pretend that fights never happened as soon as they are over. I know there will be a Round Two when Craig gets home, but I have no intention of being here when he does.

After lunch, Mom goes out. Shopping or hanging out with friends, I don't know.

"Lily, want to go to the school and play on the playground?" I ask as soon as Mom's car is out of sight.

Lily looks at me with big eyes. She's been begging Mom and Craig to take her to the school playground for months, ever since she realized she's going to be starting kindergarten in the fall. "Yes." Her voice is an excited whisper.

"Great." I force myself to sound cheerful, like this is just a fun outing that totally has parental permission. "I packed you some toys, so put your coat and boots on. Maybe we'll find some puddles to jump in."

"There's no puddles. It's too warm."

Her coat and boots are bulky and I want her to have them, but I don't want to carry them. "We're not going if you don't wear your coat and boots," I tell her. "I'll bring your other shoes and we can change when we get there if you want to."

She accepts that, and a half hour later we're hopping off the bus at the school, each with a backpack and a second bag. I'd had to leave a lot of stuff behind, but I don't want to look more suspicious than we already do.

Lily asks where my classroom is, so I lead her through the sixth-grade wing on our way to the playground. Then I take a spot in the shade to read while she runs and plays. I manage to lose track of time reading until Lily climbs up in my lap and announces that she is hungry. I look up and realize that the sun is getting low and I'm hungry, too. There's a cafe across the street from the school, and warm food smells are blowing past. I have all my saved money, so I ask her if she wants to go out for dinner.

Lily is thrilled. She loves eating at restaurants. I tell her to order anything, and she orders a grilled cheese sandwich. I order one, too, since it's the cheapest thing on the menu. When the waitress brings our food, Lily announces, "It's my birthday!" It isn't. She actually turned five a month ago, but she's learned that if you tell people in restaurants that it's your birthday, you sometimes get a free cupcake. It works this time.

We leave the restaurant and head uphill. Two years ago, I'd gone trick-or-treating with some kids from school in this neighborhood. They'd pointed out an abandoned house that they claimed was haunted. I don't believe in ghosts, so as far as I'm concerned, it's just an unoccupied building, close to the school and with a reputation that keeps people away from it. In other words, the perfect place for Lily and me to live.

I figure it's important to stay in school. For one thing, I can get food there. For another, while Mom might not come looking for me, the school would notice and would do something if I stopped showing up. I remember the drama last year when Michael's family moved and didn't tell anyone. I don't think I was supposed to know how upset the teachers were, but I'm good at eavesdropping.

Unfortunately, I'm not as good at directions. Lily and I wander down one street after another, working our way farther and farther uphill through the neighborhood. It's starting to get dark, and I'm worried that an adult will see us and start asking questions. Lily has gotten tired and wants to go home, which is the last thing I want her telling some stranger.

I'm about to give up and find a nice bush to sleep under when I see a sign saying *Redwood Lane.* This seems familiar. We're near the top of the hill, and the land is more heavily wooded. The houses are farther apart, and there are fewer streetlights. I remember the road we went down on Halloween looking like that, so I take the chance that this is the one and follow it around the hill. It's even darker on the east side of the hill with the light of the sunset blocked by the towering trees. I pull my flashlight out of my bag, and soon it illuminates the metal gate. I know where we are.

We wiggle through the gate and go down the overgrown driveway until we come to the house in a clearing. Here, I find another unpleasant surprise. The wide porch which I had planned for us to sleep in is covered in blackberry vines. We'll have to find a way inside or sleep out in the open.

"Who lives here?" Lily asks.

"Meow!" The noise makes me jump, but I quickly identify the source. There is a long- haired tabby cat standing on the fence near the house.

"The cat lives here. We're going to live here now, too," I say to Lily.

"I'm going to call the cat Kitty," Lily says with enthusiasm.

Then I say to the cat, "Hey Kitty, do you know how to get in the house?"

The cat nods and hops down off the fence. Lily and I squeeze through the rails and follow it through the tall grass to the back of the house. The back door has a cat door that Lily is small enough to squeeze through. She unlocks the door and lets me in.

It's dark inside, and I reach for the light switch without thinking.

I'm surprised when the lights come on. For a moment I worry that the house isn't abandoned after all, but looking around at the amount of dust and cobwebs, I realize that no one has been in here for a long time. Just inside the door is a washer, a dryer, and a sink. I try the sink faucet and water comes out. Even though the house is empty, the power and water are still on. I have no idea why, but it makes our situation a lot better.

Lily and the cat go ahead while I'm playing with the sink. Then Lily comes running back. "Iris, come see!"

She pulls me by the hand into a bedroom near the front door. "A princess bed!" she exclaims, pointing. "Can I have this room?"

I look in the room and see a canopy bed, a wall covered in book-shelves, and a comfy looking chair. There's a closet door in one corner. "Sure," I say, "This can be your room."

Lily immediately starts unpacking her bags. I leave her to it and continue exploring. There's a bathroom across the hall from the bedroom, and past that a kitchen, with a door onto a covered porch. The other door out of the kitchen leads to a dining room, then a living room area that leads back to the door we came in. I can hear Lily in the bedroom chattering away to the cat, so I climb the stairs to the second floor. One side is walled off into a room. Over the dining room and kitchen area, there's a loft with a railing where I can look down into the living room. Guessing that the other room upstairs is another bedroom, I try the handle.

I switch on the light and nearly scream. There's a pair of eyes right next to my face, halfway up the wall. A second later I realize that I'm looking at a mirror. The eyes belong to a doll sitting on the bed on the opposite side of the room. She's one of those really detailed dolls with a porcelain face and hands but a cloth body. She has real hair, but whatever color it was originally, it has faded to a grayish brown. Her dress might have once been purple but looks almost white from the sun. Everything in this room is sun-bleached. Large windows line the far wall. The curtains are open and the sky outside is black.

This room feels colder than the rest of the house, and there's a smell I don't recognize. The doll stares at me like I've interrupted something private. "I'm sorry," I whisper. I turn off the light, push the button on the inside of the knob to lock it, and pull the door closed.

"Lily, can I sleep with you?" I ask when I get back to her room.

"Sure!"

We brush our teeth in the bathroom across the hall and climb into the dusty-smelling sheets with the cat purring at our feet.

Lily and I both wake up with stuffy noses, probably from the sheets. The cat is gone, probably out exploring for the day. I toast us some of the Pop-Tarts I brought for breakfast, and then start cleaning the house while Lily plays outside. I find some laundry soap and wash the sheets, then knock down the cobwebs everywhere and sweep.

I make macaroni and cheese for lunch. Lily complains that she has no ketchup but eats it anyway. After lunch she shows me the "cat-shaped rock" that she had found in the garden earlier. It isn't a rock—it's actually a ceramic cat with the word *Muffin* and two dates on it. I explain to her that this was a gravestone for a kitty.

Next, I explore the garage. There's a nice car in it and even a ceramics studio. There's a kiln and shelves of dry clay. Whoever lived here had obviously made the cat gravestone. I find some half-finished hands and faces and suspect that they made the doll upstairs also.

In the daylight the place seems much less creepy, so I go back upstairs to have another look at the doll. It isn't until I try the door that I remember locking it. I don't know how to pick locks, so I feel some regret that being scared the night before cost me my own room. The smell was probably from a dead mouse or something. I'm sitting on the stairs feeling sorry for myself when I hear the cat meowing in the laundry room. She has half a dozen ketchup packets in her mouth and looks very proud of herself.

"Are you the lucky cat of ketchup packets?" I ask her, examining them. None are damaged. I rinse them off, and Lily has ketchup on her leftover mac and cheese for dinner. I end the day with a hot bath, feeling very grown up and accomplished. I've found a home and made it nice to live in. My sister and I are safe. When I get out of the bath, I find Lily has fallen asleep in the chair.

"Wake up, it's time to go to bed," I tell her. She gets up and sleepily brushes her teeth, and then we climb into the princess bed.

I look down at the cat, who is sitting at the foot of our bed. "Wake me up by seven, okay?" I ask her. "I don't want to be late for school."

The cat nods. I hope she understands.

I wake up to the cat meowing and poking her nose in my ear. My watch says it's six-thirty, which is earlier than I'm used to getting up, but close enough. Lily is still sound asleep. The cat trots ahead of me into the kitchen and meows at her food bowl. There's still a lot of food in it, but the middle is empty. I shake the bowl so kibbles from the sides go back in the middle. This seems to be what she wants, because she starts purring loudly as she crunches at the kibbles.

I heat up a Pop Tart for Lily's breakfast and give her a bottle of water and a bag of crackers to snack on. I tell her to play outside but not leave the yard. She's happy about that—she loves being outside— and our old house didn't really have a yard. I instruct the cat to keep an eye on her and then leave for school.

The walk downhill is longer than I expect, and I'm a few minutes late for school. I explain to Mrs. Forrester that I missed the bus, which she accepts, but my real regret is missing school breakfast. The hot lunch today is baked potatoes, and I'm starving. I know I have to find food to bring home for Lily, too. We only have a few boxes of mac and cheese left and not much money. A few of my classmates have gotten boxes of milk and then changed their minds. I stick those in my lunch bag. They also give me lots of bags of baby carrots and a pack of seaweed strips. The real score comes once we're dismissed.

"Anyone want some butter?" Gary the lunch guy calls, holding up a nearly full box of the individually wrapped butter slices from the potatoes. Most people ignore him, a few laugh. I start to move against the tide of people leaving the lunchroom.

"I do," I say.

He laughs and plunges a hand into the box. "How much?"

"Can I have all of it?" I'm thinking of all the things I can cook if I have butter.

"Sure, why not?" He hands me the box. It's a little smaller than a shoe box, about three quarters full. "Don't eat that all at once now."

"I won't." I tuck it in my backpack before any of the other kids notice.

The walk up the hill after school is hard. I'm tired and worried about Lily. I know leaving a five-year-old home alone all day with just a cat to watch them is a bad idea, but I don't have a choice. There are only two more months of school for me, and then I'll be home all summer. In the fall, Lily will go to kindergarten, so leaving her alone won't be a problem for much longer.

When I get home, Lily is sunburned and grumpy. The cat is still there with her, which I'm glad to see. I cook canned tuna, carrots, and rice in the rice cooker I found while cleaning the day before. Lily eats a lot of carrots and rice with butter on them but refuses to eat the tuna. She gives her portion to the cat.

I fall asleep wondering what I'm going to do about Lily the next day. I don't want to leave her outside to get sunburned again. The next morning, I wake to the sound of the gutters dripping. A thick fog outside has soaked everything. I tell Lily to stay inside today, which she doesn't complain about. I make her promise not to go into the garage or upstairs, and not to open any bottles she finds or play with sharp things. I instruct the cat to keep an eye on her, too, but I'm not sure how much good that'll do.

After breakfast, Lily goes back to bed. The cat follows me to the door and almost hits me with an umbrella that she knocks off a shelf in the entryway. I leave it lying on the floor. I don't want to miss breakfast again, and I figure I can pick it up when I get home. By lunchtime, I'm wishing I had brought the umbrella with me. Instead of burning off like the fog normally does, this has turned into a steady drizzle.

I get milk again from the lunchroom, but nothing else. Lunch is turkey and vegetable soup, so there aren't separate packages of vegetables for people to give away. The walk home is miserable—my shoes were soaked on the way to school and never got dry. Now they squish with every step up the hill, which seems steeper than it was before. I worry about Lily the whole way home. As soon as I get there, I drop my coat and shoes in the laundry room and hurry into the living room.

Lily is sitting on the couch with the creepy doll on one side and the cat on the other. The doll has my copy of *White Fang* in her lap. Lily looks up as I come in. "Hi! Hester is reading to me about the wolves."

"How did you get her? That door was locked."

The cat sighs, looks over at the doll, and says in perfect English, "Hester, we should tell her."

The doll, Hester, nods, which is the least surprising thing so far. "Please don't be scared," she says in an old lady voice. "My name is Hester Goldsmith. This is my house, and you are welcome to stay here as long as you like."

"They're ghosts!" Lily says helpfully. "She's not really a cat, and Hester haunts the doll."

I glance back at the cat, but in her place is a tall, translucent, Hispanic woman.

"I'm Valencia Rubio," she says. "Hester's wife."

"Okay…" I'm already leaning against the wall because I'm tired, but also to be as far from the ghosts as I can. I never believed in ghosts until now.

"We won't hurt you," Valencia tells me. "We're not those kinds of ghosts."

"Why were you a cat?" I ask.

"Taking physical form is not easy," Valencia explains. "I find it easier to be something small, like a cat, if I have to be solid for a long time. I can be solid in this form—"she gestures to herself—"but not for very long."

"I never got the hang of manifesting," Hester says, "I just possess things."

I know it is probably a rude question, but I can't help asking. "How did you die?"

Valencia scowls. "Some guy was having a very bad day and decided the only thing for it was to shoot six random people at the gas station, two police officers, and himself. My final thought was that I wanted to be home with my wife, so that's where I ended up."

"I'd been studying ghosts." Hester adds sadly. "I'm much older than Valencia, and I expected to die before her. We weren't able to get married back then, so I was trying to figure out how to provide for her after I was gone. I decided that I should become a ghost, and we could hide my death. When she came home dead, we didn't really change that plan. I passed away from age and illness about ten years ago. I'm glad you stayed out of the master bedroom and bathroom. I'm sure all that's left by now is my skeleton, but you would probably find it disturbing."

I decide sharing the other room with Lily is just fine with me. "How are the lights still on?" I ask. "Who pays for that?"

"My social security was set to direct deposit, and the bills were already on auto pay. I'm capable of calling the bank if they have any issues. I just—" she pauses with a bit of a chuckle—"can't appear in person."

"And what brings you here?" Valencia asks. "Why'd you two run away from home?"

I'm not sure what to say, so I tell them the truth. They listen and don't ask questions. When I'm done talking, I feel strangely empty. I hadn't realized how messed up my family is until I told someone else. Lily looks uncomfortable, and I'm not sure how much she understands.

Valencia looks over at Hester. "Well, you always wanted kids."

Hester looks thoughtful. "It's going to be hard, since we *are* dead."

"I wasn't much older than Iris when I ended up on the street," Valencia replies. "And I didn't have a house with electricity and running water to use as a home base. With our help, these kids can do it."

Hester nods. "There are resources available from the school, too. We'll need to change Iris' contact information... Do you already get free lunch?"

"Yes," I hear myself say, although it's a lot to process. Ghosts are real, and I am getting adopted by some. "Wait, what if my mom comes looking for me?"

Hester gives Valencia a significant look. "You should tell her."

Valencia looks at me. "The first night you were here, I wanted to know where you came from, so I found your mom and, well, read her dreams. She's afraid to come looking for you. She thinks you just ran away and will come home, but if you don't, she's afraid of what she'll find out, and afraid she'll be blamed for anything that happened to you."

"It's not that she doesn't love you. It's just that her fear keeps her from looking," Hester says hastily. I recognize the lies adults tell children to try and keep them from feeling sad. I don't feel sad though. I've known for a long time that I wasn't the most important thing in Mom's world. I am a bit worried that if I stay at school, she might find me there.

"Can you keep her from looking for me without hurting her?" I ask the ghosts.

"We can."

And now, I find myself standing in the school office at seven on Wednesday morning, holding an umbrella while Valencia talks to Mrs. Knight the secretary.

"Iris' mother is my half-sister. She asked me to look after the girls for a while, as she has some personal stuff going on. I wanted to give you my information so the school can contact me with anything Iris needs," she explains. She's doing pretty good about being solid, but she's a little see-through from the knees down. I'm glad no one else is in the office this early, and Mrs. Knight can't see around the desk.

"Drinking again..." I mutter. Valencia shushes me, but Mrs. Knight gives me a sympathetic look. It's something I heard my fourth-grade teacher say to her a few years ago when I didn't return any field trip forms that year. He hadn't been wrong about why.

When Valencia gives her the address, Mrs. Knight looks surprised, "Oh, 1989 Redwood Lane. That used to be Mrs. Goldsmith's house."

"It still is," Valencia says, "I'm her caretaker. She's ninety-three."

"Well!" exclaims Mrs. Knight. "ask her if she remembers Alice Shaw. I spent a lot of time in the library when I was a student here."

"I will," Valencia tells her. "She speaks fondly of being the librarian."

"Iris, why don't you go get breakfast?" Mrs. Knight suggests.

"See you when you get home," Valencia tells me, patting me on the head.

"Yeah, okay," I say, and then, because it feels right, I add, "Love you."

I duck out the door but don't go right to breakfast. I wait a moment to hear what the grown-ups are talking about once I'm out of the room.

"No offense to your sister, but I'm glad those kids have a responsible adult in their lives for a change," Mrs. Knight says. "It was good of you to take them in."

"Of course," Valencia replies. "They're family."

For the first time in a long time, that word feels like it means something.

TOGETHER AGAIN

DURENA BURNS

$\mathcal{A}$ nita didn't think she could get pregnant. She had tried four times with a previous boyfriend without any luck. It became such a scandal—for a young, unmarried woman to feel pressure about wanting to have a baby. The scandal later died down, thanks partly to the efforts of her family. Once she *was* married (at her family's urging), Anita had tried three times with her husband Hank Cole and had lost the first baby. The third try became the magic number as she was blessed with not one, but two baby boys. Her twins were born on January 2, 1924 in Helena, Arkansas.

The boys' weight came to a healthy seven pounds, with seven and nine ounces between them. The birth was exhausting for Anita, but it was worth so much. As soon as the nurses placed the twins on each side of her arms, she was entranced.

Anita found that she enjoyed parading her babies around and showing off their little faces. Their caramel skin gleamed so majestically; it was like looking at melted bronze.

Anita named her identical twins Eli and Josiah, names derived from Hebrew with the meanings of "elevated" and "healed by God" respectively. The boys were her miracle. Not just because of their birth, but also because months before they were born, her husband Hank had disappeared.

On the last day she had seen him, Hank had mentioned that two white men had confronted him with intent to harm. For what reason, Anita never found out for sure. And these same men had been seen wandering around in the backwoods of their town. A rumor had even circulated that the men had been seen carrying a full, human-sized sack.

White law enforcement did little in terms of an investigation. It became apparent to Anita that the circumstances of his disappearance were being treated as inconsequential. Anita even suspected that the officers knew exactly what had happened to her husband, but they were turning a blind eye from any leads or details presented to them.

Anita believed someone had murdered her husband.

The pain of losing him was almost too much to bear, and she would often visualize conversations she would've had with him.

"Look at our boys," she imagined her husband saying after the birth of their sons. She could even envision the smile on his face as they held the boys together and Hank would appear like any other delighted papa. *"Look at what we did, Anita."*

Anita, even with the love she had for her twins, sometimes felt inadequate because she had fewer children than her other family members. Her extended family was huge. Anita herself had six siblings, two sisters, and four brothers. There were plenty of mothers, fathers, aunts, uncles, brothers, sisters, and cousins.

Anita's mother, Katherine, felt compelled to explain to her often, "Anita, as your wise Momma, I'm here to tell you that you and those boys are *our* miracle."

Anita bore a likeness to her mother as far as skin tone and weight. She was described by those who knew her as a lovely woman with windblown, thick hair often styled with pin curls. Her complexion was a nice dark brown and her facial proportions were similar to that of a toy doll.

Though her sons were identical in looks, the twins were opposites in personality. Eli was timid, quiet, and pensive whereas Josiah was adventurous, playful, and curious. Both of them had expressive almond eyes that tugged at Anita's heartstrings each time she looked at them. Their eyes reminded her of their father's eyes. She would worry any time she saw her sons leave the house, thinking that the boys would disappear just like Hank had. Anita knew that she couldn't keep her twins in the house all day long, so she always warned them about coming home by sundown. She vowed to herself that she would do whatever it took to protect them.

Because of the Flood of 1927 and the Great Depression, the family lived in seven separate houses around the same area. Anita and the boys lived with her mother, father, one of her aunts, and her two youngest brothers. Each house was in a state of disrepair inside, but the outer paint of the structures was well-maintained. The family made sure that the exteriors of their homes were adorned in a respectable and clean manner, representing themselves as pillars of both the black and white communities.

They wanted to show their respectability to the Edwards in particular. The Edwards were an influential family, considered one of the leaders of white society in Helena. Their household had fallen on hard times since 1929, but they had enough authority and support to have people on their side, people willing to fight on their behalf.

The Summer of 1935 had hot temperatures and humidity in the town. The boys were now eleven years old, and they were tall for their age. They appeared older too, and it was always troubling for Anita that the other kids around the neighborhood would pick on them because of their closeness. The teasing made Eli and Josiah that much more determined to stick up for one another.

On a Sunday morning in July, Anita watched the twins in amusement as they scampered around in the kitchen, singing gospel songs. The family had just settled down after having walked miles home from church, barefoot. The building that housed the services for the black patrons was further away from Helena, while the main services were closer to the town square. Everyone in the house was tired except for the twins with their boundless amounts of energy.

When Josiah made a particular silly sound with his mouth, Katherine said, "Go on and take that foolishness outside."

Anita laughed, knowing her mother was just as amused as she was when she saw the smirk on Katherine's face. "Be careful," Anita hollered to Eli and Josiah as they rushed toward

the front door. "And don't be later than sundown."

She heard a quick, "'Kay, Momma, we will, bye-bye!" before hearing the sudden slam of the door.

* * *

ANITA PEERED out of the living room window for what must have been the tenth time, a concerned frown on her face. Katherine sat beside her on the couch, holding her hand and using her thumb to rub her daughter's knuckles.

The sun was just about to set, and even though it wasn't the *exact* time she expected her boys home, their absence was still worrying. That worry began to grow like a storm brewing in her gut.

"Want me to go out and look for 'em?" Anita's brother Joseph asked, walking into the living room. Joseph was the male version of Anita in appearance, except for the fact that he was tall at six foot two, and his sister was a shorter five foot four.

Their youngest brother, Douglas, appeared right behind him. Douglas had a more quizzical nature compared to his siblings. He looked similar to all his brothers and sisters, with the exception of Douglas being light-skinned. He was often mistaken for a person of mixed race.

Just as Anita was going to answer, there was an urgent knock on the front door. Anita frowned again, wondering if it was her boys, but quickly knowing in her heart that they would have just let themselves inside if that had been the case.

Her stomach felt like it plummeted once she opened the door and found one of the elderly black neighbors standing on the porch. The neighbor, known as Sweetie Dee, lived up to her nickname, as she was one of the nicest people Anita knew.

"Anita," their neighbor began. "Are your boys with you?"

"No, we were just about to look for them." Anita motioned to her brothers, who came to stand beside her.

Sweetie Dee shook her head. "That Mr. Edwards. He has his fellas lookin' around for them. He says that Eli and Josiah attacked his daughter and broke her arm." The older woman looked straight at Anita with grief-stricken eyes. "They gon' kill those boys, Anita."

The sinking feeling in her stomach grew in intensity. All the sounds around her seemed to only focus on the words Sweetie Dee had said, the words repeating in her head forcefully.

They gon' kill those boys... They gon' kill those boys... They gon' kill those boys...

With tears gathering in her eyes but with a fierce determination, Anita called out to her brothers and any other family members who heard her. She sprinted out of the house while her brothers ran past her and stayed ahead. She heard a commotion behind her, yet her steps became bigger in stride. She assumed that some other family members were following her.

Anita and her family looked in several places where they thought the boys might be. The familiar landscape and scenery of certain properties made the search more efficient, but hours passed with still no sign of the twins. The growing darkness caused the search to become more unsettling for them.

...Running on a dirt path away from their house, Eli and Josiah laughed in enjoyment, their breaths deep from exertion. They had stopped singing hours ago and were now attempting to outrun each other, wanting to see which one would be the winner in their little competition.

"I beat you, Eli!" Josiah declared, getting ahead of his brother by jumping a few times.

"Uh uh, you cheated," Eli countered. He grumbled in annoyance once he saw that his twin wasn't even listening to him, already creating a victory dance.

The boys, still arguing about who was the real winner of the race, came across a sidewalk. Ahead of them were two teenage boys and one teenage girl. All three of the children had reddish hair and were playing with marbles. Eli and Josiah quieted their voices down, lowering their heads as they got closer to the other children.

Although white and black people lived around one another in Helena during this time, black people were expected to step off the sidewalk if they came across white people standing or walking there.

Josiah was the first to reach the others, preparing to step off the sidewalk until one of the boys moved the marbles in Josiah's way, making him stop in his tracks. Eli was just a few steps behind him. The teenager to the left of the sidewalk, the one blocking the two, snickered and kept playing with the marbles. Josiah tried to walk in the other direction, still off the sidewalk, but it happened again with the girl.

Eli strode right to his brother, grabbing his hand. "Let's just turn back around," he whispered, trying to be discreet.

"Ain't you the Coles?" the teenager on the right of the sidewalk asked out loud, looking at them with piercing eyes.

"Yes, sir," Eli said politely. The teenagers couldn't have been more than two or three years older than the twins.

"You like marbles?" the same teenager asked.

"Yes, sir," the twins said in unison.

The teenager on the right stared at them longer than necessary before moving some of the marbles out of the way. "You can walk here, if you want."

Eli was skeptical, but Josiah moved forward with cautious steps. The girl again moved the marbles in their path. Josiah kept his head down, but a glare appeared on his face. Moving just a bit closer, Josiah's foot slightly hit a few of the marbles, the black spheres heading straight towards the girl...

"Anita?"

A comforting hand landed on Anita's shoulder as she turned from looking out toward the sky. She, Joseph, and their mother now stood near a stump out in the open. Katherine looked at her daughter in alarm, as Anita appeared drained and was wobbling on her feet. Joseph, still with his hand on her shoulder, also peered at his sister.

It was nearing three in the morning. The sky above had blue- and purple-looking streaks of clouds that hid the moon. The family had been searching for Josiah and Eli all night but to no avail. It was a nightmare for the whole family as they began to assume the worst. It didn't help that they had to also evade some of Mr. Edwards' posse, with one of the men trying to intimidate Anita's uncle and break into his house.

"Where my boys, Joe?" whispered Anita. The rich tones of Anita's skin appeared chalky under the now emerging moonlight.

Joseph sighed. "You're tired," he said. "Let's start again when the sun comes up."

"I'm not leaving without my babies."

"You're of no use in this state." Joseph guided his sister back toward their house. "You ain't of any help to those boys if you pass out. You need rest. We'll look for them again."

Anita struggled against his hold as much as she could. "I ain't leaving."

"Then *I'll* keep looking, but you need to go home now."

Anita stared at Joseph pleadingly. "We have to find them."

"And we will," he said in a final tone. "But I would feel much better if I took you home."

"Momma?" At last, she turned to Katherine, maybe as a way to contradict her brother.

"He's right, baby," her mother said, on the verge of tears and exhausted herself. At just fifty-five years old, Katherine was still as strong as she'd been twenty years prior, and their family was known to keep pushing on through their struggles. Still, the search for the twins was taking its toll. "And you're still *my* daughter, and I'm worried about you."

As she was led away, Anita saw white spots floating in her vision. She made a hand motion so that her brother would stop walking with her. Anita bent down to catch her breath. Katherine and Joseph stared again at Anita in unease. It was at that moment that another family member, a cousin of theirs, ran to them out of breath.

"We found them," their cousin revealed, panting as she halted in front of them. "They're near the river."

The Mississippi River flowed along the Eastern part of Arkansas, close to where the family resided. Near the outskirts of the river, a single outhouse was situated across from the fluid descent. The outhouse was dilapidated, the plywood rotting on its edges. The twins were huddled together behind the small structure, squatting down so that they remained undetected from the posse.

Still hobbling with an exhausted body, Anita fell to her knees, hugging her children fiercely and protectively. She cried hard as she held them.

Four limbs wrapped around the shaking body of the relieved mother. Renewed tears streamed down the faces of the boys as they kept their arms around Anita. A few other family members approached the trio and rallied around them like a protective shield. Each member was in different stages of relief, with many eyes filled with their own tears.

After several minutes of embracing her boys, Anita leaned back to look at them with a more critical stance. The twins had worn blue overalls with stained white tank tops and had no shoes on their feet. The tight kinks in their hair had a bit of dirt on them. Their faces were clear of any blemishes, save for the wetness on their cheeks. As Anita peered down, she let out a sob. Eli and Josiah's pants were tattered in many parts, blood seeping past the torn material.

"Sorry, Momma," Josiah said softly.

"We didn't want to cause no trouble," added Eli.

"Oh, my babies," Anita said. Her eyes had barely left the sight of their beaten legs. "Who hurt you?"

...The teenage girl tripped on the black marbles that rolled towards her as she took an intimidating step forward. She screamed in absolute pain as her arm landed awkwardly and struck the sidewalk. The twins winced as they heard the crack of her bone making contact with the sidewalk.

Apologies poured out of Eli's mouth as Josiah stared in horror. One of the older boys ran to help the girl, yelling at the twins about retaliation for harming their sister. The other teen began picking up marbles to launch at them. The teenage boys' screams must have reached the surrounding area as people emerged from the houses nearby. Several white folks who came outside took in the situation, shouting at the twins with heated threats and racial slurs. A couple of the women from the group urgently made their way to the girl, whose screams had started to lessen into whimpers.

Dodging the marbles thrown at them, Josiah was the one to grab his twin's hand this time, and the two tried to get away. They hadn't gotten very far before they were cornered by the adults.

The twins howled in pain and fear as three men brutally beat their legs with large sticks. The biggest of the men had the same reddish hair as the teens. The red-haired man's rage was evident; he made snarling sounds and his face began to match the color of his hair.

The same man shouted at them, his words chilling the boys to their core. "Y'all are gonna die, just like that Daddy of yours!"

Josiah and Eli kept attempting to run while being struck hard. Eventually, the boys were able to escape, the hollers of the adults' continuing slurs and threats still ringing in their ears...

"Sorry," Josiah reiterated, tears still falling down his face. "We were 'fraid to go home. We thought they would look for us there."

Anita kissed both of their foreheads. "I'm just so glad to find you both safe," she said, feeling dizzy. She released her sons, wanting to lessen the lightheadedness. Joseph stepped forward and squatted down to embrace her from behind. "We can't stay here," she whispered, her breaths low and rapid.

Joseph was silent for a moment, peering back at the others in contemplation. Douglas also stepped forward from the group and bent down next to his huddled family.

The two brothers stared at one another before Douglas asked, "What're we gonna do?"

"First, I'm gonna get Anita and the boys cleaned up and somethin' to eat," Joe said. He helped Anita and the twins to their feet. The family had gotten closer to the four, with various arms and hands reaching out to touch Eli and Josiah. "You stay with Momma and Pop, you hear me?" he instructed Douglas, who nodded.

Stealthily, the group separated in different directions. Joseph led his sister and nephews through a rarely traveled route that zigzagged through the yards. Before leaving, Douglas watched as Joseph supported their sister's body on his side. The last image he had of the four were the twins taking a hold of their mother's and uncle's hands.

* * *

Within the following days, there were no signs of Anita, Joseph, or the twins.

Much like Hank, the four had vanished without any clues to their whereabouts.

Douglas questioned his parents multiple times about where they possibly could be, but his Momma and Pop had no idea what could've become of them. He, along with other family members and friends, had conducted other searches. Mr. Edwards and his men had still been on the prowl and had antagonized several of Anita's family and neighbors until even he gave up looking for the twins.

By November, the sunny presence of the town had morphed into an overcast gloominess and a more cooling season. Douglas, in the meantime, had noticed that some other members of his family were disappearing too. His parents had remained, but the rest of his siblings had also begun to disappear, one by one. Douglas felt both scared and discouraged, wondering if the disappearances were planned or if something bad *had* happened. He felt useless because he was the last of his siblings to be left in Helena. Joseph's words about staying with their folks were one of the things that kept Douglas from leaving town. He felt that his parents were losing hope because of the disappearances in their family, and he figured he should remain at home at least for their sake.

It was a full year before Douglas found out what happened to his family.

Entering his parents' house in July of 1936, Douglas wiped the sweat off his forehead. He then walked into the kitchen, initially unaware of his mother sitting at the table in concentration.

Katherine, who had been reading a postcard, watched her youngest son make his way to the sink. She smiled in fondness as she watched him wash and dry his hands. Douglas made a startled noise after he spun around, facing the older woman.

"I didn't see you there," Douglas said with a sheepish look. "How was your day, Momma?"

"It just got a whole lot better," she said, standing up to hand over the postcard to her son.

Douglas gently took the postcard. His own smile bloomed as he read the contents. He looked back at his mother, and she answered his unspoken question with a single nod.

Dear Pop, Momma, and Douglas,

Sorry for the late reply. We wanted to keep you safe, and this was the only way we knew how. A reverend in Mississippi let us and our other family stay with him. Good friends of mine helped us all with jobs. We're in California now and we're happy. The twins like their new school. Everyone says hi. We miss you. We'll all be together again as a family. Just be patient. We'll send for you soon.

All our love,

Joseph, Anita, Josiah, and Eli.

LETTERS TO THE ODDITY

R.H. WEBSTER

ou were named for your father.

You were already three years old when you met him for the first time, on a pale concrete airfield under the unforgiving New Mexico sun. You recognized him from the tiny, worn picture in your mother's wallet, but he looked older and more tired when he stepped off the military troop transport.

You were afraid to let go of your mother's hand to greet him, but his blue eyes were so kind and his smile so genuine that you felt yourself smiling back, even as your long white-blonde curls blew across your face. After a moment, you reached for him and he swept you up into a tight hug, gently brushing your hair out of your eyes and kissing your temple. The silver wings pinned to his chest poked your cheek as he held you.

He had been a pilot for the three years that you were growing. He had been far away, fighting and barely surviving battles against an enemy that was technologically superior to the human race. Crossing the stars to the battlefield had taken too much time, and the enemy had seen the ships coming. Without the element of surprise, they never stood a chance. After unimaginable losses, humanity had withdrawn back to their own tiny blue and green planet.

The generals had called the defeat the Last Wars, but your father said that humanity would never be done fighting and so neither would he.

He immediately returned to work as a researcher and a test pilot. He explained to you that a new technology would open a hole in space, allowing the pilots and their machines to get to the fight in the blink of an eye.

That's when the problems started.

You see, when space is disturbed, time fights back.

* * *

REMEMBER THIS PICTURE: Matthew Collins, the man who was your father, standing on a pale concrete runway in what was left of the New Mexico high deserts. These stark blue skies had for centuries been the proving grounds of the first rockets, the raceways where humanity pushed the edge of the envelope. It was only fitting that now your father would fight yet another battle with the physical laws of the universe in the same place his forebears sweated and sacrificed.

Your father stood cocooned in a pressure suit, bright silver in the never-ending sun. It had taken three years of work and testing to get to this point, the moment of sending a single pilot through a portal.

You watched as he climbed into the prototype, clasping tightly to your mom's hand. You had just turned six years old. You and your mom had been invited by the project leader to observe the first physical test. Your eyes were so wide they almost hurt in the cool darkness of the observation booth, so different from the heat outside. As your vision adjusted to the darkness, you took in the dials and screens and technical readouts around you, eager to learn everything you could about your father's work.

The power required to maintain the portal was godawful, more power than had ever been produced on the planet, contained in a single reactor that the engineers suspected would melt down and self-destruct. The test went forward anyway; the engineers explained to your mom that sometimes things blew up, and that was part of the test process as well.

They thought you didn't understand that part of the conversation, but you did. Just like you saw the fear in your mother's eyes that she tried so hard to keep hidden from you.

You, your mother, and the observing generals and government officials were kept far from the reactors and prototypes, just in case the self-destruction was more explosive than expected.

A second reactor sat in Matthew's prototype to power the return trip. The math was in the computer, the most powerful computer that could be constructed. All he had to do was survive the initial jump, then reverse the math to get home.

The test and the task were simple. It was going to be okay. Your father had told you that everything was going to be okay. Every precaution had been taken.

* * *

MATTHEW COLLINS WAS THE QUIET, thinking type, with calm eyes that reminded you of a deep lake you'd seen in a picture book. But something in his eyes told you that like a deep lake, much lay below the surface, unspoken.

His commander said that he was the best test pilot anyone had ever seen. He studied endlessly, committing to a prodigious memory the schematic and function of every valve and line in the training prototypes. And when he climbed into the cockpit, he flew by instinct, managing maneuvers no one had ever even thought to try.

But, most importantly to you, he was a gentle and attentive dad. You learned your addition and subtraction sitting on his lap at the kitchen table. The smell of aircraft oil mixed with dust, sweat, and stale coffee consumed from disposable cups would forever be associated with first grade mathematics. Tired and still wearing his flame-resistant flight suit, he took time to make sure the numbers that swam before you on the paper made sense. He told you stories before bed, and on the rare day that he had off from work, he took you and your mother to the mountains to spend time away from the heat of the desert.

* * *

Opening the portal didn't look like something from a movie. There was no spinning ring, there was no bright light. Matthew's prototype sat on the airfield. The reactor powering the prototype glowed white-hot (but didn't explode).

You thought you saw a flicker.

The hatch of the prototype opened.

Around you in the observation booth, the generals and admirals in their stiff blue uniforms groaned. The test had failed. The prototype went nowhere. Clearly, the math had been wrong.

But the scientists standing next to them scribbled furiously in their notes, conferring in words too fast and too technical for anyone else to catch.

When the prototype opened, your father practically fell from the cockpit, pale as the white concrete and vomiting onto the scorching ground.

The displacement had been momentary at best, but it had happened. Matthew had leapt from a standstill on the airfield to the target location on the distant edge of the solar system and back again. The data recorders in the prototype showed that he had traveled across spacetime in a fraction of a second, returning almost simultaneously to the exact place he had left. The scientists all agreed that the data was consistent with the predictions.

Your father was physically unharmed, just really tired. After the required debrief, he went home and slept for fourteen hours, into the next day, practically without moving, even when you crawled onto the bed next to him to wake him up for dinner. Your mother suggested he should go to the doctor, but he refused. The test was stressful. Anyone would have slept for a day after that kind of ordeal.

Having reviewed all the data and the debriefing records, the generals and admirals called the experiment an unqualified success.

The public held Matthew Collins up as a hero.

The losses of the Last Wars would not be in vain. Humanity finally had a way to avenge their fallen parents, siblings, and children.

* * *

TIME IS A CURIOSITY. It moves fast and slow seemingly at will, running forever downhill into the future, leaving behind only images, feelings, sounds, smells that will forever haunt your dreams.

During your seventh summer, time seemed to stretch around you like the unending plains of New Mexico. The hot afternoons lasted interminable hours, punctuated only by the chirping of grasshoppers and crickets as you waited for your father to come home, sitting on the front porch of your brown stucco house, identical to the line of brown stucco houses lining the narrow dirt street on the civilian part of the test base.

The girl you were in those days faded away a little bit with each passing moment, eroded by the unending and unrelenting current of time.

You turned eight a week after school started. As a birthday gift, your mother let you keep the stray kitten you found in the commissary parking lot. No one could determine where the small beast had come from; wildlife in the area stayed sparse and small, almost invisible. Cats were not known to roam the base, and kittens didn't just flicker into existence at the whim of the universe.

The days shortened, contracting the world around you. You used a blanket to wait on the porch for your father; desert nights are often chilly. You and the kitten caught the bugs attracted to the porch lights and fed them to the family of many-lined skinks that hunted on the porch windows.

Mountains to the south and west gave the horizon a black jagged edge, framed against the pink and gold of the autumn sunset. Some nights, you saw lights on the mountains, the glitter of a distant city. Other nights, the mountains were completely black.

You asked your father about it, and he stared into the sunset, squinting. He told you that it must just be a mirage, a trick of the light and atmosphere making it look like a city might be near the mountains. The city in those mountains had been abandoned centuries ago, he said, and no one lived there anymore.

But you heard a moment of hesitation in his voice, a note of curiosity, that told you that he wasn't convinced of his own answer.

Sometimes, time seemed to eddy, to swirl about itself. Some days felt like they repeated themselves with only small changes. You practiced your multiplication over and over again, filling out grid after grid with the messy handwriting of a third grader, willing the facts to stick in your brain as your father sat on one side of you, reviewing technical specs. Your mother sat on the other side, drinking tea and knitting yet another scratchy scarf from recycled plastics that you would only wear until you were out of sight of the house and then stuff into your backpack for the remainder of the day.

Sometimes, during the long winter evenings, the cat slept in a basket by the stove.

Sometimes, the cat couldn't be found for days on end.

* * *

THE NEXT STEP was to move even larger, more complex machines through the portal. The researchers built another reactor, even more powerful this time, and attached to an even larger prototype. The military asked for another volunteer, and Matthew again stepped up to serve his people.

He would be gone longer this time, to see if he could fly from the entry point to another location and still return safely.

With every new test the scientists performed, there was always the possibility Matthew would not return. Mountains of paperwork accompanied this risk, to ensure the military and research team would not be held liable in the event of Matthew's disappearance or death.

You, of course, as his child, would have been well cared for by his life insurance policy. He made sure of that.

By the time you were eight and a half years old, you were already fascinated with the experiments your father participated in. You begged him to take you to the military base so you could see the new prototypes being built. You made cardboard and aluminum mock-ups that you brought with you to base on the days he picked you up from school. You cradled them carefully as you jogged alongside Matthew, struggling to keep up with his longer strides, your pale blonde pigtails swaying down your back.

You had an undefinable sense that something was strange when you followed him into the command headquarters to sign the last stack of paperwork before the second test. You sat straight and tall in the chair next to the desk, trying to patiently wait for this part of the day to end so you could see the completed portal prototype up close one final time.

The waiting was the worst part. The boredom of waiting for the papers made time seem to swirl in one spot, looping on itself and mixing past, present, and future in a haze of beige and gray carpeting that smelled of cheap, industrial cleaners and over-heated coffee in an unseen office coffee maker.

Matthew placed the pen to the paper and scratched his signature. When he made a small sound of confusion, you looked up from your cardboard model. Craning, you could see that his signature was not on the line, but lower and to the left of where it should have been.

He pinched the bridge of his nose, squeezing his eyes shut like he had a headache. A moment later, he shook himself and wrote his name again, this time in the right place.

Time felt linear again as he passed the paperwork across the desk. The woman who accepted the papers asked if he was okay, and he simply nodded. He offered her no explanation, and she didn't ask any follow-up questions. No one questioned the hero, Matthew Collins.

He took your hand and led you to the hangar.

That night, the cat fell asleep curled up in his basket, smaller and younger than the day before.

* * *

THE SECOND TEST went off without any noticeable hitches. Matthew was more prepared for the flight, and it didn't affect him as negatively. He stepped from the cockpit, confident and well. He smiled at the observation booth and gave a thumbs up. You waved back, though he probably couldn't see you through the darkly tinted windows.

No one mentioned that he came back with a scar on his left cheek. It was barely visible, just a thin white line, clearly healed for many years. No one else noticed the flash of surprise in his eyes as he saw you exiting the observation booth.

THAT NIGHT, you cried as he held you on his lap, telling you stories. Your tears were reflected in the swimming blue depths of his eyes, so familiar and yet somehow strange. He held you tightly, as if he had never hugged you before, pressing gentle kisses to your head as you sniffled. When you asked for the story about his old dog Pepper, your favorite of all his slightly tall tales, he said he didn't know the story.

Your young developing brain couldn't have comprehended what your gut sense knew was the truth: the man who had returned through the portal was not the father you had known.

In an attempt to understand why he came back different, you asked him what he saw when he went through the portal, and he smiled sadly down at you.

"It's like high noon on a summer day," he said, "but there are a thousand suns and they burn every cell in your body."

"Is that why you're crying? Because it hurts?" you asked him.

He smiled even as a tear slipped over his cheek. "Part of why," he said. When he smiled, the small white scar on his cheek disappeared, and for a minute he looked like the father you'd seen that morning.

* * *

MATTIE, my dear, our family is both blessed and cursed. They are blessed with the most incredible courage in the face of unyielding difficulty, but this blessing curses them to be on the front lines of history. This strength lives deep inside you, as it did for your father. It prepared you for what comes next. When you are the most scared, and most alone, you use that strength and use it to find your way forward. Never forget this, no matter what happens, no matter who you are.

* * *

AFTER THE LAST SUCCESSFUL TEST, it was time to open a portal big enough to move the fleet. Multiple pilots were placed in their fighters, each equipped with a reactor, each carefully briefed by Matthew Collins himself, each steely-eyed and ready to face whatever the universe could throw at them.

Invisible to the naked eye, the portal stretched wide and swallowed the fighters and the pilots within them. You, clasped tight in your mother's arms, waved goodbye to your father as he flickered from existence. You were going to turn nine years old in three days.

* * *

IMAGINE THIS: You throw a stone into a puddle, and there will be a splash. Water is displaced from the stone. There's a tear in the fabric of the surface as the water separates to allow the stone to pass through. As the water rushes back to fill the void, there's a blip.

Any child knows, even ones raised in deserts, that the bigger the stone, the bigger the splash, the bigger the ripples, the bigger the blip.

Now, throw a boulder into a small stream, and some of the water will be displaced completely in the splash. It will land in other parts of the river and will become a part of the water there, merging into a new surface, absorbed into a new fabric. Some of the splash may go upstream, may go earlier in the river's path. Some may go downstream, skipping a section of the river completely.

In the same way, disturbed spacetime snapped back to fill the void that had been opened to allow the pilots and their machines to pass through.

Containment failed on the portal field, and the splash of displaced time reached the onlookers who had come to say farewell to the pilots. In a split second, you saw the same thousand burning suns your father had mentioned in his stories to you. You felt the arms of your mother desperately tighten around you before she vanished, leaving you alone in a cold void. The last sound you remembered hearing was her desperate scream as you were ripped away by the tidal forces of time.

Because when space is disturbed, time fights back.

* * *

BY SOME MIRACLE, you survived to wake up in a cold, sterilized hospital room. The woman staring down at you was wearing glasses, something humanity hadn't needed for many decades before you were born. She was kindly, gentle as she spoke to you, asking where your family was and how you had ended up alone in the middle of a New Mexico desert. You were practically nine, so you didn't know how to answer perfectly, but you put on a brave face and told the nice nurse all you could. Her smile turned brittle as you told her about the Last War, the machine your father piloted to fight the enemy, and your mom who was probably out in the desert looking for you right now. She made several notes on an old brown clipboard and then left the room quickly.

There were pilots here in this hospital, too. It was easy to tell; pilots for generations had refused to give up the comfort of their flame-resistant flight suits and the metallic wings on their chests. You studied the faces, trying to find someone you knew from visits to the hangars. You didn't recognize any of them, but one looked a little bit like your father, with honey-colored hair and rich blue eyes. He had the same kind smile, but unlike your father, he sneaked you bits of hard candy when the nurses weren't looking.

They never found your mother or father. After the uncertain reaction from the nurse, you decided to never tell them about the burning suns you saw.

The nice pilot and his wife took you in and raised you in their home in nearby Albuquerque. Living in a city that was destroyed so long ago was weird at first, but by the time you started middle school, it felt like home. By high school, the brown stucco house on the military base, the cat by the stove, your mother's scratchy scarves and your cardboard models of your father's prototypes seemed more like a dream than reality.

By college, explanations of the event began to become clear.

* * *

JIM AND MARY, the kind pilot and his loving wife, are waiting downstairs. They've been there for every milestone, every lost tooth, every school event, to the point that I think of them as Dad and Mom. My father and mother are faded memories now, eroded by the ever-moving flow of time around me.

After nearly six years of graduate school research, I am finally beginning to understand what happened, what freak accident landed me here. My theories are still in the process of being proven, but it's obvious that spacetime is a fabric, a cohesive unit. Disturbing a patch of this fabric doesn't happen just in the single location of the occurrence but echoes across all of spacetime.

I can't help but wonder if the city I saw in the mountains as a child —the same city I would eventually grow up in—was a refracted image visible through a ripple in spacetime.

Around large bodies of water, engineers can build seawalls, locks, dams to control ripples and waves. I can only assume that the scientists working on my father's project tried to do the same thing, but spacetime proved more difficult to control.

The larger the disruption to the fabric of the universe, the larger the ripples. Containment fields only worked to a certain point. And when they failed as my father left for war, I was carried back through time in the ensuing wave.

How I survived, God only knows.

I see myself in the mirror, understanding my very existence to be an oddity in this time, coming of age three hundred years before I was ever born. There is no way to generate enough power to get back to my father and mother, to the time of my birth. The technology of this era is still so analog, the men circling the moon are using push buttons to change programs in their computers. There would be no way to create a reactor powerful enough to open another portal, even if I could recreate the math.

The only way to fix this would be not to go to the launch at all. I glance at the notebook on the small table in my bedroom, filled with a letter to myself—to the girl that I was so many years in the future. Perhaps, if the letter can make it to my parents, it can serve as a warning about the accident.

But as I'm here, dressed in my finest for my graduation ceremony this afternoon, I think it won't work. I never saw the notebook as a child, and I have to assume that it must get lost in the centuries to come.

I close the notebook and slide it into a drawer on my vanity, determination making me straighten with squared shoulders.

It was my father's courage and determination that landed me here. Being from the future doesn't mean I know what's going to happen next, but…

What I do know is that I was named for my father. And I hope I can make him proud.

PETA BABKAMA LURUBA

MIKE X WELCH

An earlier version of this story was featured in the independently
published collection ENANTIODROMIA

I will now recount the beginning of my journey to you. You might not believe me when I tell you that I was born millennia ago; but I assure you, just as I am sitting here in front of you in the year 2022, everything I am about to tell you is true.

My real parents were nothing to me. I don't have any recollection of them. I don't recall a life before being a slave girl in Aram's house. Aram was a brewer who lived in Mesopotamia, in the city of Lagash, over 4,000 years ago. We spoke a mixture of Sumerian and Akkadian, as both languages were used widely in the city at that time. For whatever reason, I was the only slave the family had.

Aram was like my father. I came to be in his service around the age of five. Salamu, his wife, was a mother to me in every way possible save one. She was kind to me, but she was foremost the mother to her sons. Her oldest was the cruel Ahu-Mash; five years older than me, he held dominion over the house once Salamu was gone and Aram was away, which was always. Her middle son, Ahu-Essuru, two years his brother's junior, was a dullard and lived up to his name. Essuru means "bird" in Sumerian; and he was as wise as a bird, which is to say not wise at all. Lastly, her youngest son was the kind-hearted Ahu-Bassu, who was just one year older than me.

Today, we would call Aram a master brewer. Back then, he was nothing less than the finest maker of beer in all of the Akkadian empire, Assyria…the world! He had amassed considerable wealth and renown, but he was a humble – and simple – man. He was devoted to Salamu, who was in turn devoted to her family. I was fortunate enough to have been part of that family. We were assets, yes, but extremely valuable ones that no wise merchant would ever misuse.

From an early age, I was tasked with helping to prepare the family meals. By the time I was ten years old, I could slaughter a lamb or goat without the animal feeling a thing, such was my tutelage and my skill. The sight of blood never bothered me. Foolish Ahu-Essuru would watch me sometimes. His simple gaze annoyed me. I never knew what he was seeing in his mind – a person, another animal, simply the blade and the blood – it was difficult to divine his thoughts.

Ahu-Mash, however, was an open book. He stared at me. He would fondle himself and leer at me when no one was watching. I would go days without bathing just to avoid his gaze. When I brought my concerns to his mother – our mother – Ahu-Mash would call me a liar. Salamu would tell me not to worry; it was normal male behavior, and he would grow out of it. Above all, he was the only member of the family intent on reminding me I was a slave. Ahu-Mash often told me that he recalled a time before I was in his house, that I was given to Aram as payment of a debt. Ahu-Mash would tell me that I was worth nothing, not even the money I represented. Plainly, he both hated and desired me.

My only refuge—aside from hiding in Salamu's fringed skirts— was Ahu-Bassu. Bassu and I played together, and he showed me kindness. Our favorite game was for Bassu to carry me around on his back, spinning me in circles until we both fell down dizzy. Bassu did his best to protect me. Many times, he would place himself between me and Mash, who of course always had Essuru trailing in his wake.

Everything changed during the dry season of my eighth year of life. Bassu carried me on his back, running at full speed in long straight lines. We ventured onto the moist riverbed of the Tigris. The river had been dammed far north of our city so that our recently deceased king could be buried under the riverbed. Salamu, a short distance away from us, called for Bassu and me to get out of the riverbed, as one never knew when the waters would return. Bassu turned with me still on his back, both of us laughing and laughing, and began running back to the banks. He slipped and we both tumbled into the mud – me doing a neat somersault and landing on my back. Bassu was on his chest, his face covered in mud. His white teeth shone when he looked at me and we resumed giggling.

A shrill scream from Salamu interrupted us.

I can remember the sound like it was yesterday: a low bass rumble that seemed to come from the sky, accompanied by screams from the women along the riverbank. Bassu and I were not the only children who had strayed into the wet mud.

The smile fled from Bassu's face as he looked upriver to see what the noise was. Salamu went by me in a blur of bright garments, shouting *"Go!"* Bassu was about two meters from her, still on his chest, propped up on his elbows, stunned by the wall of water coming his way. I rose from the slippery mud and covered the distance to the bank in a sprint, then turned to look back from the safety of dry land. Salamu had made it to Bassu and was hauling him up roughly with both hands. I looked to my right and saw the surging brown-white waters spiked with shattered wood nearly upon them. I looked back to Bassu in time to see Salamu, holding her son by his wrists, plant her feet and swing him desperately toward the bank.

The river swallowed Salamu while Bassu was still in the air.

I leaned over the riverbank and held out my hand for Bassu. I'd like to think that I would have saved him from drowning—her toss had been short by a mere foot or less—but before I could reach him, I was knocked roughly out of the way. Mash stood over me—one of his feet pressing my ankle down into the soft clay of the riverbank—and easily hauled Bassu out of the water. Soon, a panting Essuru arrived, stopping at the scene to double over and put his hands on his knees as if *he* had nearly drowned. Last came Aram. He shuffled forward, looking up and down the raging brown river with wide, searching eyes. He called for Salamu with increasingly hoarse cries.

No one ever recovered her body. The family tomb soon had a chamber with her name, but there was nothing inside.

* * *

IN MY THIRTEENTH YEAR, Bassu started to look at me differently. Mash ruled the house; Aram was either borrowing or paying back money, drinking his wares among rowdy "friends," or whoring. Sometimes, he was actually brewing—anything other than tending these rapidly maturing children. Aram was lost to me when Salamu was swept away as surely as if they'd been embracing in that riverbed. When the Tigris reclaimed that which it had only been briefly denied, I lost everything.

Mash almost certainly blamed me for the loss of his mother. My simple presence at the river had been enough to earn his resentment for a lifetime. He barely forgave Bassu, who carried the guilt of her passing like a yoke for the rest of his days. Bassu was still kind but distracted, and he was struggling with becoming a man. He almost never smiled after his mother was gone.

I knew the day that Bassu truly saw me for the first time as a young woman. He happened upon me as I was finishing my bath. as he was arriving for his. We had, of course, seen each other without our clothes on many times growing up. But he was maturing, as was I, and so we both stood there dumbly. A light smile raised the corners of his mouth for the first time in a long time. After a moment, other things were rising as well. I blushed and looked away, turned a bit to the side to hide my nascent breasts. Bassu seemed to take this as a

234

signal and walked toward me. I froze, but he extended his hands and gently guided me out of the bathwater. He boldly appraised me as I stepped toward him, and my modesty evaporated as I judged his form as well. He was smooth, hairless but for his pubic area and under his arms, lean but with a well-muscled torso. I had always loved his face— to have his smile return reminded me just how much I had loved and missed its presence. Our bodies pressed together in an embrace, his sex pressing stiffly into my stomach area, such was the difference in our height. He took my chin in his hand gently and guided my mouth to his. We were able to share one lingering kiss before the sound of Mash's shouting startled both of us; we flew apart like two magnets whose polarities had suddenly reversed.

"What are you two doing?" Mash demanded, stalking to the bath area. He knew very well what we were doing; he had almost certainly seen our embrace. I hastily gathered my clothes and held them in front of me, my modesty back in full force. I would sooner have displayed my nude form for the drunkards in Aram's tent than show it to Mash.

Mash dispensed harshness to his brother, demeaning words and gestures that bullies have used to shame their targets since before man was truly man. He positioned himself between Bassu and me, his back to my now shivering form. Mash harangued Bassu until, humiliated, he finally fled with whatever dignity he had left wrapped in the tunic fixed awkwardly around his waist. At last, Mash turned his gaze to me, and his mouth went from the straight line of anger to a crooked one of manipulation and lust.

"Do you want me to tell Father about this?" His words oozed threat, laced with a certain intensity. "Do you want to be sent to another family, one that will have use for a whore as well as a poorly-skilled butcher?"

"No, Mash," I replied, unable to meet his eyes. I could see the tell-tale bulge in his tunic, and I'd known his intentions before he even touched me.

He took my hands away from my chest, where they clung to my wet clothes, and caused me to reveal myself to him. "My, how you have grown this season, *little sister.*" The Sumerian phrase he used was similar in meaning, but miles away in context. "Come with me now."

Mash took my hand and pulled me after him, not roughly, but certainly not with any degree of tenderness. He placed me against a nearby palm tree, face-first, and, after a furtive look around for unwelcome spectators, raped me for what felt like an eternity.

* * *

I DON'T WANT to recount how many times Mash caught me unawares, or alone, or simply sent the others away, then attempted to violate me. I would fight him and at other times run away. If I raised too much commotion, others would check on us. Mash seemed to enjoy it when I fought; he became especially cruel and threatening, goading me to fight him more often. I would threaten him with the consequences of raping me and bearing a child with a slave of his own house. Some months he was easier to convince than others. Mostly, I had to avoid him at all costs.

In my seventeenth year, I began to hear something that sounded like whispers in the air around me. I would swat imaginary insects away from my head. I thought I was perhaps injured, that one of Mash's violent slaps had damaged my hearing in some way. For most of that first year back, I was convinced that I was losing my sanity. When the ethereal voice clearly spoke my name, I stopped questioning and chose to start listening.

Later that year, in between completing my ever-increasing chores and dodging Mash, I was able to determine what the voice was trying to tell me. It would take the voice almost a month to get a word pronounced correctly, as if it were learning Sumerian by overhearing bits and pieces of conversations. I lay in my bed many a night trying to interpret what it was saying, trying to preempt it as one might a stammering child. The message eventually became clear: *Come to your mother's tomb after the midnight hour.*

It wasn't common practice for slaves to visit the necropolis that surrounded the temple, which itself was the center of the city.

Certainly, slaves had tasks that took them in proximity to the graves and tombs, but I didn't have any that would. And even if I had, nothing would have required me to visit this area in the dead of night. Traditionally, respect was paid to the dead when appropriate, but it was rare for a person to linger over a grave outside of the initial mourning period. Akkadians did not believe in a strict afterlife, meaning we believed there was a netherworld, if you will, but whether you were good or bad had no bearing on your status or destination there. We simply thought of those who had left life as existing in a dimmer version of our own world.

I stole away from the house the first night after the message was clear, confident that I wasn't going to be noticed or followed. Everyone was asleep. By now, Mash had adopted his father's habit of drinking heavily after dusk, which thankfully rendered him sedentary and tired. Essuru could often be heard talking deep into the night, but I wasn't concerned with him; the idiot was more often in conversation with himself and wasn't paying attention to anything going on around him. Bassu, sweet boy that he was, dutifully went to bed at an early hour to be able to rise promptly and do his chores around the house. Besides him and me, no one else was going to perform them.

I made my way to the family tomb. Tombs were not sealed in those times; they had doors that were closed but unlocked, allowing families to add on to or reuse the chambers as needed. Besides the immediate antechamber beyond the entrance, there were only three chambers in the small building. Aram's parents' mounds were in one chamber, there was one unoccupied chamber destined to be Aram's, and lastly there was Salamu's barren chamber. A small, guttering torch I had purloined on my journey was my only companion. I set it in the small indentation within the chamber. Inside, there was a small platform – about the size of an adult's bed mat – raised from the sandy earthen floor. It was upon this dais that I sat, shivering in the evening cold, waiting for the voices to tell me what to do next.

In the deathly silence, I heard the Sumerian word for blood: *uri*. It was repeated over and over, building to a cacophony in the stifling air of the tomb. I looked around the chamber, searching frantically for something I could cut my skin with.

A sizzling rift appeared in the air about a foot above my head. It was only there for a moment, and out of it dropped a small rock shard. I had to avert my face to avoid it landing in my eye; it bounced harmlessly off the top of my head and dropped to the ground. A scent lingered in the air: light, sulfuric.

I leaned down to pick up the tiny rock shard, which was not much larger than a grown man's thumbnail. After a moment of childish fear, I steeled myself and sliced neatly through the skin of my left forefinger.

Blood seeped from the small slit in my finger. In the air around me, a chant started: *Peta. Babkama. Luruba.*

My blood dropped to the dais. The chant continued. I thought of how difficult it had been for the voices to collect the full sentence that had brought me here – *come to your mother's tomb after the midnight hour* – and how much more difficult it must have been for the voices to chant these three words over and over without practice. *Peta. Babkama. Luruba.*

It was a common enough phrase in our tongue – travelers who wanted to enter the city would ask *"peta babkama luruba anaku"* at the outer gates, which were closed against invaders: *open the gate for me so that I can enter here.* I struggled to consider how it applied to this situation, until on a whim, I flung my bleeding finger in the direction of the wall of the chamber, close to where Salamu's head would've rested had her body not been lost to the Tigris.

The chanting had stopped.

I tried again. This time I spoke the words myself. "Peta babkama luruba."

A sizzling portal opened in front of me, shimmering and ethereal. The hole was about the size of my head, jagged but round. In it, I saw a shifting, translucent visage.

It spoke. "You have done well. Now we can speak. We will only have as much time as there is blood. There is another world, which you are seeing now. We can join and then travel between our two worlds. There is much we can do if—"

The portal fizzled to a close. Again, the smell of sulfur tickled my nostrils, stronger this time but fleeting.

Without a moment's hesitation, I sliced the sharp edge of the tiny rock across my middle finger this time and flicked the blood in the same direction. "Peta babkama luruba!"

The same-sized portal opened, and again the ethereal visage filled most of it. It immediately started speaking, and I realized that the bulk of our conversations were likely to be interrupted regularly. "—can do if we work together. The blood works from your side, other methods from ours. The words are not as important as the intent. We can save you from—"

I was already drawing the shard across my finger as the portal closed. I flicked the blood and said the words.

"—from the danger you are in. You must learn how to make the portal from your side without blood. You must keep what you learn to yourself and never allow another to see. This is the most important thing. Always at this—"

Again, I caused the portal to reopen. My fingers were stinging, but I hardly noticed.

"—at this same time. The place isn't important to us. The time is. Time here is like place there. Come tomorr—"

The portal closed, and despite cutting all my fingers and the top of my left foot, despite whether I sobbed or whispered or nearly shrieked the words, the portal did not reappear.

I found myself wandering back to the house through the cool desert night air. Goosebumps, as we call them now, covered my flesh, but I didn't feel the cold. I was too excited. The stranger's words reverberated through my head. I distilled their message into this: *We know what you are enduring; we want to help you; keep this a secret.*

Sleep finally claimed me about one hour before I was to wake. Still, I rose energized, my mind's eye repeating the spectacle while I did my mundane chores. The adventure caught up with me around midday, and I found myself nearly unable to continue. I nodded off while slaughtering a young lamb and wounded it badly. It screamed in agony before I recovered my senses enough to perform the kill properly. Still, the lamb's lament had roused Mash, and he stomped over to the animal's pen. He started to berate me – I don't even recall his words – but at once I stood, dropping the lamb's fresh carcass to the dirt (a definite *faux pas* back then). Mash's eyes moved immediately to the dripping knife in my hand, then back to my face. For the briefest of moments, the balance of power between us mercifully shifted, and I realized what freedom might feel like.

Then he slapped me across the face with all his might, and I fell to the ground next to my slaughtered lamb. I couldn't will myself to rise. I simply moaned into the dead lamb's cooling wool. Mash stalked away with uncharacteristic slowness, stopping only once to look over his shoulder at me. Whether he did so out of disgust, triumph, or fear that I might be coming after him with the knife, I would never know.

I WENT BACK to my mother's tomb that night, and the next night, and the night after that, and again and again. My eighteenth year brought with it no changes that I could share with anyone – in this dimension, at least. My chores were the same or worse, the threat of Mash was the same or worse, Aram was more distant or entirely absent for long periods. Bassu and I admired each other from afar but did not act on our feelings. Essuru remained stupid.

In Salamu's tomb, however, everything had changed. Qareen had taught me how to open a portal we could speak through by using a set of reeds I blew certain notes into. We could not pass items through this portal, but it stayed up until I closed it using another tone from the reeds. Utilizing the few Sumerian and Akkadian letters I had learned, I had scratched arcane instructions into the walls with a rocky stylus. I did my best to use a vague shorthand that only I might understand. The voice cautioned me repeatedly against this practice, but had no power to stop me directly. Qareen and I communed during every hour I could steal away from the house. What I learned about her world was astonishing.

They existed in a different dimension from ours. Bear in mind, we didn't use words like "dimension," or any of the advanced physics terms I might currently use to convey these experiences. We were able to converse adequately using my language, which Qareen had gleaned an understanding of by watching our dimension. They were able to open portals into our dimension using reagents on their side, which enabled them to snatch objects to study: rocks, coins, water, jewelry. One could easily imagine troves of missing objects – "Husband, where is my necklace?' 'I have no idea, wife.' – being studied on Qareen's side. Qareen herself had no set appearance. She was ethereal in that she had no solid shape when viewed from our dimension. That she occasionally presented as a face to me had more to do with my own mind trying to conjure familiarity out of chaos than the reality of her form. She lacked gender, too, from what I understood of her kind; clearly, I was projecting my lack of a mother figure by thinking of Qareen as "her."

I came to understand that many of her people latched on to specific humans and bonded with them for life. Her people did not die in the sense that there were physical functions that would stop, resulting in a dead body that would decay. Her people came into existence without warning, and they could just as easily disappear; if there was a rhyme or reason to any of it, Qareen had not yet discerned it. She could confirm that they were not bound by human timelines – for example, she knew of several of her kind that had latched on to different humans over those humans' lifetimes. These beings acted as what we would consider "guardian angels" nowadays.

Eventually, Qareen related to me that while it was rare for a being from her dimension to cross into ours, it had certainly happened. The only way to do this, that she was aware of, was for the being from her side to combine with the human on my side. She told me that it was difficult for her to explain what would happen to the combined entity after that, as the beings on her side could no longer easily tell who had integrated. They could view humans from their dimension; they could not see one of their own on our side. I boldly suggested to her that humans who had fits or claimed to see visions were possibly the results of these combinations. She seemed troubled by the concept and did not have a definite answer. She desired to combine with me but was now concerned about the effect it might have if my suggestion was true. .

I asked Qareen if we bonded and then I died, would she die with me? Qareen was silent for long minutes, then said that she had heard of beings from her world bonding with humans, then returning to her dimension after the human died. These beings almost immediately sought a new human to bond with, as if having been bonded and then torn away from the flesh was too much for them to bear. Qareen admitted it was known that information tended to leak from one human to the next as humans shared the same entity from Qareen's realm. Looking back, this explains some humans' insistence on experiencing "past lives" and the theories of collective, ancestral, or racial memory. Back then, however, this made me consider that bonding with me might benefit Qareen more than it would benefit me. But I had grown to love and depend on her, so I realized that I didn't care.

I told her that whatever the price, I would be willing to accept her into me. She had saved me. She gave my monotonous existence hope. I felt empowered simply knowing that she – and her ilk – lived and spoke and watched and desired communion with humans. She gave me perspective. Distant was the near-weekly danger of Mash, the loss of Salamu. Even the unfulfilled promise of Bassu's affection seemed small by comparison. I lived for nothing but Qareen.

Late in my eighteenth year, my fate was sealed over the course of one week. I was lying in bed, dreading the start of my chores for the day. I was still tired from being awake most of the night; I now functioned on three to four hours of sleep a night at the most. I remember that Mash started shouting my name. He was not calling me to him so much as trying to locate me. I cowered under my animal skins as flashes of what I'd done wrong ran through my mind – a gate left open, a cracked earthen jar and beer lost, a message not relayed, any number of gaffes my sleep-deprived self might have committed. At last, his voice boomed outside of my bedchamber, and he stepped in. He was furious, his eyes wide and his chest heaving.

"Do you know what you have done?" he demanded.

All I could do was shake my head no, my skins pulled up to my chin.

Essuru and Bassu soon flanked him, Essuru grinning malevolently and Bassu, confused, looking from me to Mash and back again.

"You left the pen open again. All our animals are gone. Gone!" Mash roared.

I didn't doubt him. It was not the first time I had made that mistake. Bassu had caught my errors before and saved me from Mash's wrath, but this time he could not.

"Brother," Bassu tried to interject.

"No!" Mash screamed into his younger brother's face. "You will not defend this whore any longer!"

Essuru giggled nervously, distracting Mash. Bassu took the opportunity to place himself between Mash and my bed, where I had scrambled to a seated position but still covered my nakedness with the skins.

"We will get the goats back. Essuru can work on finding the lambs – they can't have gone far—"

Mash struck him across the face. Blood flew from Bassu's lip and landed on the wall. In my head, the words started, unbidden. *Peta. Babkama. Luruba.* If I were to but speak them aloud, Mash would nearly die from fright at the sight of a portal.

"This will not continue," said Mash. "You will not coddle this whore any longer. You must know her for what she is. She is not some pure creature you will someday run away with. That is not her fate, to marry the son of a rich man. She is a slave! I have lain with her! And she *loved* it! Whore, tell him how much you loved my cock!"

Bassu put his hands up defensively and backed away from Mash, which immediately angered me; why wasn't he defending me?

I rose up on my bed mat, dropping my skins and declaring loudly, "Mash, you will never be a man! No one is a man who forces himself upon a young girl! Your cock means as much to me as the rest of you

– nothing!" And then I made the mistake of my young life, such was my fervor and wounded pride at Bassu's inaction. "All of you – all of you are boys! You will never know what burden a woman bears. You could never hope to be my equal in knowledge or decency! And you cannot possibly conceive of what destiny lies before me. Just know that it doesn't involve any of *you*!"

Silence came over the entire room. Bassu bowed his head, wounded, as I had intended with my words. Essuru looked stricken. Mash grinned obscenely; however, his eyes fixed on the top of Bassu's head.

"Did you hear that, little brother? You will never be a man to her. Not her future. And *never* decent," Mash hissed. "I think we, all of us, need to teach her a lesson." Behind him and to the side, Essuru started to rock back and forth in excitement.

I realized what Mash meant to do, and I tried to dash out of my chamber. I barely made it off my bed mat.

Mash shouldered Bassu aside – almost gently – and grabbed me around my torso in mid-air. My naked legs churned in space and I rained my fists down on Mash's back and shoulders, but I had no strength compared to him. He slammed me down hard onto my bed mat, which itself was nothing more than woven reeds over a hard, baked clay floor. The air went out of my lungs and my head rang from the impact. My vision danced with vivid points of light.

"Show her, brother," Mash urged Bassu. "Essuru!" Mash indicated me with a flick of his head. Essuru, dullard though he was, understood and complied. He gripped my wrists and held my arms down, above my head. I was still stunned and breathless and could not resist.

Mash took hold of one of my ankles. By now, I was starting to regain some clarity. I opened my mouth to speak and Mash used his free hand to cover it. I thrashed my body as much as I could. "If you do not fuck this whore with us, brother, then you'd better not try to stop us!" Mash sneered in Bassu's direction.

Bassu took one step toward the tangle of limbs that his brothers and I presented, and Mash brutally backhanded him. Bassu sunk to his knees, holding his face in his shaking hands, before rising to flee from my room.

* * *

BY THE TIME it was over, both of them had assaulted me. Mash took over the duties of subduing my arms while Essuru disrobed and quickly climbed on top of me. Upon touching my right breast, the moron came furiously all over my thighs before having the chance to enter me. To this day, I can still remember his asinine laughter as he looked down at my legs covered in his semen.

Mash derided him, forced him to use his own tunic to clean my legs, and then sent Essuru out of the chamber. Still pinning my wrists painfully to my bed mat, he pivoted his body into position and attempted to enter me. I was able to close my thighs and resist him long enough for him to tire. He slapped me hard across the face, spit on me, and then left. I wiped his spittle from my stinging cheek and wept.

I spent the rest of that day in bed, shirking my duties. Not one of the boys spoke to me for the remainder of the day. Not one of them checked to see if I was even alive. I did not sleep; I simply bided my time.

That night, as had been my habit for more than the past year, I stole out of the house around the midnight hour. This time, I chose to bring every possession I had in this world and a bit of bread and some dates. I was never going to set foot in this house again, whether I remained in this dimension or not.

Upon arriving at the tomb that had become my only refuge, I communed with Qareen and told her of the day's events. She told me that she had watched helplessly. If she had intervened in any way, I would have been branded a sorcerer and killed. She asked me to make a small blood portal — something we hadn't done in months. Absent anything to cut myself with — I had worn the rock shard down to a useless sliver long ago — I bit the corner of my thumb hard. I squeezed until sufficient blood had pooled on the surface on my skin, then flicked it into the air and mouthed the words.

Peta. Babkama. Luruba.

I had barely finished the last word when a sizzling portal appeared in midair, and from it dropped a beautiful bronze ceremonial dagger. The portal disappeared practically before the dagger had cleared its edges. It clanged on the dais next to me before I snatched it up in my right hand.

Qareen intoned, "This will protect you. You cannot allow such an assault again. To do so might kill you."

"*Allow?* Would that you had dropped this into my hand before one of them so much as touched me..." I stopped. Railing at Qareen would not help anything. She was helping me the only way she could, and I chose to trust that she had my best interests at heart. I channeled my resentment back toward the boys who had been like brothers to me. Especially Bassu. I expected nothing less of Mash and nothing at all from Essuru. But Bassu had wounded me far deeper than I could ever express.

For a long time, I beheld the dagger, admiring its beauty, imagining its lethality.

Qareen was singing to me, something she had been testing out lately. Previously, she had been incapable of carrying a harmony that was anything short of grating to my ears. On this night, however, she managed to land on a melody that soothed me. I laid down on my dead mother's dais and, cradling the shiny dagger between my breasts, drifted off to a peaceful sleep.

* * *

I WOKE WITH A START, hearing my name called. I was disoriented – unsure of which way was up – there was no torchlight in the tomb. I felt the weight of the bronze dagger in my hand still, and that reassured me. Again, I heard my name voiced – closer now – from immediately outside the tomb.

Bassu.

Before I could act, he was inside the tomb, carrying a torch. That meant it was night again – I had slept through the entire day – and he had probably been searching for me for hours.

"I'm…here," I called quietly.

Qareen opened a tiny portal from her side and babbled at me, confusing her words in her haste. I made out only "No, he cannot see!" before Bassu appeared at the entrance to his mother's chamber. His eyes moved up to Qareen's portal as it fizzled to a close, hopefully believing it was some trick of the light. His brow creased in confusion, then relaxed as he looked at my face. He set the torch in the holder outside of the threshold.

I can't imagine what I looked like to him in that torchlight, my hair askew and unbrushed, making my bed on the dais of the mother who had died saving him. His mouth worked, but no words issued. His cheek was swollen from Mash's blows. Bassu's shoulders relaxed for a moment, and the hint of a smile began to grow. He raised his eyes to take in the chamber itself.

His relief was gone the moment he viewed the walls. He took one last, tiny step into the room and read the writing on the wall. Confused, he looked to me for answers. His eyes widened with fear as he saw the dagger clutched to my chest.

He turned to leave.

I sprang off the dais, not thinking of anything but stopping him. I wanted to explain to him what he had seen, how it was a blessing and a miracle and something we could share – certainly Qareen would welcome him into her confidence - and I would forgive him for hurting me, for I loved him with all of my heart and always had. I landed on his back and clung to him, mimicking the game we had played as small children where he would spare my delicate, bare feet from the sharp rocks of the desert.

He made a small sound, a lover's moan, and then fell forward hard onto his face. He did not put his hands out to stop the fall, and I rode him down not realizing that I had embedded the dagger in his back. The blood was already pushing against the hilt of the dagger, trying to get out; I had pierced his heart.

I pulled the dagger out, hysterically saying "no" over and over, unable to believe what I had done. Blood spurted from the wound once, twice. His tunic turned red before my eyes. Bassu's legs twitched for a moment, causing me to rise to a standing position over him. By the time I reached my full height, he was still and remained that way.

Qareen opened a portal behind my left ear, startling me. "We can join. If you say the words now, I can combine with you. I will give you the strength to continue. You must simply open yourself to me." This was something that we had discussed many times with hopeful tones.

I stood dumbly for a moment, unable to wrench my eyes from Bassu's bloodied body.

"The boy's lifeblood soaks into the earth and is lost to us. Now is the time," Qareen prodded me. She did not come across as malevolent, simply expedient and pragmatic. Unspoken was the understanding: we would not have access to this much blood again without committing another murder.

In a daze, I stepped back from his body and spoke the words: *Peta. Babkama. Luruba.*

A massive portal opened underneath Bassu's form. His body slid into the void, traveling into her dimension like so many tiny trinkets had before. Blue-white ethereal wisps floated up from the portal, illuminated by Bassu's guttering torch. They appeared as thousands of individual strands of the same material, like smoke but lacking even that much worldly presence. As they inched toward me, I relaxed my body and my mind. I spread my arms out, my right hand still holding the bloody dagger.

Qareen entered me.

I remember thinking *this is what drowning must feel like*. That this was what Salamu felt by giving herself to the river to save her child. That I was saving no one but myself now.

I could not breathe. I could not move. It seemed that every individual cell of my body was under attack, unable to fight back. And I reminded myself – in a detached sense – that I didn't *want* to fight back. My body had to accept Qareen wholly, without battle and without reservation. There was no pain, just the feeling of giving in to the void, to surrendering my life to a cold, infinite future.

Before I knew it, I was on my knees and able to breathe again, able to move my limbs. I was panting. The portal was closed, the stink of sulfur heavy in the close air of the tomb. I realized instantly that Qareen was a part of me now, that there was no longer a "me" and a "her," but that we were combined into an inseparable new being. I had my memories, my desires, my fears, my hopes for the future. I still felt the raw grief and guilt from Bassu's violent demise. Melded with these sensations were new understandings, new perspectives that had to have come from Qareen. Again, they did not seem like someone else's, but rather mine, newly realized.

I knew everything she knew – even if the workings of her dimension made little sense at the time - and she knew everything that I had known: pain, lightness, hunger, fatigue. Dazed, I made my way back to my mother's dais and fell onto it, exhausted. I slept.

I woke to the sound of my name being called once again. This time I was neither startled nor disoriented. Mash was outside the tomb. Bassu must have known that I was stealing away in the night to his mother's tomb, but he had kept this secret to himself until today. I could imagine him telling Mash that he would fetch me from here, seeking to deflect his sadistic brother's wrath. Briefly, I remarked on the clarity of this knowledge; surely this came from Qareen and not my intuition. I was at peace with this bastion being violated by the likes of Mash now. The usefulness of this place had reached its end, and I had plotted my revenge already.

Mash threw open the outer door loudly. There were two sets of footfalls, so I guessed that he had dragged the idiot Essuru behind him as usual. No matter—I could deal with him as well. "I know you're in here, little whore," Mash snarled.

I placed the dagger on the ground, left of the dais, where no one entering the chamber could immediately see it. "I'm in here, Mash," I called as seductively as possible. Part of me was cautiously curious about what was to come – despite the melding of our consciousnesses, Qareen had never directly experienced the touch of another. I had no time to tamp down this perverse sense of arousal. I needed it as a weapon as surely as I needed the blade.

Mash stood in the doorway of the chamber, then turned and handed his torch to Essuru, who stood behind him and out of my line of sight. Bassu's neglected torch stood in the holder outside of this chamber, so Mash did not need his. "I expected to find my brother in here with you." Mash feigned confusion.

"He was here," I said, coyly letting my gaze fall to my own lap. I started to scoot forward on the dais, which caused the woolen shawl covering my legs to hitch up. "I don't know where he is now. But I'm glad you're here." All these statements were the truth.

"Ah," Mash said. He needed little encouragement. He pulled up his tunic, revealing his partially erect manhood.

In response, I opened my shawl and fully revealed myself to him. I let it drop quietly on the floor to my left, and my hand remained there, dangling off the dais in casual repose. Essuru murmured and rocked back and forth in the doorway. I did not care.

Mash was on me in an instant, his manhood pressed against my pubic mound. His mouth closed on one of my nipples.

Qareen's sense of revulsion matched mine, and I steeled myself for the next action. As Mash switched his mouth to my other breast, I brought my right hand over to grip the shaft of his member.

I grasped the dagger in my left hand and swept it up under his testicles, sacrificing no momentum. The blade sliced upward cleanly, leaving his genitals free in my right hand. Mash rocked backward on his heels, his mouth gaping.

Hot blood spurted onto my naked stomach.

Essuru couldn't see what had happened and remained in the doorway, confused as to why his brother was no longer on top of me. Mash turned left, then right, unable to locate a flight path in his shock. He realized that the door was to his left and turned to leave, his hand on the wall of the chamber to support himself.

I sprung up and, with a single motion, sliced the tendon of each heel. Sweeping the dagger back in the other direction, I cut the thick tendons in the backs of his thighs. Mash's butchered penis dropped out of my hand and hit the ground with a wet slap. He went down hard on his knees in front of Essuru, who emitted a high-pitched screech. While he watched, I reached around the front of Mash and swiftly sliced his trachea open, being careful to avoid cutting any arteries. I wanted him silent, not dead. Yet.

For all his stupidity, Essuru had the sense to drop the torch and flee without another moment's hesitation. He would be my herald, then, babbling what he had witnessed through the narrow city streets.

I hooked my arms under Mash's shoulders and dragged him backwards fully into his mother's chamber. I dropped him roughly, and he lay on the tomb's floor, motionless. His eyes were wide, unblinking, fixed on me. I can only imagine what he saw: an unabashedly naked avenging angel, covered from shins to chin in his blood, holding a grisly bronze dagger that she had no right to touch let alone wield, staring down triumphantly at him.

Mash's upper body still worked. He snapped out of his shock and began to rock side-to-side on his shoulders in an attempt at escape, gurgling emphatically. I straddled him, sitting down roughly on his stomach and knocking the wind out of him, then went to work with the dagger. As his body convulsed with pain, blood spurted sporadically near his ruined throat. I made shallow, lengthwise cuts on his torso, arms, and face. Anywhere his flesh remained unblemished was my canvas. Whenever Mash attempted to raise a hand to strike at me, my blade met that hand instead. Soon he fell to weeping and tried to cover his face from my assault; the only sound he made was a wet sputter from the red chasm of his throat. Mash was turning white as milk.

I don't know how much time passed, but it couldn't have been long. My arms should have ached but didn't. I made small games with myself, swinging my arms to-and-fro, slicing his flesh in unplanned, random patterns. His blood stained most of my form - my forearms resembled garnet gauntlets; my legs clad in a scarlet skirt. Mash was no longer gurgling or moving. I whispered the words: *Peta. Babkama. Luruba.*

There was a sickening rush as a portal opened underneath Mash's prone body. The tomb tilted away, and I became enveloped in blackness. Where Mash's body went, I cannot say. I only know that I regained my equilibrium after what felt like a day of tumbling into the void.

I was in Qareen's world now and utterly gone from mine.

* * *

I FELT NO FEAR THERE, despite the absolute gloom. I was able to see my own body, my own hands in front of my face. All else was black. I could walk, but I was unable to say if I truly went anywhere; there were no landmarks, no waypoints to measure my progress.

I called out to Qareen, then remembered that she and I were one now – there would be no assistance coming from outside of us. But the answers came quickly enough.

It came to me like a memory. It was certainly not anything that I had ever experienced, so it had to have been Qareen's. I knelt in the boundless black, reached my hand out, and came back up with an indescribable object. There were no – and still are not any - words in a human language that can describe it, not by color, shape, texture or weight. I knew only that it was the reagent needed to open a portal between the two worlds. All that was required was to think of what I wanted to see.

A small window opened in front of me, close to the level of my neck. I had assumed the portals from Qareen's side were made at the relative position of her feet. That was wrong. Through the portal – which was about the size of my chest, if I had to estimate – I saw into Aram's house. My perspective was from a dozen feet high, in the courtyard. This was the most heavily trafficked area of the house; I'd traversed it many times a day in the course of my chores.

It was daylight, and I saw two figures in the courtyard. Aram was seated on a stone bench, not unlike the dais his body would reside on

252

within his tomb. Aram was older, grayer, and slumped in a posture of sadness and defeat. He leaned his head on his left fist, his elbow on his knee. Near his sandaled feet sat a man whose head was shaved. This man turned his head sharply as if he'd heard a sound, and I could tell it was Essuru.

Aram looked like he was on his deathbed, and Essuru looked like a thirty-year-old man. I had only been in Qareen's world for what felt like hours, and at least fifteen years had passed in the world I had known.

I wondered how long the portal would stay open, and it promptly closed. I recalled Qareen telling me that reagents on her side allowed her people to open portals through which they could snatch items from our world. However, this portal did not appear to be one. This was a watching portal.

I walked a few steps further, then bent down anew. This time, I thought only of acquiring what was needed to open a portal strong enough for me to reach my hand between worlds and snatch something up. I came up with an object which – again – defied description utterly. I knew only that it was different from the first object. I remembered Qareen telling me when we first met that intent was important. That explained the difference in objects I picked up; what I intended to do determined what object I came back up with.

I thought of Aram's same courtyard, and a portal was conjured, again slightly below my head – perhaps at chin level this time. What I saw was utterly different.

The stones were still present; the dais that Aram had been sitting on minutes ago was still there. It was chipped in some places, in others rounded by years of wind and sand. I reached my hand through and found that the portal zoomed in to the location I indicated. If I reached for a pebble on the ground, the portal focused on that area and brought me millimeters away. If I focused on a bee sunning itself on a sandstone brick of the house, the portal brought my hand close enough to be stung. I pulled my hand back, almost exiting the portal completely, which would have caused it to close.

I stopped when I saw movement in the upper right portion of my view – the doorway of the house leading to the back courtyard. Out of it staggered an ancient man. His head was bald save for a few wisps of white hair behind his ears. His beard was white. He leaned heavily on a cane. His stricken face looked up directly to my portal.

Essuru.

His mouth moved and I recoiled immediately, causing the portal to close - much to my relief. But it was not quick enough. His mouth was forming my name. He had spit the first syllable out as the portal slammed closed. Lost behind my despair at having seen him – and him having seen me! - was the fact that clearly, several more decades had passed. How that simpleton had survived to a ripe old age was of the least curiosity. I turned my thoughts inward – the only way to speak to Qareen directly – and pleaded for guidance within this pitch-black netherworld.

Relief came almost instantly, but to be fair, time seemed to have no meaning in this dimension. There was no sun nor moon to track across the sky. No meals endorsed the hour of waking or rewarded a workday completed, and yet, I had neither hunger nor thirst. My body threw off no waste nor wanted for anything; my mind yearned for the sustenance of answers.

A voice – similar to that of Qareen's before she joined with me – spoke into my left ear. Answers started flowing in what a modern human would call an "information dump." Soon voices surrounded me – on my left, my right, in front of me, behind me, even above and below. They each provided some bit of insight that addressed or validated what another voice had said. If something confused me, the confusion was addressed seconds – or less – later. Things like:

Time is place.

To find when, find where.

Only take objects which will not impact time.

You will not be able to take those objects.

You cannot stop time.

Time is events. You cannot prevent an event.

You may visit Jesus, or Hitler, or Ran Min. You cannot prevent what they do.

These names meant nothing to me, of course. I had no understanding of their significance, nor *when* they would be significant. I came to understand, gradually, that this dimension was essentially for observation of the world I had come from. So far, none of the occupants had indicated there were other worlds other than Earth on which to spy. My thoughts turned to my own well-being and whether or not I could ever return home.

Time will not move forward for you here.

You must not occupy a time in that world twice.

You can go through a portal any time you like; you are different than we are.

I realized that Qareen and her kind were bound to that dimension. That their only escape – if they even desired to leave – was to merge with a human. The dark dimension was the sea, and they were like the myriad fish within. And in merging with Qareen, I had become like a fish who could survive in both environments.

One denizen addressed me at length. The other voices quieted, but whether this was in deference or simple utility, I could not say.

You have merged with one of ours. There is no division in you. And so, you can be here and live, and you can be there and live as well. Your physical body will not age here, nor will it need sustenance. Any time spent there will age you, and your hunger, thirst, and bodily needs will return. You may bring articles with you from there to here; in fact, we would appreciate you doing so. You will only be able to bring objects that do not affect the flow of time. You cannot bring a human here to stop or to cause their death. You cannot interrupt the destiny of the world. We choose not to interfere with lives even if we make contact with those lives.

"Wait," I retorted, "how can you say that? How was my destiny not interrupted by bringing me here?" There was silence, and I thought on this. "I am not ungrateful. Qareen has saved my life. She certainly saved me from years of rape and subjugation and unhappiness."

Finally, the answer came: *Coming here was always part of your destiny.*

I felt the being move away, although by what means, I cannot say. While they were speaking to me, I glimpsed movement in the void but nothing I could define as a face or a body. Formless beings, moving about in a formless void. And here I was amongst them, where I would not age, and could presumably travel throughout time. Identifying *where* which time was located was the challenge.

That I would have to be careful with my earthly visits was plain; I would age at a normal rate each moment I spent outside of this dimension. But I was free to roam the earth in search of my destiny. *My* destiny. I had never given the concept much thought, even after meeting Qareen. Now she and I were one, our two destinies merged into one. It was time to discover what that destiny was.

I opened a portal and slipped through into earthly light.

OLDS

CARI DUBIEL

"Fuckin' Olds." Wells slams the lid of his CompuPad.

Eryn flinches and reaches for the baby. He's on one of his rants again, his voice rising.

They've been married for over a year now, and she still hasn't figured out how to respond to his outbursts. He's not an easy man to be with. His temperament changes like the sun. Her first approach had been to soothe him, to tell him everything would be all right, but that didn't work. It only made him more depressed, sulky. When she tried the opposite – ignoring him – he'd begun to lash out. Now any response, it seems, will damn her.

"They're at it again." He swivels in his chair, looks down at her. She's sitting on the carpet below him, the baby in her lap. "Now it's a curfew. And sanctions on alcohol."

"You have your customized vape pen," she says mildly.

He rolls his eyes. "Yeah. They're supposed to be aligned with your genetic code or whatever. But they're probably putting something in them to control us. They've already got us under a microscope. I wouldn't put it past them."

Eryn hasn't told Wells that she has her own THC pen. She'd had her genetic code sequenced the last time she went out for a general practitioner appointment. The doctor, who appeared in her upper forties and on the last legs of her duty tour, smiled gamely at Eryn when she described the anxiety she'd been having. "It would help us to have your DNA sequenced anyway," the doctor had said. "When I'm not here anymore, you'll want to share that information with your new practitioner."

Wells gets up from the table and stalks across the kitchen, his pants leg whispering past Eryn and Gus on the floor. He pulls a bottle of mead from the fridge and pours it into a glass. She watches bubbles form in the yellow liquid before he knocks it back.

"It's not even noon," Eryn says.

"They're going to take it away from me," Wells says. "I have my rights. For now."

* * *

HE STUMBLES off in a haze a few hours later. Eryn checks the clock – he was supposed to report at News Headquarters by nine in the morning. The sun is already past the middle of the sky.

It's time for Gus's nap anyway, so she bounces him off to the darkened room, turns on the fan, sings to him until he falls asleep. Then she slides out the nursery door and back into the main section of the apartment.

This is Eryn's favorite time of day. When she can be alone. When she can sit on the couch or on the porch and stare out at the lake.

Wells is always angry about something – mostly new policies from the Olds, but he will also rail against society in general. Not a good look for a man assigned to Journalism. People in that office are supposed to be neutral, reporting news as they see it, not with a political lens. Eryn has never seen someone be removed from their Calling before, and she wonders what would happen to her husband if he were reassigned. He might be moved to Trash Duty, or to Farms. Or even Bottling – something mundane.

She'd been relieved when she was assigned to Child-Rearing. Her body had always craved motherhood, even when she was a young girl. Her own mother had been so compassionate, always there for her scraped knees and falls off her hoverbike. Eryn hadn't wanted to let her go, not even at the assigned time. Eryn's parents had chosen to take their Ascension on the same day – at the time, Eryn had celebrated her father's sixtieth birthday, knowing she had six more months with her parents before she had to say goodbye to them forever. But those six months had gone by all too quickly, and she cried her eyes out at the Ascension, watching as they said goodbye to Earthly life for good.

After they were gone, she was alone – until Wells.

Eryn shifts on the couch, watching the lake through the front window. The water's crystal surface shimmers in the bright sunlight, people on their Recreation Day cruising along in boats and kayaks. The weather is perfect: not too cool, but not too hot either. When Gus wakes up, she might take him for a stroll.

"Your perfect genetic match," the letter had said, assigning her to Wells Franklin Carter, he of the hot temper and the pillowy lips. One thing was for certain: even if they weren't compatible personality-wise, they were a tornado in bed. She got pregnant only a month after the Joining Ceremony.

She knows he doesn't like their life. He'd be so angry if he knew that she sometimes thanks the Olds. Thus far, Eryn has been protected from so many terrible things. War, pain, disease. What's the point of a long life if it's pockmarked with blemishes?

She pulls out her remote device and taps the button to open the windows. Fresh air rolls in as the panels retract. Eryn takes a long, deep breath, savoring the moment.

* * *

GUS IS awake when the mail comes. "Hey there, Eryn," the mail carrier greets her. "How's your day going?"

She balances the baby on her hip, taking the bundle of papers and letters. "Not too bad. How about yours, Uli?"

He tips his hat. "Not too bad, not too bad. Got a few more houses on the rest of this road, then it's quitting time."

"I love that for you."

They exchange a quick bow, and Uli jaunts down the street to the next living pod.

Gus fusses, and she bounces him a little as she sorts through the post. There isn't much to impress her. Mostly ads, along with an invitation to a birthday party for one of the other children in Gus's neonatal group. Gus is rapidly approaching his first year, but Eryn isn't interested in holding a celebration. She's still thinking about her parents and how much they would have loved to get to know Gus. She knows she shouldn't be so hung up on them – knows they've Ascended for a reason – but she wishes she could have them all in the same room, all at the same time.

There's a letter from the Council offices. She wonders if it's an invitation for her to join another birthing group. Surely the Council was pleased with her addition of Gus to the population. He is truly a perfect child, she thinks as she holds him close, inhales his strawberry-scented hair. She's spent the extra credits on special shampoo for his golden curls. He's worth every sacrifice.

Eryn places Gus on the floor and hands him a soft toy, then slits open the envelope from the Council.

Then she drops it. Now she is on the floor too, beside Gus, a hand pressed to her mouth.

* * *

"You're kidding."

Whatever buzz Wells had when he left, it was gone when he returned. Eryn has made dinner – it's part of her job as a Child-Rearer, and she takes it seriously – but Wells doesn't seem to care. He's too fixated on the letter from the Council.

"I'm not. They want me there on Monday morning."

"Who's going to take care of Gus?"

"You, I suppose?"

It wasn't a coincidence that Wells had been handed a letter that day too. From Journalism. Wells was no longer contributing to the mission, it said. He would be reassigned within the next few weeks. He should expect a letter from the Council with his next assignment.

"This doesn't make sense." Wells paces the kitchen. Eryn cannot stop smelling the ketchup and mustard and garlic and onion. She's made him burgers from the replicated meat she'd picked up on her last market visit. One coupon per family – but she figured today was as good a day as any to make them, especially since they'd gotten such big news. "Will they reassign me to Child-Rearing?"

"And if they do?"

Eryn doesn't want them to. Raising Gus is her Calling – she's sure of it. She couldn't stand being away from the scent of him, the softness of his skin, his curls.

"I'll challenge it." Wells picks up a bun and slaps a burger onto it. "I'm a good journalist. I look at every angle of a story. That's why they don't like me – because I make them look bad." He takes a savage bite and stares back at Eryn. "They don't want me to expose them and all their corruption."

Gus breaks into tears then.

Eryn presses her lips together. "Do you not want me to do it?"

Wells scoffs. He sounds like a horse. "It doesn't matter what I want."

* * *

SHE DECIDES TO GO.

Her closet does not contain any appropriate clothing. In school, they had worn uniforms; she has never owned suits or dresses. Eryn wears soft pants and flowing tops: Mom clothes, as they might have said a generation ago. She is a mom, but she is more than that.

In the end, that's why she made the decision.

Her own parents approached their Ascension with dignity and grace. They accepted it as what it was, had planned for it. Eryn always thought she would be the same way – but now she has Gus.

And if it takes being on Council to have more time with him, she will do it.

She wonders sometimes whether her parents grieved for her. Knowing, as they did, that they would lose her too.

Uli brings her an assortment of items she's ordered: a black dress, a black jacket, a red dress, a tan pantsuit. She tries on all these things, inspecting their fit, analyzing whether the Olds will take her seriously when she wears them. Eryn experiments with different types of makeup, lining her eyes with kohl, worrying it's too sexually provocative, then retreating to a soft brown shade. Ultimately, she can't hide the fact that she's so young – a child, really.

She takes a photo with her son and posts it on the feeds. The compliments flow in. *You're gorgeous. Gus is getting so big. Your Calling fits you so well. Such a beautiful family.*

Is this a family or something else?

* * *

"WHAT DID THEY SAY?"

Eryn discards her jacket and hangs it on a chair. She sighs at the house. It's all a mess. Cereal squashed into the carpet. Toys spread on every surface, including the kitchen counter.

At least Gus is okay. He's in his bouncy chair, gnawing on a plastic teething ring. "Did you put it in the freezer?" she asks Wells.

He stares at her. "What?"

She points at Gus. "His teething ring?"

"Why would I put it in the freezer?"

"It feels good on their gums." She can't believe she has to explain this stuff to him.

But she doesn't have time to write him a manual on how to be a parent. He already got his reassignment. There are plenty of resources online. She's jealous.

Eryn opens the cooling unit and peers inside. "Meals haven't arrived yet?"

Wells rolls his eyes. "Sorry I'm not best buds with the mail guy like you are."

She doesn't know what that means, so she ignores it. "So what do you want me to make? We have leftovers from last week and some snacks from the Center."

"I don't care." He slumps in a chair across from her jacket. Eryn takes a breath. The hustle of her day is still spinning through her mind. It is jarring to see him in her position, exhausted but hopeful that the night will be better. "I think the meal notifications are being sent to your mailbox. Maybe we should redirect them."

Wells sounds like he's been defeated, and Eryn wonders who has defeated him.

* * *

SHE NEVER DID TELL him about her day, and she doesn't really want to.

She nurses Gus and puts him down, then retreats to the living room. Wells is sprawled across the couch, snoring.

Eryn never knew what living was, not really. She wonders if her parents ever knew, either. Today she felt alive. Buzzing with electricity. Her mind on fire.

She'd gone through a series of different security clearances, including a genetic scan and a retina print, before they finally admitted her to the Council chamber. It was one of many in the country, of course, but this was the one for their district. One person on Council reported to the National High Council.

She wasn't a member yet. Not really. Even though her DNA had signified she was an excellent candidate. Neesa, the woman who showed her around, said she'd have to go through a series of physical and mental tests before being fully confirmed. The woman was extremely tall and graceful, wearing a type of dress that Eryn had never seen: slim-profile, but made of a thick fabric that shimmered when she moved. Eryn wondered if Council members were permitted to order from different catalogs.

Neesa was Old, although not much more so than Eryn's parents were when they Ascended. Eryn couldn't tell her exact age. "We stop counting after sixty," Neesa told her. "It isn't prudent for us to track our years lived. Past sixty, we are only here to serve others. Nothing else matters. Do you have more questions, dear?"

She had so many, but it wasn't the right time.

Wells opens his eyes, blinks. She's still watching him. Sleep creases his brow. She thinks he's going to say something, but then he rolls over.

WELLS TUGS on her waist in the middle of the night. She's tired – Gus has already woken twice – and her breasts ache. But he is insistent, and she feels guilty.

He whispers to her, breathing into the shell of her ear. She lets him touch her and take her. It's the least she can do.

He's nearly finished when he cries out. "Oh, God, it should have been me," he wails. Then he buries his face in her neck.

She goes to the bathroom to clean up.

NONE of it is as bad as she'd thought – although she's not sure if she ever thought it would be bad.

She goes to chambers once a week to train. There are special groups she must join through the feeds and mail she needs to read. She isn't a full member and won't be unless she passes the tests – but it will be some time until she is old enough to pass them.

Eryn is privy to information she cannot give to Wells. She knows now about community money, dispersal of resources, knowledge used to make decisions. He is moody, often leaving her alone with Gus on days she isn't at chambers. She doesn't mind. It feels almost like she is back to her old self, before she was split in two. She greets Uli at the mailbox and brings the meals in, prepares them. She welcomes her husband home as if he were still reporting stories.

He softens a bit. Maybe he feels guilty for the way he's behaved. They move together in a careful dance, touching when it makes sense, hiding when it doesn't. One night, after Gus is asleep, they sit together on the couch. Wells produces a bottle of wine. "Where did you get that?" she asks, marveling at the forbidden item.

He smiles. "I get around."

They pop the cork out, and it's surprisingly smooth down her throat. She's never tasted alcohol before. It's sweet, like grapes, and gives her a fuzzy feeling. It also makes her tired, and as her vision spins, she places her head on his shoulder. He allows it. He's warm, and he smells like the wine.

She reads more. On chamber days, they tell her it's part of her job. Part of the training. She's reading about her country's history, what things were like before Society. Wars, strife, hungry people, people who froze to death on the streets of cities. There's an understanding now, a common thread that weaves all people together. She reads novels from the time before, getting lost in the stories, conflict driving characters to do terrible things. All of it is very interesting.

Time slides past her. Past them.

One day, Wells doesn't come home.

* * *

"Will I go back to Child-Rearing?"

Eryn hefts Gus on her hip. She didn't have anyone to leave him with, so she had to bring him to chamber.

Neesa purses her lips. She looks at Gus like he's an insect. "It's an unknown. We don't usually run into scenarios like these."

Wells is dead. At least in the eyes of the government. His tracking chip has turned off, although it's possible he has gouged it out of the back of his neck. Eryn doesn't put this past her husband. She isn't sure what she hopes, although she is glad she doesn't have to listen to him chew his food anymore.

"People don't leave the unit?"

"Oh, no, they do. But not when the spouse is a Council trainee."

Neesa opens a CompuPad and swipes across its surface. "Policy isn't clear on it, either."

If my parents were still alive, they could take Gus. The thought zaps Eryn, unexpected and unasked for. She winces. "So I won't be able to take my spot when I'm of age."

Neesa shakes her head. "It's really unknown. There are other viable candidates, Eryn. I think it's for the best if you return home with your son. We'll be in touch."

* * *

THE NEXT ENVELOPE Uli brings her contains the information.

Eryn sags against the wall as she reads it. *Confidential information... you signed an agreement... any leaks will result in penalty of death.*

Ascension to occur at standard age.

Uli doesn't leave. He's peering at her from the doorway.

"Don't you have mail to deliver?" She wipes at tears that drip from her cheeks.

"I'm sorry," he says. "That looks like it's... not good."

"Nothing is good." She snuffles. "Nothing is bad. It just... is."

Gus toddles into the hallway. He's starting to walk, but he's not adept yet. He sees her, and his little eyes light up—but then he loses his balance and his diapered rear hits the carpet with a thump. He starts to cry. She scoops him into her arms, bounces him, inhales deeply. He gives her life.

"Are you sure?"

"You don't have to stay," she tells him. "I'm fine. I'll be fine."

"You look like you need a friend, though." Uli reaches out a hand, brushes her shoulder.

She flinches. "I know my husband is gone, but you don't... I'm not..."

"A friend," he says. "I'll see you tomorrow."

* * *

GUS GETS OLDER. So does Eryn.

He is so smart. He learns his ABCs. Can count to 100. He starts school. Eryn takes as many photos as she can of him and them together. They are a unit, she and he, a matched pair. Genetically compatible. When he is at school, she reads, writes, plants flowers. Uli introduces her to strangers. She joins the unit neighborhood beautification committee. She makes friends, surrounding herself with people she has chosen.

Time moves both slowly and all at once. Gus loves to read, and she shares the novels from the Before Times with him. They talk about the conflicts, how things were different back then, how people suffered. Gus agrees with her that the stories are more interesting, not like the bland streaming series they watch on their screens and CompuPads. He is turning into a man, her son. Someone who can form opinions and hold discussions.

Gus excels in school. He's not a rebellious teenager, not like some of the kids he knows. He keeps to himself, searching for the balance between clinging to Eryn and building a relationship with her. She watches him teeter, both of them knowing what's coming, even as he strives for independence. She stays out of his way.

The years slip past. He learns to drive. Gets his chip—she cries. Gets his letter from the Council—she cries again. He'll be a trainee like she was long ago. He won't Ascend. He'll be on the Council, making decisions for their community. She loves that for him, even as her stomach pinches with jealousy and maybe fear.

Gus is tall, taller than her, but still golden-haired. He'll be a wonderful politician. People will look up to him, revere him. As he gets older, his hair will turn gray, and artists will paint his portrait. Eryn wishes she could be there to see it.

He gets an assignment for a spouse. Eryn will be a grandmother, even if she's not here to meet her grandchild. Her Ascension Day is coming, approaching fast. She can't avoid it. Her life has been full, but she has not had enough. She will never have enough of her son.

Two days before the Ascension, her doorbell rings. It's probably Gus—he said he would come over and spend the next few days with her. Gus's new spouse has the name of Vella, although he hasn't met the woman yet. They've chatted a few times, and he tells Eryn he's excited but nervous.

The door swings open. She doesn't recognize the man behind it.

She blinks a few times.

His face is lined, his hair white and gray. He's stooped over. She's never seen someone so old.

He looks familiar. A ghost of a former life, buried in her subconscious.

"Dad?"

Her father draws her into his arms. And he can't be real, but he is real. Flesh and blood. He is frail, and another man stands behind him, ready to catch him if he falls. *Wells.*

"How... how did you..."

Wells takes her hand, across her father's shoulder. He's older, too, but there's a spark in his eyes she's never seen before. A lit fire. Within his palm is a small pill. "Prevents the drug from taking hold," he says into her ear. "You go into a deep state. Think Juliet."

"Oh my God." It is all too much. She falls to her knees. She is buckling. "How... how did you?"

Wells steps forward and takes her hand, transferring the pill to her. "I went deep undercover. I managed to get an assignment within the Council chambers under an assumed name. They underestimated me. I'll be breaking the story within a few weeks. I know they'll come for me, but I wanted to see you first." He looks down, maybe even penitent. Eryn's shaking.

"Your mother's gone," her father says. Eryn still grips the pill. It's hot in her palm.

"I'm sorry." She shakes her head. "I'm so sorry."

Wells interjects. "I killed the camera feeds. One of us will come to the house and take your body for disposal, once they finish their inspection." His voice cracks. "Eryn, I failed you. I didn't realize how much I loved you until I left."

She can't react to this revelation. It freezes her. "It's not safe for you to be here. If they see you... Dad..."

His smile is crinkly. "I'm an old man. They can't do anything to me."

Her father smells like bourbon and smoke. Eryn can only wonder what he and Wells have been up to for this long time. And she knows why they haven't come until now. They couldn't put Gus in danger, couldn't destroy Eryn's charmed life. It had been charmed except for the knowledge that she'd lose her son one day.

Wells… she doesn't know what to think about him. All the harm he'd caused her.

She grabs them both and wedges herself between them, the pill still lodged tight in her hand.

"Did he get his assignment?" Wells asks.

She's never loved him. There's an ache deep inside her.

Eryn nods. "Council."

"Of course." His baritone has gotten deeper, rumbling in his chest. "It should be him."

T.C.C. EDWARDS

T.C.C. Edwards, or just Chris, comes from Waterloo, Ontario, and has been enjoying the life of an expat teacher at a university in Busan in South Korea. He lives just outside Busan with his wife and two young sons, and enjoys going on long hikes around the hills and mountains of Korea.

He edited and wrote short stories for four anthologies published by the Busan Writing Group, *Nothing Too Familiar, Convergence, Peripheral Portraits*, and *Headquarters*. He also wrote a one-act play for *Fleeting* by the Daejeon Writing Group. More recently, he wrote a short story for the Writing Bloc anthology *Deception*. His forthcoming work is the long-in-progress sci-fi novella *Far Flung*, to be published within the next two years.

He has a writing blog, writeorelse.com, where he muses on the life of an author. He can also be reached through his page at https://www.facebook.com/tcceauthor

SUSAN K. HAMILTON

Susan K. Hamilton is the award-winning author of epic, dark, and urban fantasy books including *Shadow King, Darkstar Rising*, and *The Devil Inside.* Her short stories have been featured in the *Escape!, Deception*, and *Passageways* Anthologies from Writing Bloc. She is currently branching out into a new genre--women's fiction--with her upcoming novel, *Stone Heart.*

Horse-crazy since she was a little girl, she pretty much adores every furry creature on the planet (except spiders). She also loves comfy jeans, pizza, and great stand-up comedy. Susan lives near Boston with her husband and dotes on her very opinionated mare.

Follow her on Twitter for book updates and other random musings: @RealSKHamilton.

DAVID LEE

David Lee is a retired high school counselor/teacher who worked in California/Washington State schools for over forty years. Most of that time was spent at the Riverside Unified School District's Educational Options Center, an alternative site for expelled and troubled students.

Mr. Lee is the author of "Hummingbird," a short story in the Writing Bloc's *Deception* Anthology. He has also had numerous articles published in Reno's "The Good Life" magazine. He writes most frequently on his blog, "Musing on the Mayhem," which can be found at *davidrlee.blogspot.com*. Here, since 2007, he has been recording his thoughts on modern life.

Married almost forty-four years to Jackie, the love of his life, he is the proud father of five exceptional children and "Papa" to six (soon to be seven) amazing grandkids. Mr. Lee hails originally from El Paso, Texas, attended the University of San Francisco, and lived in the Riverside area of Southern California for the better part of 30 years. He and Jackie now reside in Reno, Nevada, with their golden retriever, Annabel, and two black cats, Winston and Sadie.

KAYTALIN PLATT

Kaytalin Platt is an author and graphic designer living in Philadelphia, Pennsylvania. Platt was raised on a farm in rural Deer Park, Alabama—a place which offered inspiration for her short stories *Eleanor* and *Only God Can Tell.*

Platt's parents contributed in growing her personal quirks and writing passion. Her mother encouraged her creativity and her father —when he wasn't putting her to work herding cattle, planting crops, building fence, or welding—encouraged her to do something with what she made.

Platt's debut novel, *The Living God*, was published in 2019, with the follow-up arriving in 2021. She has several short stories appearing in Writing Bloc anthologies, and the third installment to her *Equitas* series arrives late 2022.

S.E. SOLDWEDEL

S.E. Soldwedel received his MA in creative writing from the City College of New York (2007). His journalism degree from Michigan State University (2002) came in handy during a ten-year career at the *New York Post*, Hearst Magazines, and *Rolling Stone*. He lives and works in the Bronx, where he teaches English Composition at Lehman College. There, he also earned his MS Ed. in Teaching English to Speakers of Other Languages (2019). With that, he tutors local immigrants and refugees.

Soldwedel's fiction is a distillation of noir, pulp, science fiction, and adventure stories. In 2019, Inkshares published his debut novel *Disintegration*. It takes place in the Broken Circles story universe, upon a mirror Earth. This is the setting of his short story "Teardown" and his forthcoming novel *Integration*, from which "Bitter Fruit" is excerpted.

PETER L. HARMON

Peter L. Harmon is the author of *The Happenstances...* Young Adult
Book Series, the editor of the *Horror From The High Dive* horror
anthologies for High Dive Publishing, and a writer of many other
things including a best-selling book of dad jokes, *A Daily Dose of Dad
Jokes*, that he wrote with his buddy Taylor Calmus the "Dude Dad." To
find out what he's up to next, follow him @PeterLHarmon on Twitter
and/or Instagram.

DEBORAH MUNRO

Deborah Munro is a California native who is now working across the world as a biomedical engineering faculty member at the University of Canterbury in New Zealand. The first seventeen years of her career was spent working as an engineer in industry, designing orthopaedic implants and medical devices.

Munro has always loved writing and began her first novel, *APEX*, in 2015 as part of her Certificate in Novel Writing online program through Stanford University. She entered her novel manuscript in late 2016 to an Inkshares.com competition and won a publishing contract with them for *APEX*, which is now going through the editing process. Deborah is also the author of two other short stories, 'Ambition' and 'Picture Perfect', which are featured in the Writing Bloc anthologies *Escape! & Deception*.

ALY WELCH

Aly Welch lives in Western New York with her husband, author Mike X Welch, and their twin sons. When she isn't writing, she enjoys acting, karate, and yoga. Welch also loves exploring the woods, and still hopes to find magic behind every tree and under every rock.

Her story "Alpha" was first published in the *Deception* anthology (Writing Bloc, 2019), and appears in her *Silly Little Monsters* story collection (Writing Bloc, 2020). Her debut urban fantasy novel, *A Better Me*, will be released this spring.

DANIEL LEE

Daniel Lee is a multi-disciplinary creative and author of the novel *After Death*, which won First Place in the Nerdist Sci-Fi Contest and is forthcoming from Inkshares.

His short fiction and poetry has appeared in *The Santa Clara Review*, Writing Bloc's *Escape!* anthology, and High Dive Publishing's *Horror From The High Dive* anthology.

He lives in Los Angeles, where he makes his living as an editor of film and television advertising. See more of his work at **Dan-Lee.net**.

JASON POMERANCE

Jason Pomerance is the author of two novels, Women Like Us, (Quill/Inkshares, 2016) and Celia at 39 (Writing Bloc, 2019). His four part novella Falconer appears on Nikki Finke's Hollywooddementia.-com, and his short stories have appeared in the Deception and Escape anthologies, both published by Writing Bloc.

A long-time WGA member, Jason has written movie and TV projects for numerous studios and production companies. He lives with his partner and their beagles in California, where he surfs (badly) and is at work on a new novel.

JANE-HOLLY MEISSNER

Jane-Holly Meissner, an Oregon-based author, has been scribbling stories into notebooks, online, and in the Notes app on her phone for most of her life. She lives with her four children, three cats, two dogs, and her husband in a state of barely organized chaos.

"Mildred" is Meissner's third published short story, and is related to her story "The Cleansing" which appears in Writing Bloc's *Deception* anthology. Her first novel, *Fae Child*, was published by Inkshares in 2020.

EVAN GRAHAM

Evan Graham is a world building addict and connoisseur of dread who moonlights as a science fiction author.

His debut novel, *Tantalus Depths* (Inkshares), arrives in bookstores nationwide this summer. *Tantalus Depths*, along with multiple stories featured in Writing Bloc anthologies (*Escape! Deception,* PASSAGE-WAYS: *Nine Tales, Nine Unique Literary Worlds, & Family*), are set in Graham's *Calling Void* universe.

Graham has a bachelor's in Education Studies from Kent State University, and resides in rural northeast Ohio.

JENN NEWMAN

Jenn Newman grew up in the suburbs of Massachusetts. Not one for big changes, she is still there. She shares the company of her wonderful husband Eric, her fabulous identical twin boys, and two rescue pups. By day she tackles the world of Human Resources, and by night she pretty much just wants to curl up with a glass of wine and watch Twilight (don't hate).

Starting out long ago in the world of fan fiction, Jenn discovered a passion for creative writing. With the encouragement of a high school friend and accomplished author (you know who you are), she began to dabble in competitive short story writing through NYC Midnight, recently making it to the third round of a competition and thoroughly enjoying each round of torture.

With a collection of never-finished manuscripts filling the binders in her office, Jenn looks forward to continuing one of her favorite works in process and sharing it with the world someday. Her ultimate goal is for Stephen King to consider her talented (for those of you not familiar with his definition of being talented – write something, get paid for it, pay the light bill with the money). For now she has accomplished a magnificent feat – being published alongside a wonderful group of writers in this anthology.

BYRON GILLAN

Byron Gillan has written for the Buffalo News amongst multiple news outlets. He favors fiction, with a preference for Horror and Science-Fiction.

Gillan currently resides in Western New York with his dog Winston. When not immersed in world building, he loves spending time with his family, and donating his time to various non-profit organizations.

KELSEY RAE BARTHEL

Kelsey Rae Barthel grew up in the quiet town of Hay Lakes in Alberta, a sleepy place of only 500 people. Living in such a calm setting gave her time to imagine grand adventures of magic and danger, inspired by the comic books and anime she enjoyed.

After graduated High School and moving to the city, she decided to turn her hobby into something more and worked hard to evolve her writing. Her hard work bore fruit and she was able to publish her first urban fantasy adventure, *Beyond the Code*.

Since then, she has written articles for websites, a magazine, had her work featured in a short story anthology, and is currently working on a sequel to her debut novel.

JASON CHESTNUT

Jason Chestnut is a writer, musician, avid reader, and gamer. He has published numerous short stories and co-created the supernatural time travel comic book *Zero Town* with artist Angela Guyton. *Family* is his second Writing Bloc Anthology appearance.

After taking some time off from writing to complete his degree in Information Technology, he is currently completing the first volume of *Zero Town*, developing a second graphic novel, revising his long-gestating pulp space opera *To Live and Die in Avalon*, and recording demos for a full-length album of songs written during lockdown.

Chestnut lives in Asheville, NC with his fiancé Melanie, a punk rock photographer, and their two dogs Foxy and Pascal.

ESTELLE WARDRIP

Estelle Wardrip lives in northern California, behind the redwood curtain. She shares a home with her mother, two cats, two dogs, two horses, varying quantities of goats and poultry as well as approximately thirty fruit trees. When not teaching children or working on her small farm she likes to write.

She has written many stories, and this will be the second one published with Writing Bloc. Her first story, "Loyalty" appeared in Writing Bloc's *Deception* anthology. She is happy to be working with such a talented and friendly group of people and looks forward to publishing more in the future.

Inspired by stories such as "Watership Down" and "The Jungle Book," Estelle seeks to present tales from unique perspectives and unexpected settings. She also incorporates her love of art, nature and science into her work.

DURENA BURNS

Author **Durena Burns** currently resides in Southern California. Having an active imagination since she was a small child, Burns has loved putting together that imagination through writing stories. Her other interests include singing, dancing, watching TV, and working in special education.

Much like the theme of the *Family* anthology, Burns' work tends to focus on family dynamics. Her book *Call Me Whitehead* is about her late great uncle's experiences as a black man during the Vietnam War through her perspective. Her other work has appeared in the Writing Bloc anthology *Escape!* titled "I Wish It Happened."

R.H. WEBSTER

R.H. Webster grew up in rural Alabama, reading everything she could get her hands on. She started writing her first novel at the ripe old age of 13, and while that particular work remains incomplete, she never lost the dream to one day become a novelist.

Webster now lives in sunny El Paso, Texas with her other half and two adorably demanding rescue terrier mix puppies, Charlie and Rosie. She released her first novel, *Lucky*, in 2018 and the sequel, *Striking It Rich*, in 2020. Both are available in paperback & ebook wherever books are sold, and on Audible.

MIKE X WELCH

Mike X Welch lives in Western New York with his wife, the author Aly Welch, and their twin sons. His adult daughter lives in Seattle. In addition to his day job, Welch is the Project Manager of Books for Writing Bloc. In this capacity, he has helped shepherd two Writing Bloc anthologies into existence: the one you're holding, *Family*, and the inaugural volume of PASSAGEWAYS: *Nine Tales. Nine Unique Literary Worlds*.

His work has appeared in the two original Writing Bloc anthologies (*Escape!* & *Deception*) in addition to the *Hell Hour* anthology (Abomination Media). His self-published collection of horror stories, ENANTIODROMIA, has been met with universal acclaim. His next appearances will be in the *Horror from the High Dive 2* anthology (High Dive Publishing), and an entry in the PASSAGEWAYS: *Mythos* anthology (Writing Bloc).

Welch is currently at work on his debut novel, the long-awaited *PROOF: Protection of Occult Figures*, due to be published in 2023 if he ever finishes writing this author bio and the cat gets off his keyboard. Visit www.mikexwelch.com

CARI DUBIEL

Cari Dubiel's short work has been published in several anthologies, including *History and Mystery, Oh My!* (2015) and *Day of the Dark: Stories of Eclipse* (2017), as well as the Writing Bloc anthology *Escape!* (2019). As lead editor for Writing Bloc, she has produced and edited eleven works, with more on the way. Cari also reviews trade publications for *Booklist*, and she has edited both academic nonfiction and traditionally published fiction.

Her novel *How to Remember* won Library Journal's Indie Select Award in 2021 and the Hugh Holton Award from the Midwest Chapter of the Mystery Writers of America in 2017. Her short story collection *All the Lonely People* became an Indie Select title in 2016.

Cari is a co-host of the Indie Writer Podcast, which is produced by Writing Bloc, and a board member of Northeast Ohio Sisters in Crime. Previously, she served on the National board of Sisters in Crime as the Library Liaison. She's represented by Lynnette Novak of the Seymour Agency.

Cari is also a librarian and may be buried in her library's reading garden because she's been there so long. She has a husband, two children, two cats, two betta fish, and way too much work to do.

WRITING BLOC INDIE PUBLISHING TEAM

Writing Bloc was founded in 2018 by Michael Haase, who wished to create a community of like-minded writers for sharing ideas and discussing the state of writing and publishing. The Writing Bloc community connects on Facebook, Twitter, and Instagram, and we have a newsletter list. Writing Bloc is now led by Jacqui Castle, Becca Spence Dobias, and Cari Dubiel, with assistance from G.A. Finocchiaro, Kaytalin Platt McCarry, and Mike X Welch.

Our podcast, the Indie Writer Podcast, is available on Podbean and anywhere you prefer to stream your content.

Our publishing arm distributes quality content from our members. We publish short story collections and anthologies, mysteries and thrillers, science fiction, horror, and contemporary romance.

Visit our website at www.writingbloc.com
Twitter: @writing_bloc
Instagram: @writingbloc
Facebook: @writingbloc

ALSO PUBLISHED BY WRITING BLOC